Robin Hood

Also by Antonia Fraser

King Arthur and the Knights of the Round Table

Robin Hood

ANTONIA FRASER

Dolphin Paperbacks

For Stella, Blanche, Atalanta and Thomas now

This edition published in Great Britain in 1993
Published in paperback in 1994
by Orion Children's Books
Dolphin paperback edition reissued 2001
by Orion Children's Books
a division of the Orion Publishing Group Ltd
Orion House, 5 Upper St Martin's Lane, London WC2H 9EA

A catalogue record for this book is available
from the British Library

ISBN 1 85881 093 0

Printed in Great Britain by
The Guernsey Press Co. Ltd, Guernsey, C.I.

CONTENTS

1

CHRISTMAS EVE IN SHERWOOD FOREST

IT WAS Christmas Eve, and in the great forest of Sherwood the snow lay thick upon the ground. As the shadows lengthened towards evening, a stealthy figure could be seen creeping from tree to tree. He had a bow in his hand and a quiver of arrows slung across his back; at intervals he stopped short to examine the tracks in the snow.

In spite of the bitter cold and the late hour, the hunter was not alone in the forest. Hidden in the shade of a great oak, two men were watching him, hooded and cloaked against the weather.

'A plague on this Saxon knave,' said the taller of the two in an angry whisper. 'We have followed him nigh on an hour, Dickon Barleycorn. He must surely make a kill soon.'

'I would I were at home in Nottingham by my own fireside, Walter,' sighed his companion. 'Instead of tracking a miserable peasant through the forest of Sherwood.'

'Stop your whining, Dickon,' snarled Walter of Weybridge. 'Men say that you have a Saxon mother, and the Saxons are all craven in the face of danger. 'Tis lucky that we Normans are here to rule them.'

At that moment, before Dickon Barleycorn could protest against the slur, the hunter whipped an arrow out of his quiver, fitted it to his bow and aimed boldly across the clearing. There was a noise in the undergrowth and a huge stag bounded out into the open. A second arrow felled him to the ground, and with a cry of triumph, the hunter ran forward and plunged his dagger into the great beast's heart. The next thing he knew, his arms were roughly pinioned from behind and he was struggling helplessly in the hands of his pursuers.

'Let me be!' gasped the hunter. 'Let me be, I say!' But the Sheriff's men were broad and burly, whereas their prey was thin and shrunken, with such fragile stick-like arms that it was remarkable that he had managed to draw a bow at all.

'Not so fast, my fine fellow,' said Walter of Weybridge with an ugly sneer, securing the arms and legs of his captive with a rope. 'Now, sirrah, tell us your name and place of dwelling.'

'They call me Nat the Weaver,' said the prisoner sullenly, 'although since the Sheriff's men have taken my loom from me I have been out of work.'

'Perhaps you do not know that all the deer in this forest belong to His Royal Highness Prince John, and that the punishment for poaching them is death?' continued the man-at-arms, ignoring the prisoner's gibe at the Sheriff.

'Prince John is only the Regent of England,' cried the hunter, 'while our true King Richard is away on the Crusade. King Richard would never have let his people starve, as Prince John has done. He would not have punished me for shooting one beast among so many, when my wife and our six children have not tasted meat for three

2

months.' The wretched fellow sank to his knees. 'Have mercy on me,' he gasped. 'Do not drag me before the Sheriff. Tomorrow is the Feast of Christmas: for the sake of your own wives and children, will you not pardon a desperate man?' At his appeal the younger man faltered, and said in a softer voice:

'Are your wife and children indeed starving? Perhaps some bread . . . my wife has enough to spare . . .' His voice trailed away, as he saw the furious face of his companion.

'You soft fool!' snarled Walter of Weybridge. 'Are you a woman, Dickon Barleycorn, to be taken in by every tale of woe that you hear? It is forbidden to shoot the Prince's deer, and the punishment for the crime is death by hanging. Now let us leave this icy forest and make all speed to the Castle of Nottingham. This whimpering cur will make a fine Christmas gift for our master the Sheriff. He will be hanged on Christmas Day, as an example to the rest of his kind.' So saying, Walter of Weybridge raised his hand to strike his prisoner contemptuously in the face with his glove.

THE GREEN-FEATHERED ARROW

Suddenly he gave a howl of pain, and letting go of his prisoner, started cursing and shouting, as he shook his hand this way and that. Dickon Barleycorn and Nat the Weaver stared in terror and amazement at the long arrow, tipped with a green feather, which transfixed Walter of Weybridge's palm!

'What are you staring like that for, you moon-faced idiots?' shouted Walter. 'Have you never seen an arrow before? Pluck it out of my palm, Weaver! And you, Dickon

Barleycorn, after the man who shot it! What does the Sheriff pay you for, to allow murderers to roam his forests, shooting arrows at honest men?' Dickon Barleycorn stared fearfully into the bushes. It was quite dark now. Only the white carpet of snow gleamed across the clearing. He took one step towards the undergrowth, while Nat the Weaver broke the arrow painfully out of Walter's horny palm.

'Not so fast! Gently there, you baboon, you clumsy dolt!' Walter alternately cursed Nat the Weaver, and shouted at the faint-hearted Dickon, who was becoming increasingly reluctant to take a single step away from his companions.

The second arrow landed with a faint hiss at Walter of Weybridge's feet, just grazing the toe of his shoe. The man sprang back with more curses, and hastily pushed Nat the Weaver in front of him. As if to punish him for his cowardice, the third arrow came from behind and whistled past his ear, narrowly missing it. By this time Dickon Barleycorn's knees were trembling so much that he could hardly stand.

'We are lost,' he groaned. 'We are surrounded by our enemies. Woe is me, I shall never see the light of day again. To think of dying on Christmas Eve in the depths of Sherwood. I have seen my dear wife for the last time. . . .'

'Cease your moaning,' said Walter between set teeth. 'We are caught like rats in a trap in this clearing. If we want to get out of here alive, we must make the shelter of those trees.'

Scarcely had he finished speaking when three more arrows in quick succession buried themselves in the very tree which he had indicated. Walter and Dickon loosed a

4

few arrows wildly into the darkness; they were answered by a mocking laugh, and a hail of arrows, from every point of the compass – or so it seemed to the terrified men. Walter lost control of himself and fired arrow after arrow into the trees, the bushes, and anywhere where he thought he could detect a movement. His quiver was soon exhausted. Dickon Barleycorn's hands were shaking so much that he could not draw a bow at all – he kept dropping his arrow in the snow and scrabbling hopelessly for it with frozen, trembling fingers. Nat the Weaver watched them both with melancholy resignation. Walter had untied his hands, but his ankles were still bound. In any case there seemed no particular point in fleeing from the Sheriff's men, only to die at the hands of a bandit.

'It seems that I am to die soon in any case,' he thought. 'I may as well meet my death here in the open as like a wounded rabbit in a hole!'

When Walter saw that Dickon was incapable of handling his bow, he shouted at him to hand over his arrows.

'Drop that quiver,' said a voice from the darkness. At once Walter seized an arrow and fired it in the direction of the speaker. Once again that high mocking laugh sounded, which struck a chill into Walter's heart, and four carefully aimed arrows landed in a circle at his feet.

'I shall not miss next time, Walter of Weybridge,' said the voice. 'Throw that quiver as far as you can away from you. Then untie your prisoner.'

'Do what he says, Walter,' said Dickon Barleycorn anxiously. 'Otherwise we shall soon all be as dead as doornails. Oh, my poor wife, my little children . . .' Dickon Barleycorn started to moan and lament once more.

'Coward!' cried Walter of Weybridge. 'Have you no spirit left in you? Your Saxon blood betrays you. Wait till the Sheriff hears of this. We have waited the whole day to catch a thief in the forest, and now you want to throw away all our work and make us return empty-handed. Never!'

'I am afraid that we shall not return to the Sheriff at all unless we obey,' said Dickon in a tone of piteous fear. With these words, he bent down and untied Nat the Weaver's bonds. Then he plucked the quiver from Walter's hands and threw it as hard as he could away from him. Nat the Weaver rubbed his ankles and stood irresolutely, not quite knowing what to do next.

'Take to your heels, Nat,' said the unseen voice. 'And if I were you I would not show my face in Nottingham for some months, until the Sheriff's anger has cooled.'

Nat did not need to be told twice. He raced off as fast as he could across the clearing, into the trees, and was soon out of sight. Walter and Dickon stared gloomily after him at the footprints in the snow.

A ROYAL SNOWMAN

'Well, now, what happens to us?' said Walter of Weybridge at length. 'We have lost our prisoner. Are we to lose our lives as well?' There was no answer. The wind blew a scurry of snow in the faces of the Sheriff's men, but otherwise nothing moved in the forest. No arrows sped from the trees, no voices from the darkness. Walter and Dickon stood in silence in the middle of the clearing. At last, after about a quarter of an hour, Dickon, who seemed to have recovered his spirits somewhat, observed:

'We had best be getting back to our master and tell him what has happened. The night is cold, and I have a mind to be home by my own fireside before midnight.' As they followed the path through the forest, which threaded its way through deep rifts of snow, Dickon examined the footprints closely.

'This was Nat the Weaver,' he muttered, 'running away from us at a fine pace, too. See how he has only left the print of his toes in the snow. Ah, here is another track – someone walking at a more leisurely pace, methinks. And yes' – exclaimed Dickon in excitement – 'here is where his horse stood. He mounted the horse and rode off down the path which leads to Abbotsburg.'

Dickon Barleycorn touched Walter's arm.

'Walter,' he said sadly. 'All that time there was only one man in the woods. He must have raced round and round us in the darkness. The footprints tell their own tale. We have been properly outwitted.'

So saying, Dickon Barleycorn looked timidly at the Norman, to see if he was going to administer another rating for his cowardice in the face of danger. Would Walter of Weybridge really complain to the Sheriff of his faint-hearted behaviour? It would mean a severe rebuke, a night in the dungeons, even. He was agreeably surprised when Walter of Weybridge replied quite calmly:

'Well, take care that you do not let that get to the Sheriff's ears. I shall tell him we found the footprints of twenty men. We were outnumbered ten to one.'

Dickon Barleycorn swore fervently that he would never let the Sheriff know the truth. They plodded on together in silence.

'Friend Dickon,' said Walter at last.

Dickon Barleycorn thought wonders would never cease – here was Walter of Weybridge, the most feared man in the Sheriff's troop, calling him 'Friend'!

'Something is troubling my mind, friend Dickon,' went on Walter. 'When we were in that devilish clearing, being fired at, for all the world like two nesting birds, did nothing strike you about the voice of our enemy?'

'It was a very terrible voice,' replied Dickon, shivering once more at the memory. 'It was the voice of the devil, or perhaps of a giant, or perhaps a monster come out of some cave, or a bear, or a—'

'Peace, fool!' Walter interrupted him angrily in something like his old manner. 'Cease your babbling. It was a voice like any other . . . or perhaps not *quite* like any other, for no two voices are alike, and I have a feeling that I have heard that voice before, and not so long ago either!'

'Oh, Walter,' cried Dickon admiringly, 'if you could only remember where you heard it.'

Walter of Weybridge suddenly stopped in his tracks and gripped Dickon by the throat. 'Swear that you will not blab about what I have to say, until I give the word!'

'I swear,' gasped Dickon. Walter released him abruptly.

'Well then,' he said slowly. 'Did it not strike you that the voice of our tormentor was uncommonly like that of . . . ROBIN HOOD?'

For a moment neither spoke, while Dickon Barleycorn stared at Walter in astonishment and fear. Who had not heard of Robin Hood, the only son of the powerful Earl of Locksley, who had departed on the Crusade with King Richard many years back, leaving Robin as a ward of the Sheriff of Nottingham? It was not only the broad lands and rich manors which he was to inherit on his twenty-first birthday that made Robin Hood famous in the county of Nottingham. For Robin's adventures were the talk of the neighbourhood. He was always in trouble with his guardian, the Sheriff, for some scrape or other – some madcap wager, or a race through the forest, or a midnight attack on a neighbouring castle, or the rescue of a beautiful damsel who was being married off against her will to a rich baron. Wherever there was romance and adventure to be had, there was Robin Hood to be found. Moreover, he was a fearless rider and an intrepid swordsman, generous, high-spirited and reckless; above all, he was the finest marksman with a bow and arrow for many miles around.

Robin Hood was of Saxon blood: and he loved to harry the Norman barons with his pranks. He made no secret of his hatred for Prince John, the Regent of England, during the absence of the true King Richard the Lionheart. Openly he would declare that Prince John divided the nation into two by favouring the Norman lords above the Saxon people, whereas King Richard had united the country by treating Norman and Saxon alike. Naturally his contempt for the corrupt and base barons of Prince John's court, so boldly expressed, aroused their hatred. Three men in particular had reason to fear Robin's outspoken tongue – the three greatest villains in the land, who oppressed the poor, and made England a place of misery for those who were not rich and strong. They were Guy of Gisborne, the most powerful baron in the neighbourhood of Nottingham; Oswald Montdragon, the Prince's evil counsellor; and thirdly, none other than Robin's own guardian, the Sheriff of Nottingham himself.

'It is true that Robin Hood has often tried to help the poor people of Nottingham in their wretched plight,' said Dickon Barleycorn, reflecting on all this. 'Last winter, when it was cruelly cold, he brought firewood to my wife's mother, when her widow's hoard of gold had been taken from her in taxes.'

'What the Sheriff takes one day in taxes, Robin Hood gives back the next out of his own pocket, in charity,' said Walter of Weybridge. 'For my own part I think he is a fool. The Saxons deserve to starve if they have not wits enough to feed themselves.'

'Yet even Robin Hood would not dare release a prisoner of the Sheriff's,' exclaimed Dickon Barleycorn. 'Why, he could be put in a dungeon for that, or even punished by death.'

'So he could, friend Dickon, so he could.' And Walter of Weybridge smiled grimly. 'Moreover, I do not think our master the Sheriff would break his heart over the prospect, either! Have you forgotten that it will soon be Robin Hood's twenty-first birthday? Then all his rich lands pass out of the Sheriff's hands for ever. Unless, of course . . .' Walter left the sentence unfinished, but Dickon was in no doubt as to his meaning. He gaped at him in open-mouthed astonishment. To think that the Sheriff might acquire all Robin Hood's broad lands for himself if something happened to Robin before his birthday! Dickon's simple mind was quite dazed by the thought.

The moon was up by now; and just as they reached the edge of the forest, the two men saw something strange and white glimmering in its pale light.

Dickon Barleycorn started back in fear.

'It's an enormous snowman!' he exclaimed, looking

behind him, as if he expected somebody to materialize out of the shadows of the forest. 'And – look, Walter – it has an arrow right through the heart.'

'And a crown on its head,' added Walter. ' 'Tis a royal snowman, Dickon, transfixed with a green-feathered arrow. Evidently our enemy, who stole Nat the Weaver from us, has no love for Prince John.'

He was right. Traced in the snow at their feet were four ominous words. DEATH TO PRINCE JOHN.

'Forward to Nottingham,' said Walter. 'We must tell this tale to the Sheriff.'

NOTTINGHAM CASTLE

Nottingham Castle frowns upon the city of Nottingham from a high hill. In the great hall the warm blaze of the fire contrasted with the gusts of snow blowing across the windows. The Sheriff's men-at-arms were lounging round the glowing logs, talking idly of Christmas, their families, their wives, and the evil weather. One or two looked up when Walter of Weybridge and Dickon Barleycorn stumbled in, with the snow powdering their cloaks, and their teeth set against the wind.

'Walter of Weybridge is scowling mightily,' observed Rob Cuttle out loud. 'Where is that fat peasant you were going to bring our master for his Christmas Eve supper, Walter? You know that Prince John comes hither soon for Robin Hood's birthday celebrations, and the Sheriff has promised to have a fine list of offenders mouldering in his prisons for him to see. Particularly poor wretches who have been driven by hunger to steal some of the royal deer out of Sherwood Forest.'

'Hush, Rob,' said his companion, nudging him. 'Here comes the Sheriff. And by his looks he is no sweeter-tempered than Walter of Weybridge. See how he frowns.' Rob Cuttle bent down in great confusion and pretended to be fondling one of the great dogs stretched out asleep in the fireplace. It was true: the Sheriff's plump face was creased with annoyance.

'Well, Walter of Weybridge,' he said peevishly. 'Show us your captive. The hour is late, and I have waited up for you. Where is the saucy fellow who has been stealing the royal deer?' The Sheriff looked round, as if expecting to discover the prisoner in one of the dark corners of the hall.

'Captive!' burst out Dickon Barleycorn, before Walter could say anything. 'Why, we nearly ended up captives ourselves!' And he would have spilled out the whole story if Walter had not motioned him to be silent, with a furious gesture.

'I should like to tell you my story in private,' said Walter to the Sheriff. He shot a significant look at the curious faces of the soldiers gaping at them. The Sheriff nodded importantly and swept out of the hall again, closely followed by Walter. Dickon Barleycorn trotted along behind, but found the arras of the Sheriff's chamber falling heavily in his face. He had to go sadly back to the fire, and be plagued with questions from his comrades which he did not dare answer truthfully.

THE SHERIFF TAKES COUNSEL

Meanwhile the Sheriff was striding pompously up and down his room, stamping his feet and exclaiming:

'I never expected *you* to fail me, Walter of Weybridge!

Half a dozen prisoners for His Highness to see hanged – that's what I promised him – and now it is three weeks till he comes, and I have only got one old woman who stole some of my chickens. Not much of a catch for a royal hanging!'

'I think I have news of a more important entertainment for His Highness than the hanging of six common criminals,' said Walter of Weybridge in a low voice. He bent closely to the Sheriff and whispered in his ear:

'The news I have concerns *Robin Hood*.' At these words, the Sheriff's petulant babyish features contracted with rage again.

'All news about Robin Hood is bad news,' he snapped. 'Don't mention that boy's name to me, Walter. He has quite spoilt my Christmas by rescuing, yes, *rescuing* some miserable scoundrel out of Guy of Gisborne's dungeons and sending him home to his family with a bag of silver florins in his pocket. All because he had the impertinence to think the fellow was innocent! As if a mere lad could know better than Guy of Gisborne who is innocent and who is guilty. Guy of Gisborne has just ridden here hot foot to give me the news, and is asking me, if you please, to do something about it. As if I can do anything that I haven't done a million times – that is to say, rebuke the boy, threaten to take his horse and bow away from him, while all the time he is laughing at me behind my back because it is only three weeks till his birthday, and then he will be out of my care for ever. Good riddance,' added the Sheriff viciously.

'Then of course not only Robin Hood will be out of your care,' said Walter smoothly, 'but all his rich lands and manors.' Before the Sheriff could say anything more, and his mouth was half open already in another stream of complaints, Walter whispered in his ear:

'I have proof that Robin Hood is a traitor! What say you to that?' And he outlined briefly the events of the evening in the forest, finishing with the royal snowman which had been found with the arrow through its heart. This time Walter of Weybridge had really succeeded in gaining the Sheriff's attention. Without another word, his master rang his handbell three times, and bade his servant fetch Guy of Gisborne and Oswald Montdragon, who were to be found fuming with rage in the inner chamber. Walter found himself pushed into the background while the two statesmen pondered over this latest iniquity on the part of Robin Hood and how best it could be used to ruin him.

'Treachery!' murmured the Baron of Gisborne, smoothing his beard thoughtfully. 'But we should have to have better proof than a mere surmise before we convinced His Highness Prince John. . . .'

'If we could convince the Prince,' said the Sheriff pensively, 'it would be death, or at any rate outlawry, for our bold Robin.'

'And in either case, that means he forfeits all his estates,' finished Guy of Gisborne. The three men gazed at each other thoughtfully. There was a moment's silence.

'There is a way to provide proof,' said Oswald Montdragon slowly, at last. Then he suddenly noticed that Walter of Weybridge was watching him with ears and eyes agog.

'Be off, knave,' he cried. 'You have done your work, now go.'

'You have done right well, Walter of Weybridge,' added the Sheriff more kindly. 'Take this bag of gold, and give a few pieces to that moon-faced Saxon varlet who went with you. Mind, not a word of all this to anyone.' Reluctantly Walter of Weybridge bowed his way out of the Sheriff's chamber, but as he lifted the heavy arras, he paused for a moment, and heard the one whispered word, 'Shooting-match'.

2

A NARROW ESCAPE

THERE WAS a rousing cheer from the children in the market square of Nottingham as the young man on the fine horse galloped into the square and leapt lightly from the saddle.

'Hooray for Robin Hood!' cried one shrill voice. Robin of Locksley bent down and patted the boy on the cheek.

'Why do you cheer me, boy?' he asked gently.

'Because you saved our father from the wicked Sheriff and his men,' said the boy boldly. Robin looked round quickly. There was one fellow lounging idly against the tavern wall, and a few dogs sleeping in the midday sun, but otherwise the main square of Nottingham town was remarkably empty.

'Is your father Nat the Weaver, then?' he inquired softly. The boy nodded, and the two smaller children with him piped up together:

'Yes, we are the Weaver's children, and our father has fled into the forest. He sent word to us that he had been saved by brave Robin Hood and his green-feathered arrows.' And all the children started to cheer again, all six of them, down to the smallest tugging at his brother's hand. Robin Hood pulled a handful of florins out of his jerkin pocket and pressed them into the boy's hand.

'Buy yourself some bread,' he said. 'Perhaps one day I will be able to help you further.' He smiled cheerfully. 'After all, it is only five days until my birthday, and *then* we shall see how Robin Hood uses his inheritance to save the poor of Nottingham from the Sheriff and his men.'

Was it mere coincidence that the lounger by the tavern pulled his hood over his face at these words and sidled into the tavern itself? Perhaps if Robin had looked closer he might have recognized the scowling features of his enemy in the forest – Walter of Weybridge. But a merry shout from the far corner of the square distracted him.

'Will Scarlett!' cried Robin joyfully. 'What brings you to Nottingham? Why, Will, I have not seen you since Michaelmas when you wagered me a pint of ale that I would not split a peeled wand at four-score yards with my new bow.'

'I can split a wand at five-score now, Robin,' said Will Scarlett, clapping Robin on the back. 'And that is why I have come to Nottingham this day.'

'To Nottingham?' Robin looked puzzled. 'Why, there is precious little marksmanship in Nottingham these days – unless it be in the Forest of Sherwood,' he added under his breath. 'No,' he went on, 'the Sheriff has set his heart against tournaments and all merry-making of that sort. He grudges the expense,' he added bitterly. 'There was a time when there were fairs and shooting-matches at Nottingham every quarter, and the people came from miles around to try their skill. That was in King Richard's day, before my father went on the Crusade.'

'Look yonder, Robin,' said Will Scarlett with a smile, 'and see if those days are not come again.' As he spoke there was a great noise of shouting and laughing, and a

17

crowd of people ran into the market square, with the Sheriff's herald in their midst.

'Patience, good people,' said the herald fussily, adjusting his ruffled clothes. 'All this commotion for a shooting-match,' he muttered.

'The first we have had for many a long year,' shouted one sturdy fellow. 'When King Richard went on the Crusade he took all the gaiety of England with him. Alack, he now lies a prisoner in the hands of his enemies, far away in a foreign land.'

At this moment, the herald managed to get his trumpet free, and blew a long shrill blast on it.

'Oyez, oyez,' cried the herald, clearing his throat and extending a long scroll of parchment in front of him. 'Good people of Nottingham, be silent to hear the words of the noble Sheriff of Nottingham. Be it known unto all of you here present, that the Worshipful Sheriff, out of his great goodness and mercy towards his people of Nottingham . . .'

'What a mouthful of words!' whispered Robin Hood. The herald glared at him.

'Silence!' he shouted. 'Be it known unto all you here present, that the Worshipful Sheriff has decreed that on Shrove Tuesday, that is to say, in a week's time, a shooting-match will be held here in the square at Nottingham!' A loud huzza broke from the townspeople, and Will turned excitedly to Robin.

'There, that is what brought me to Nottingham,' he cried. 'Much the Miller, who takes the flour to the castle, brought the news privately a week or so back.'

They were interrupted by another peremptory blast from the herald's trumpet.

'Forasmuch as' – he shouted above the hubbub – 'Forasmuch as it has pleased the Worshipful Sheriff to celebrate in this manner the twenty-first birthday of his beloved and right noble ward, Robin, son of the Earl of Locksley, commonly known around these parts as Robin Hood.' More huzzas greeted this announcement, but Robin stepped back in amazement. 'His beloved ward!' Those were not the words in which the Sheriff generally addressed him. 'Scrapegrace! Troublesome knave!' and 'Saucy boy!' were his usual terms. And why should he go to the expense of arranging a shooting-match when he particularly disliked archery, since he was too portly to draw a bow with comfort?

But there was a fresh surprise to come. A third time the herald reduced the crowd to silence with his trumpet, and this time, in the most splendid language at his command – which was, indeed, splendid – he announced that His Royal Highness the Prince John, Regent of England, had graciously condescended to honour the shooting-match with his presence during his visit to the midlands of his kingdom.

'Strange,' murmured Will Scarlett. 'I cannot help thinking there is more to this shooting-match than meets the eye.' But Robin Hood did not heed him. He threw his cap into the air and shouted cheerfully:

'This is the first good news I have heard yet about Prince John. Off to the meadows, Will, and let us set to practising our archery.'

Will Scarlett shrugged his shoulders. He knew that it was a waste of breath trying to argue with Robin once his mind was made up. Part of Robin's charm was his trusting nature. He never willingly believed evil of anyone.

A Warning

As the two lads crossed the square, a fellow on the edge of the crowd tugged at Robin's striped sleeve and muttered:

'I would have a word with you, Robin Hood.'

Robin paused, and then gazed at him closely. 'Dickon Barleycorn, is it not?'

The man nodded and flushed. 'I reckon your worship knows my face well enough after that punishing we took in the forest,' he said in a shamed voice.

Robin patted his shoulder in a friendly fashion. 'Tush, Dickon, not a word of that here. The whole countryside seems to have heard of that little exploit. The Weaver's brood of children shout it abroad from the market square. I fear my arrows were recognized.'

'The Sheriff too has heard of it,' said Dickon. 'And Master Robin, I warn you, he means mischief. That very Christmas Eve the Sheriff, together with Guy of Gisborne and Oswald Montdragon, plotted against you. Master Robin, I fear that no good will come of this shooting-match. Whatever you do, do not go near it.'

Robin laughed merrily. 'I thank you, friend Dickon, for your kindness,' he said, 'but Robin Hood was never yet frightened away from a shooting-match by threats. Did the Sheriff send you to me with that message, eh, Dickon? No doubt he has some plot to win the prize himself.'

Dickon looked Robin Hood straight in the eye. 'I know you have good reason to reproach me,' he said, 'for it was I who helped to catch Nat the Weaver. But for all the fact that I serve the Sheriff, I do not like his evil ways. Perchance it is my Saxon blood which rebels, for I am half Saxon by birth. It was Walter of Weybridge who warned me about the shooting-match, for he overheard something about it.'

But although Will Scarlett nudged his friend and bade him take heed, Robin, with another friendly smile at Dickon Barleycorn, dismissed the warning lightheartedly, and mounted his horse as if he had not a care in the world. It was as well that he could not overhear Guy of Gisborne, who at that very moment was sitting in his castle, weaving a dark conspiracy.

'I'll be revenged on young Robin Hood,' he vowed. 'However long it takes me. No one flouts Guy of Gisborne with impunity!'

The Robbers' Valley

The day of the shooting-match dawned bright at Nottingham. The air was frosty but clear, and there was hardly any wind to alter the course of the marksmen's arrows. Robin Hood licked his finger and tested the breeze. He observed to Will Scarlett that it was the fairest day for marksmen there had been this side of Christmas, as they rode slowly towards Nottingham from the manor of Locksley. The road lay through the great forest of Sherwood and Will gazed enviously at the fat bucks grazing amongst the trees.

'Oh, how I long for a shot at one of the royal deer,' he said wistfully. 'What a life we could lead in this forest, Robin, with venison to feed us. We could practise our marksmanship all day, and ride about the unexplored paths of the forest. I wager that we should have many merry adventures together.' Little did Will Scarlett know how soon his wish was to come true.

Suddenly Robin gave a startled exclamation, and pointed along the stream they had been following to a waterfall which flowed precipitously down the rocks.

'This is a new path to me,' said Will Scarlett wonderingly. 'I have never set eyes on that waterfall before.'

The two lads decided to investigate it further. To their amazement, they found that the waterfall in fact concealed the entrance to a narrow path, greatly overgrown. Slithering down it, they found themselves suddenly emerging in a spacious valley.

'We must have stumbled on the Robbers' Valley, which they sing about in the old ballads,' exclaimed Will Scarlett.

'A score of men could hide out here for months and never be discovered,' said Robin Hood. 'This valley may be useful to us one day.'

Robin was anxious to explore the rest of the valley, but the more prudent Will reminded him that they would miss the shooting-match altogether if they tarried much longer, so reluctantly Robin remounted his horse, and clambered up the steep path back into the Forest of Sherwood. Will and Robin vowed to each other to keep their discovery secret, and rode on, mightily pleased with what they had found.

Prince John is afeard

Nottingham was all noise and confusion and merry-making when they arrived. Famous marksmen had travelled from all over the midlands to compete for the rich prize of the silver arrow with golden feathers which the Sheriff was offering to the finest marksman in honour of his ward's twenty-first birthday. Although on the next day he would have to hand over all Robin's money, lands, farms, meadows, fields and manors, the Sheriff's podgy face was wreathed in smiles. Perhaps there was something slightly strained at the back of his smile, as he plucked at the fur which edged his blue robe, but if there was, Prince John at least did not detect it.

'A splendid show, Sheriff, a splendid show,' he said genially. 'I am glad to hear that Nottingham is rich enough to hold a shooting-match in my honour.' The Prince's face creased into a foxy smile as he added, 'Perhaps I may increase the taxes due from this wealthy city next year.'

The Sheriff tried not to let his annoyance appear. Momentarily he cursed Guy of Gisborne for his plot. But he managed to smile bravely.

'Your Highness is too kind,' he murmured. Then he continued in a sharper tone, 'Perchance Your Highness, in gazing at this brave sight, over-estimates our wealth, and under-estimates our generosity.'

Prince John showed no sign that this shaft had gone home. He continued to play with his beard and smile amiably at the crowds, occasionally bowing his head graciously to acknowledge the cheers of the people. To the Sheriff's watchful eye, these did not seem as frequent as they might have been, perhaps because the Saxons outnumbered the Normans among the spectators. He nudged Guy of Gisborne, who was standing by, and whispered hotly:

'Tell your men to mingle with the crowd and raise a cheer or two for His Highness. Methought I heard one or two ominous cries for King Richard!'

Guy of Gisborne took the hint, and a minute later a chorus of rousing cries arose from one quarter of the square. This piece of by-play did not pass unobserved by Robin Hood and Will Scarlett, the one gaily attired in a striped jerkin, the other in his traditional red.

'I vow I'll pay the Sheriff out for that trick,' murmured Robin. 'Call forth some of the brave Saxon lads who are loyal to our true King.'

Obediently, Will Scarlett put his two fingers in his mouth and gave vent to a curious warbling bird's whistle, which had been the secret rallying-call of Robin Hood and his friends since their boyhood. Immediately half a dozen stout lads sprang to Robin's side.

'Who's for King Richard?' cried Robin. 'Friends, will you raise a cry for our rightful King?'

'Aye, Robin,' answered Alan-a-Dale, a handsome upstanding young man with a guitar on his back. 'We'll stand by you, never fear.'

Thus it came about that not long after a few tame shouts had been raised by Guy of Gisborne's men for Prince John, a lusty cry of 'Richard the Lionheart! Richard for England!' seemed to spring from all corners of the square at once. The Prince went pale, and clutched at the Sheriff's robe.

'Treachery!' he exclaimed in a tremulous voice. 'There are traitors here, Sheriff. Did you not hear that cry? You swore to me on the Rood that I should be safe here in Nottingham.'

'Your Highness . . .' began the Sheriff in great agitation, but he was interrupted by Guy of Gisborne, who stepped forward and with a significant glance at the Sheriff, said smoothly:

'Your Highness, as one of the most loyal barons in your realm, may I speak the truth freely to you? It is true that there *are* certain traitors around Nottingham, a few Saxon scoundrels. But while my right arm still has strength, I swear they will not harm a hair of Your Highness's head.'

The Prince cast a grateful glance at Guy of Gisborne's commanding figure and wiped the sweat from his pale brow. 'Ah, loyalty, how rare true loyalty is,' murmured the Prince.

Guy of Gisborne gave a smile of triumph and whispered to the Sheriff:

'This fits in well enough with our plan, forsooth. The Prince now sees traitors all round him. It will not be difficult to rouse his suspicions against . . .'

'Hush,' murmured the Sheriff, waving a fat hand. 'The match is about to begin.'

The Shooting-match

The heralds blew a long blast on their trumpets and the competitors for the first of the archery prizes stepped forward. Neither Robin nor Will raised their bow: they intended to save their strength until the final competition for the silver arrow with the golden feathers. But Robin's band of friends acquitted themselves nobly in the various contests. To Robin's joy, they worsted the Norman marksmen time and time again. It was Alan-a-Dale who snatched the coveted prize from one of Guy of Gisborne's soldiers in the last contest but one. The Norman baron's face darkened as he saw the defeat of his man.

'You young Saxon whippersnapper. I'll pay you out for

that, never fear,' growled Guy of Gisborne. He lost no time in whispering in the Prince's ear:

'A very dangerous fellow, that young Alan-a-Dale, for all he looks so young and guileless. Only last Lady Day he refused to pay his taxes to Your Highness, and declared he owed no loyalty to an upstart Regent.'

Prince John, who had calmed down somewhat, immediately turned pale again and groaned faintly. 'Are there many of these treacherous youths in these parts?' He glared at the Sheriff and muttered, 'You have indeed led me into a hornet's nest.'

'Not many, Your Highness,' said Guy of Gisborne. 'But there is *one*. . . . Alas, I hardly dare speak more, he is so dear to the Sheriff's heart. . . .' Guy of Gisborne cunningly left the sentence unfinished.

At that moment Robin Hood's slim, muscular figure could be seen, conspicuous among the crowd by his striped jacket. Pretending that he did not want the Sheriff to see him, Guy of Gisborne nudged the Prince and pointed.

Prince John's eyes grew round as saucers. 'By Our Lady,' he breathed. 'Never would I have thought it possible! The Sheriff's ward! Robin of Locksley!'

Guy of Gisborne shook his head sadly and murmured, 'It is a great grief to our dear Sheriff's heart.'

Now all attention was concentrated on the contest for the silver arrow, the last contest of the day.

Forty stout archers stepped forward in answer to the herald's command. Among them were Robin Hood, Will Scarlett and Walter of Weybridge, wearing the badge of the Sheriff's service, as well as a host of other young men eager to try their skill. They lined up, five at a time, for the first round, which would leave eight men to compete for the prize in the final attempt.

When Robin Hood's turn came, he was three inches nearer to the centre of the target than any of his companions. Walter of Weybridge displayed a certain Norman skill, too, with his shot, and Will Scarlett acquitted himself well.

'It would be a fine thing to win the silver arrow on the eve of my birthday,' said Robin to Will. 'But if you win it, Will, I vow I will not bear a grudge against you, for we learnt archery together.'

'If I win, Robin,' cried Will gaily, 'I will bestow it on you for a birthday gift.'

So saying, he stepped forward and loosed his arrow: amid the applause of the crowd it landed a bare inch from the bull's-eye. Then it was Walter of Weybridge's turn, and the man-at-arms, with the practice born of long years in the Sheriff's service, landed his arrow a fraction of an inch inside Will's. A great sigh of regret went up from the common people, who hated the Sheriff's retainers. Finally, Robin Hood stepped forward, and with careless grace, loosed his green-feathered arrow at the target. A moment's silence, then a great shout went up.

'A Hood! A Hood! Robin of Locksley wins the day!'

THE MYSTERIOUS ARROW

Even as the shout died away, a series of things occurred all at once so quickly that afterwards no man could rightly remember which happened first. One moment Robin was standing with his bow loose in his hands, gazing joyfully at the target, with its centre transfixed by his green-tipped arrow. The next moment a great crowd had surged round him, intending to chair him to the royal box in triumph. The moment after that, all in the twinkling of an eye, an arrow was speeding truly and surely towards the royal box itself!

Had Oswald Montdragon not flung the Prince aside, the arrow would surely have embedded itself in his heart! As it was, the arrow transfixed the back of the box, where it quivered in the wood. Not one person present failed to notice that the arrow had – green feathers!

'Treachery!' cried Guy of Gisborne. 'To arms! Seize the traitor! 'Tis Robin of Locksley who has attacked our Prince in this dastardly fashion. Behold, the green feather of Locksley!' Plucking the green arrow from above his head, he waved it outside the box for all to see.

'Save me, save me,' murmured the Prince, in a hoarse voice of terror, as he crouched behind the broad figure of the Sheriff. Tears of fright began to trickle down his face. Now half a dozen Norman soldiers flung themselves at Robin Hood, as he stood, half-dazed by the quickness of events, in the centre of the square.

'Guard yourself, Robin,' yelled the faithful Will. 'Look behind you!'

Robin Hood sprang back, just in time to avoid the onrush of the soldiery, and with only his woodsman's dagger to protect himself, he began to hack his way violently through the menacing Norman crowd which surrounded him. Twice it seemed that his body would fall beneath the weight of their onslaught: for how could one youth prevail against a dozen soldiers? But still Robin kept himself free, although his left arm was bleeding from a nasty wound, and his breath was coming short and fast.

At the third rush, with one desperate twist of his body, Robin managed to free himself temporarily from the clutches of the soldiers, and despite the blood pouring from his wound, he sprinted valiantly across the square, to where he saw Will holding his horse.

'Good people of Nottingham,' yelled Will, 'show your loyalty to the Saxon cause. Keep back the Norman varlets!'

The Saxons needed no further encouragement. With a mighty roar of 'Norman knaves!' they flung themselves in the faces of the oncoming soldiers, and just gave Robin enough time to fling himself on the back of his horse, and be off at a whirlwind gallop, which scattered men, women and children, Normans and Saxons alike.

FLIGHT TO SHERWOOD

The next minute, amid frantic cries of 'After him! Seize him, you craven curs!' from the Sheriff, Guy of Gisborne and Oswald Montdragon, the Normans had mounted their own horses and were in full pursuit.

Robin and Will cleared the town gates with scarcely a minute to spare before the guards were alerted, and the gates clanged shut. However, their shutting delayed Guy's men considerably. By the time the gates had been opened amid much cursing and swearing, Robin and Will were only specks of dust on the horizon of the road which led to Sherwood.

'Whither away, Robin?' panted Will, spurring his flagging horse to fresh speed. 'My mare Polly is nigh exhausted, and you are faint from your wounds.'

'To Sherwood,' grunted Robin. 'We can hide out there

. . . you remember' – he stifled a groan, and managed to gasp – 'you remember the Robbers' Valley?' before he fainted dead away over his horse's neck.

It meant an instantaneous decision for Will Scarlett. Either he had to stop and succour Robin, which would almost certainly mean capture for both, or else he pressed on alone, for it was equally certain that Robin could no longer ride a horse. Will Scarlett's pride revolted at the idea of falling into the Sheriff's hands. But loyalty to Robin came before pride – one check on the reins of his galloping steed, a lightning swoop, and Robin's lifeless body was slumped over his saddle, while Robin's riderless mount galloped on beside him. For a mile they rode thus, until they reached the crossroads, where one signpost pointed to Sherwood and the other road stretched on out of sight. Then Will Scarlett brought down a great whack on the rump of Robin's horse and swerved down the forest path. Robin's horse gave a startled neigh of anger and fear, then bolted down the left-hand road. Soon it was out of sight.

'Poor Troubadour!' whispered Robin between clenched teeth. 'Never was he used so before! But God bless you, Will, for your kindness. You could have been in Yorkshire by now, without me.'

Will Scarlett glanced down and saw Robin's deathly white countenance.

'You know that I would never leave you, Robin,' he said. He slackened his speed slightly and gazed round him at the trees and undergrowth which was growing thicker with every step his horse took. As if to encourage him to spur his exhausted horse once more, the faint shouts and hallooing of the Sheriff's men reached his ears.

'On, Will,' gasped Robin. 'Press on, and pray that stout Polly will not fall beneath our weight!'

So Will spurred Polly once more and the gallant mare made one last effort. The three of them galloped forward, until they seemed to be right in the heart of the forest. But either some memory of the morning's journey still lingered in Polly's memory, or else fortune favoured Will in his hour of need; for quite by chance he found himself riding by the withered oak tree which marked the turning to the waterfall and the hidden valley. With a cry of joy, he wheeled Polly down the disused track. Pushing their way through a curtain of leaves and branches, they found themselves bursting through the barrier of greenery which hid the entry to the valley. Polly half-slid, half-clambered down the last slope, and the journey was over.

Will leapt from his saddle and lifted Robin gently down. He lay gasping on the turf, as Will tenderly staunched his wound with strips of linen from his own shirt. All was silence around them, save for the birds, high above their heads in the trees, and the occasional rustle of foliage as one of the famous royal herd of deer sprang away in fear from the strange sight of two mortals in the deserted glade. As the afternoon drew on and the shadows lengthened, the two Saxon heroes were still undisturbed.

The Sheriff's men, after pursuing Robin's horse vainly some distance, had then returned to comb Sherwood Forest fruitlessly for some hours. They found no trace of their prey, and at length Walter of Weybridge was forced to call a halt.

'God knows we do not want to get caught in this devilish forest at nightfall,' he cried.

31

Dickon Barleycorn, who had reluctantly accompanied him, agreed fervently.

'Back to the Sheriff,' continued Walter. 'Either the devil has swallowed up Robin Hood or else he has fallen into a quagmire in the forest. Either way, we are well rid of him!'

So saying, Walter of Weybridge wheeled his horse and headed angrily for Nottingham. Little did he know how soon he was to hear more of Robin Hood.

3

OUTLAW!

THREE WEEKS LATER the deserted valley of Sherwood had become a hive of activity. Rough log huts had sprung up and a merry fire glowed and sparkled in the centre of the glade. Warming his hands in front of the flames sat Robin Hood, almost recovered from the effects of his wound and the hectic flight to the forest. Nor was Will Scarlett the only brave lad there: for when the news of Robin's flight spread through the midlands, there were half a dozen stout archers, including young Alan-a-Dale, who decided to join them and flaunt the authority of Prince John and the Normans.

A week after Robin first fled to the forest, the bushes which led to the hide-out were disturbed by a strange rustling.

'Who's there?' cried Robin, drawing his bow, ready to launch an arrow at the first sign of an attack. The grass divided, and forward at his feet pitched a half-naked figure in a dead faint. This was clearly no spy, no Sheriff's man – this bundle of filthy rags, concealing a body which did not seem to have had a decent meal for months. Curiously, Robin lifted up the matted hair which concealed the face of the unconscious man, and immediately recognized Nat the Weaver. Robin touched his shoulder gently, and called for one of his men to bring water. Nat groaned and stirred. Then he sat up, and attempted desperately to kiss Robin Hood's hands and feet.

'Save me, Robin, save me!' he cried. 'The Sheriff's men have been hunting me since dawn. Their dogs tracked me right to the shores of the stream on the far side of the forest. Then I managed to throw them off by plunging in and swimming down-stream as far as my strength would take me. I plunged over the waterfall, and found myself floating past your camp. Now I fear I can go no farther. If you cast me out, I shall surely be torn to pieces by the Norman hounds.'

Robin made him sip the water, and summoned a hearty meal to be prepared for their visitor.

'Eat first and talk later, Nat,' he said. 'But you need have no fear. I have never yet surrendered a Saxon into the hands of the Normans. You may live here with us as long as you please. The Forest of Sherwood is free for all who call themselves friends of Robin Hood.'

'You are indeed Lord of Sherwood,' said Nat, gratefully gobbling hunks of bread and venison. 'Ah, how good the royal venison tastes. I shall never forget how you saved me from Walter of Weybridge on Christmas Eve. I swore then that I would help you in any way I could. Let me join your band, Master Robin, and you will find me the best and truest servant that ever a man had. I have known this forest since I was a boy and perchance my forest lore will come in useful.'

In this manner Nat the Weaver joined Robin Hood's band, and had it not been for the thought of his wife and children, still within the city of Nottingham, at the mercy of the Sheriff, he would have felt happier than ever before. For the first time in his life he tasted good wholesome food, plentifully served and washed down with great draughts of ale and mead. For life in Sherwood was gay and carefree, with much merry-making and feasting to while away the time when the men were not out trapping or shooting food. Only Alan-a-Dale would sit all day, strumming gently on his lute, with a far-away look in his eyes.

'He is pining for the lady Lucy,' murmured Will to Robin. 'There never was such a faithful lover as Alan. I vow that for all his handsome looks, he has never loved but one lady since childhood. Alas, she is the greatest heiress of the North, and he is but a penniless squire.'

At that moment a shout from Tom Turpin, who was guarding the entrance to the valley, distracted Robin and Will from the spectacle of Alan-a-Dale's melancholy.

Ahoy, there!' he shouted. 'Someone is coming this way!'

Robin sprang up and leaped nimbly up the steep bank, drawing his sword. There was a loud rustle in the undergrowth, the sound of a horse neighing, and the next moment Much the Miller, purple in the face with heat and exhaustion, burst through, dragging a fine steed behind him.

'Troubadour!' cried Robin joyfully. 'Why, my faithful horse! I never thought to see you again!'

'I found him wandering in the Oakley marshes,' panted Much. 'He was riderless, and had not eaten for days. The Sheriff's men made several attempts to catch him, but he eluded them all.' Then Much looked grave. 'Master Robin,' he said, 'I have grave news. A week after your flight, a herald entered the main square at Nottingham

35

and declared you and all your companions here to be outlaws, in the name of Prince John.' Robin stifled an exclamation. 'There is worse to follow,' continued Much, 'for he then declared all your lands forfeit, and the wily Sheriff forthwith confiscated them to his own use, giving a manor to Guy of Gisborne and a farm to Oswald Montdragon.'

'Zounds!' shouted Robin. 'I will have my revenge for this! How dare that Norman upstart lay hands on my property! As for that craven, lily-livered Prince – it was an evil day for England when he clambered on to the throne which rightfully belonged to his brother.' And Robin viciously spiked the turf with his drawn sword, as if he were stabbing the Sheriff.

'Master Robin,' pleaded Much, 'you have not heard it all yet. This very moment the Sheriff is combing Sherwood for you, with a band of soldiers fifty strong. He has sworn to the Prince that he will not return to Nottingham without capturing Robin Hood.'

And Much, still panting heavily, flopped down on to the turf, quite exhausted. Not so Robin. He put the bugle at his belt to his lips and blew a mighty blast upon it, which brought all his comrades running from their tasks. Even Tom Turpin deserted his watch-post, and Alan-a-Dale cast his lute aside at the sound of the danger signal.

'Men of Sherwood!' cried Robin. 'This day a grave injustice has been done to me by our so-called ruler, Prince John. You all know the circumstances of my birthday tournament at Nottingham and how a dastardly plot was hatched to drive me from the town. Now this same sheriff has taken all my estates, which I hold from my father, and appropriated them for himself. Moreover,

Prince John has declared me, and all of you with me, to be outlaws!'

At this a great outcry of 'Shame!' and 'Injustice!' and 'Norman dogs!' broke out. Tom Turpin spat upon the ground and swore to knife the villain who had dared to outlaw an honest Saxon. It needed no further words from Robin to persuade his band to arm themselves for the fight against the Sheriff. In a trice they were all girded with swords, bows and daggers, and were mounting their horses to gallop out and attack the Sheriff. But just as Robin had swung himself lightly on to the back of Troubadour, Will Scarlett called a halt.

'Men of Sherwood!' he exclaimed angrily. 'Have you no heads on your shoulders? Do you imagine that with the best will in the world a dozen of you can defeat fifty men-at-arms? Outlaws, indeed! You are behaving like foolish Norman zanies. We must meet force with cunning, if we are to defend our stronghold and our lives!'

Robin's brow blackened at Will's blunt speech, but a moment's thought told him that his friend was right.

'Faithful Will,' he said, patting him on the shoulder. 'Where would we be without your good counsel? Speak your mind.'

The men of Sherwood gathered round Will Scarlett, who outlined to them his plan for outwitting the Sheriff.

Robin revenges himself on the Sheriff

Meanwhile the Sheriff of Nottingham was riding along the main bridle-path of Sherwood, surrounded by his retainers, all armed to the teeth. Walter of Weybridge rode beside him, and Dickon Barleycorn trotted along a yard or so behind. Dickon's spirits, never high, had sunk very low indeed at the thought of another foray in the forest against the redoubtable Robin Hood. His tender conscience reproached him.

'Surely my Saxon blood should curdle against this outrage,' thought poor Dickon. 'Am I so poor-spirited that I have not the strength to desert the Sheriff's service and throw in my lot with brave Robin Hood? Alack, I fear I was born a coward, and a coward I shall die.'

With these gloomy thoughts to accompany him, Dickon Barleycorn plodded along behind the Sheriff. As they penetrated deeper and deeper into the forest, the trees grew thicker, and Dickon began to hear strange sounds in the bushes. He looked fearfully round, but there was no sign of anyone.

'Walter,' he said timidly, plucking at his companion's sleeve, 'methinks we are being watched.'

'All the better,' said Walter of Weybridge cheerfully. 'The sooner we join battle with these Saxon rats the better. There cannot be more than a handful of them, all told, and we shall cut them down mercilessly, as they deserve.'

'A splendid plan,' said the Sheriff complacently. 'Dead men can tell no tales, eh, Walter? And once Robin Hood is dead there can be no chance of the Prince finding out who *really* shot that arrow out of the crowd!' With an evil chuckle, the Sheriff dug Walter in the ribs with his plump elbow.

Suddenly, Walter checked his horse in the middle of the path, leapt from its back and examined the turf at his feet closely. On the green turf of the forest were one or two red spots, which laid an unmistakable trail down a narrow path to the left of them.

'The blood of an animal!' he cried. 'Someone has killed a deer not long since, and has carried it on his back along this trail. I dare hazard a guess that we are on the tracks of Master Robin now!'

The Sheriff wheeled his troop and led them down the narrow defile. Walter continued to examine the red trail in front of them closely. He was the first to see the carcass of a huge deer lying in the clearing ahead of them, and with a shout of joy he ran forward to examine it. Then he brandished an arrow in the air – an arrow, moreover, with the unmistakable green feather in its tip.

'What do you say to this?' he exulted. 'Robin's own arrow! And the carcass is still warm. It looks as if it had been thrown down in a hurry, by some varlet who heard us coming. See where his tracks lead out of the glade by that path!'

'Forward, men,' shouted the Sheriff, waving his own sword in a passable imitation of Walter. Whereupon the whole band, fifty strong, galloped lustily down the path, waving their swords and shouting Norman war-cries. The path broadened suddenly, and the Sheriff increased his pace. His horse was going at its very fastest speed when suddenly, quite without warning, there was a terrible whoop. The next moment, a figure in a green jerkin swung down upon the Sheriff out of the tree above his head and bore him, cloak, fur hat and all, off his mount to the ground. The Sheriff shrieked in horror, but his shrieks were lost in the general confusion and amazement. For scarcely had the Sheriff been unseated, when a red figure swung down upon Walter and bore him, also struggling, to the ground. A hundred devils seemed to be swinging like monkeys out of the trees, with wild shouts and cries, bearing the unprepared band off their horses. Most of the Sheriff's men were so terrified by these apparitions that they turned tail and fled for the safety of the town.

In vain the Sheriff yelled insults at them, and urged them to come to his rescue. With Robin's muscular fingers at his throat, he could only manage a strangled groan, which terrified his retainers still more. Robin's band were left with only twenty men to cope with, and even some of these were crazy with fear at the sudden assault. The only ones with the courage to resist were Walter of Weybridge, and strangely enough the Sheriff himself. Desperation gave him strength, and he battled with Robin mightily, using his blue cloak to muffle Robin's attacks and suffocate his face. At one moment Robin was lying on his back, with the Sheriff and three of his bravest men grappling with his arms and legs. It was Will Scarlett who saw his predicament, and wresting himself free from Walter of Weybridge, rushed to Robin's rescue.

'Thanks, Will,' gasped Robin. 'Ah, sirrah, have at you!' he cried, as Walter of Weybridge tried to take advantage of his exhaustion and smite him from behind. The fight was keen and savage: Tom Turpin received a dangerous cut on his forehead, which sent him fainting to the ground, and would have put him at the mercy of the Sheriff's brawniest man-at-arms but for Robin's prompt action in felling the enemy from behind with a blow off the flat of his sword. Robin himself was bleeding profusely from a dozen scratches, and his old wound was beginning to pain him, but his spirits and energy were such that he seemed to be in two places at once – rescuing his men here, there and everywhere. Alan-a-Dale, for all his elegant looks, fought like a tiger, and succeeded in holding five Normans at bay at once.

'Surrender, you Norman curs,' he gasped. 'Surrender, else you die!'

The Normans weakly flung down their weapons and begged for mercy.

'Cravens!' yelled the Sheriff. 'What can one man do against five. . . .'

His protests were cut short by Will Scarlett, who engaged him in such a ferocious duel with his sword that the fat Sheriff had no more breath to exhort his men, but had to concentrate on saving his own skin. Relentlessly, the Normans were beaten down by the superior Saxon fighters. Soon only a handful of them remained fighting: the rest had been struck down or pinioned, or had turned tail like their companions and fled from the battle. Of Robin's band, only Tom Turpin and Dan Shepheard were seriously injured.

'Do you surrender?' cried Will Scarlett to the Sheriff, forcing him back against a broad oak tree, and putting the point of his sword at his throat. The Sheriff rolled his eyes round for help; but now only Walter of Weybridge was fighting, and he was being sorely pressed by Robin.

'I surrender!' he gasped. 'It is a crime to treat the Sheriff of Nottingham so, but I have no choice.'

Grimly, Will Scarlett took his sword from him and bound the Sheriff limb by limb with a hefty length of rope. Then he threw him down among the other trussed Normans, who lay on the ground, cursing and swearing at their fate. Walter of Weybridge, too, had to surrender, for he could not fight on alone. However, he was arrogant enough to declare:

'If I had had a dozen men of my own spirit, or even half a dozen, you would never have defeated me, Robin of Locksley.'

'It is true that you prefer foul methods to an honest fight,' retorted Robin, as he bound the Norman's hands behind his back.

'Robin,' cried Alan-a-Dale eagerly, 'here is a piece of good fortune, indeed! A bag of gold hanging on the Sheriff's belt which would feed one poor family for a week!'

Robin's men set to, to search their prisoners, and found that most of the men-at-arms had a bag of gold hidden on them somewhere, whereas the Sheriff was positively loaded down with money-bags.

'All wrung out of the honest people of Nottingham by taxes, I'll be bound,' said Robin aside to Will. 'Well, we will see to it that the money goes back where it belongs.' Dextrously he cut the money-bags from the Sheriff's belt, and added them to the growing heap of canvas, with here and there the gleam of a gold coin. The Sheriff went purple in the face with rage, and his temper was not improved when Robin and Will hoisted him up into his saddle, still with his hands tied behind his back.

'Back to Nottingham, Sheriff,' said Robin gaily. 'You will reach it all the quicker for being the lighter of your money-bags. Your horse is tired, methinks, and cannot easily carry an extra burden.'

The Sheriff struggled impotently, but his twists and turns only resulted in his falling out of the saddle again on to the ground. Robin hoisted him up once more, and gave his horse a smart thwack on its rump. With a startled neigh, the horse set off back along the path at a fine pace, with the Sheriff bumping and swaying on its back.

'My compliments to Prince John,' shouted Robin merrily. 'And tell him to come and look for me himself next time.'

Then he hoisted the rest of the Sheriff's gang on to their mounts, and gave them in their turn a merry send-off. Once the sorry band of men-at-arms were out of sight, Robin and Will happily counted out the money they had gleaned.

'Enough and to spare, to buy you a fine new jerkin to reward you for your pains,' Will told Tom Turpin, who was nursing his wound on the bank. 'And you too, Dan Shepheard, a pair of fine leather boots for you.'

Robin's men contrived a stretcher on the backs of their horses and conveyed the wounded men back to the camp, where bandages and ointments were applied. In spite of their cuts and bruises, the men of Sherwood were jubilant at their victory, and Robin ordained that there should be a noble feast that evening to celebrate it.

OSWALD MONTDRAGON'S PLOT

While the merry men feasted in Sherwood, there was fury and anger in the Castle of Nottingham, at Robin Hood's impudence in defeating the Sheriff. Prince John watched the mournful procession toil up to the gates from his window.

'I fear me the Sheriff has failed in his mission,' he murmured to Oswald Montdragon, the most evil of his counsellors.

'The Sheriff is a fool,' replied Montdragon contemptuously. 'Your Highness would do well to entrust the Shrievalty of Nottingham to someone more fitted to occupy the position.' And Montdragon cast a meaning look at the Prince, who pretended not to notice it.

'He is a loyal fool,' replied Prince John. 'He seeks only

to serve me, and not himself.' The Prince in his turn cast a meaning glance at Oswald Montdragon.

By now the Sheriff's procession had drawn quite near, and Prince John could see clearly the woeful expression on the Sheriff's face, his hands tied behind his back, and his belt hanging empty of his moneybags. The Prince swore mightily, and demanded that he should be brought to see him immediately. The Sheriff tottered into the royal chamber, perspiration on his brow. He sank on his knees, and begged the Prince's mercy.

'They ambushed us, Your Highness,' he cried. 'No man could have done more than me to capture the knavish Robin Hood.'

Prince John tapped his foot angrily. 'Then why did you fail, Sheriff?' he exclaimed. 'You swore to lay hands on this criminal, and I believed you. Now you have left a dangerous man at large in my forest, with no means on earth of trapping him. If fifty men cannot capture a handful of Saxon adventurers, there is no guarantee that five hundred will, unless we burn down the whole forest.'

Oswald Montdragon stepped forward and with a vindictive glance at the Sheriff, whose position he coveted, he said boldly:

'There is only one way to catch a thief like Robin Hood, and that is to lay a trap. You say this Robin Hood is supposed to assist those in distress?' Oswald shot the question at Walter of Weybridge. The man-at-arms nodded sullenly.

'Excellent. Then we shall provide him with someone in distress to assist. With your permission, Your Highness, may I call forth the Maid Marian?'

Now there were at Court a dozen or so wards-inchancery, young maids whose fathers were dead, and whose great estates made them rich heiresses. The youngest of these, and by far the most beautiful, was Marian of Whitby, the golden-haired daughter of the dead Earl of Whitby. Forthwith she appeared before the Prince, her eyes modestly lowered before such august company. Prince John, who had been well primed in the part he was to play by Oswald Montdragon, gazed at her sternly.

'Marian of Whitby,' he said. 'We have received some grave tidings concerning you.'

Maid Marian started back in dismay. 'Your Highness,' she stammered. 'I know not what they may be. God grant it is not some sad news concerning my mother, the Lady Hilda.'

'Nay,' interposed Oswald Montdragon smoothly. 'The Lady Hilda is still in good health, but if you do not answer our questions . . .' His sentence trailed away significantly.

Marian turned pale, for since the death of her father she had had no relation in the world save her widowed mother, who dwelt in a convent near York and whom she had not seen for some years.

When Oswald Montdragon roundly accused her of treachery towards Prince John, she was so dismayed and confounded that she scarcely knew what to answer. He invented a whole string of trumpery charges and swore that unless she admitted all of them, both she and the Lady Hilda would forthwith be cast into prison.

'Oh, how can I prove my loyalty?' wept poor Marian.

Oswald Montdragon smiled cruelly.

'I am glad you are so reasonable,' he said, 'for there is

one way by which you can save yourself and your mother. If you were prepared to help us with a certain little matter, we might pardon you.'

Oswald Montdragon started to whisper in Marian's ear. The maid grew pale with terror and disgust at the dastardly plot which was unfolded, but she feared to cause some terrible harm to her mother if she protested.

'May Our Lady show me some way to thwart this evil plot,' she thought.

Robin Returns to Nottingham by Moonlight

While Oswald Montdragon plotted at the Castle of Nottingham and the Sheriff raged in vain against his defeat in the forest, there was much rejoicing at Robin Hood's camp. Wine flowed, and many were the toasts which were drunk to the health of the absent King Richard and Robin's father. It was Will Scarlett, ever thoughtful, who first raised the question of what was to be done with the gold which had been snatched from the Sheriff's money-bags.

'There is a princely fortune here,' he said, kicking the glittering heap with his foot so that the coins sparkled in the firelight. 'These ill-gotten gains do not belong to us, and we cannot rightly keep them. Surely the money should go back to those from whom it was stolen in taxes and levies – the poor people of Nottingham!'

'An excellent plan, Will!' cried Robin, leaping up and shovelling the coins briskly back into the sacks. 'This very moment we will restore what has been stolen to their rightful owners. Why, there will be such rejoicing in the poor homes of Nottingham tonight, as has not been seen since King Richard sailed for the Holy Land. We have robbed the rich to pay the poor, and the Normans will be white with rage when they learn to what use we Saxons have put their booty.'

Forthwith Robin mounted Troubadour, and slung a sack of gold on his back. Will Scarlett followed, with Alan-a-Dale bringing up the rear. The rest of the band remained behind, exhausted by the afternoon's battle. But Robin always had unlimited energy for a fresh escapade.

The three adventurers rode silently through the forest until they had left the trees behind, and the moon above their heads showed them a distant prospect of the city of Nottingham. In order to arrive unobserved, they guided their horses on to the grass verge, so that they made no sound as they bore down on the town. The town guards were sleepy at this late hour, and paid little heed to the three unknown travellers who muttered that they were merchants from the West Country. The gates swung back, and for the first time since the fateful day of the tournament, on the eve of his twenty-first birthday, Robin Hood set foot in Nottingham.

'First to the Weaver's family,' whispered Robin, 'for they must be our chief concern. Nat fears that his brood of children have scarcely enough bread to keep body and soul together. The wretched fellow sits all day in the forest and pines for news of them.'

'Beware, Robin,' whispered Will. 'I fear the house may be watched. 'Tis common knowledge by now that the Weaver has joined your band. The Sheriff's men may be looking out for Nat to return and visit his wife.'

But Robin only tossed his head angrily. 'You are forever

counselling caution, Will,' he answered impatiently, his voice rising slightly.

It was Alan-a-Dale the peace-maker, who soothed the two angry men, and persuaded Robin to make the Weaver's house his last port of call, so that if there was any need for a quick getaway, they would not have wasted all the gold. Then, in the cold moonlight, while all Nottingham slept, Robin, Alan and Will stole from house to house in the poorest quarter of the town, and laid a sack of gold coins on each door-step. To each sack they pinned the following note:

'Greetings to the poor people of Nottingham from Robin Hood, who has robbed the rich to pay the poor.'

'What a joyous surprise when they awake!' whispered Alan gleefully.

Now all the sacks save one were gone, and Alan was beginning to look restive. He kept glancing wistfully in the direction of the gate, until Will asked him outright what ailed him.

Alan-a-Dale blushed.

''Tis the Lady Lucy,' he confessed. 'I would fain leave some message for her at the house of her maid, Matilda, which lies just beside the gate. Have we time enough to spare?'

Robin Hood clapped Alan on the shoulder.

'All the time in the world!' he exclaimed airily. 'Together Will and I will find the Weaver's family. We will meet you at the gate in ten minutes' time.' So Alan left the two adventurers to fulfil the last part of their mission alone.

ATTACK AT THE WEAVER'S HOUSE

No one had observed the dark shape which lurked in the shadow of the gate, a shape that hardly seemed to breathe, and yet managed to dart silently from building to building, on the track of Robin Hood. For one second a white face was lit up by the moon, as the stranger crossed from one shadow to another: if Robin Hood had turned round then, he would have recognized his old foe, Walter of Weybridge! Fortunately, Walter was all alone; he had been bent on some nefarious errand of the Sheriff's when he overheard Robin and Will arguing. He had no time to summon help; in any case, he wanted to capture Robin Hood alone and gain the large reward which had been offered for the capture of Robin when Prince John outlawed him. So he dogged his enemies patiently, and waited for his chance to strike.

It came at last, when Robin and Will disappeared into the house of the Weaver's family, leaving their horses tethered outside. It was the work of a moment for Walter to cut the horses loose with his knife and send them flying off with two cruel bows of his stick. The noise of hooves on the cobbles brought Robin and Will rushing out of the hovel in which the Weaver's family were housed. Too late! Polly and Troubadour were galloping madly across the square, and right in the path of the outlaws, with a smile of triumph, stood Walter of Weybridge, drawn sword in his hand.

'Have at you, verminous bandit!' he shouted, brandishing his weapon and running at Robin. 'Awake, guards, awake! The terrible outlaw, Robin Hood, is here! Seize him!'

While the terrified Weaver's wife and her children crouched in the doorway, the people of Nottingham started to pour out of their houses, some in nightgowns, some in hastily pulled-on jerkins, some holding candles and all rubbing their eyes, wondering what all the noise was about. Half a dozen soldiers ran out from the gate house, only to see a stalwart man-at-arms grappling desperately with two muscular fighters in green jerkins. They paused in bewilderment. But when the muffled words 'Robin Hood' reached them, they needed no second bidding to dash forward, and try to apprehend the most dangerous criminal in the north.

The people of Nottingham suddenly became alive to the fact that two Saxon heroes were about to be captured by Norman cut-throats. With hoarse cries of rage, they flung themselves in the way of the soldiers, and so clogged their path that the men-at-arms, already weighted down by their mail, could make no headway.

All this time Robin and Will were struggling to get free of Walter and the two traitor Saxons who had broken from the ranks of the crowd, in the hopes of sharing in the reward if they helped Walter. In vain Robin and Will looked round for Troubadour and Polly – this time they did not even have one horse between them! And they could not hold off the Normans for ever.

It was at this moment that Alan-a-Dale, having delivered his missive to Matilda, emerged stealthily from her house, to find himself on the edge of a huge foray. His first thought was for Robin and Will – for no member of Robin's band would have dreamt of fleeing to save himself while their leader was in danger. Luck favoured him: for all at once he spied two terrified horses, sweating and panting by the gate, none other than the missing Troubadour and Polly. It was the work of a moment for Alan to seize their bridles and calm them with gentle soothing words. But now, how to contact Robin and Will, and let them know that he had their horses safe and sound? He looked desperately round him: the crowd was getting thicker and any moment reinforcements would arrive from the castle. There seemed no hope of breaking through, and in any case he was sure to be recognized as one of Robin's band. Just as he was deciding to throw caution to the winds and try to cut a passage through, he spied the eldest child of the Weaver, who had slipped away from his mother and was surveying the fight from the steps of a nearby house. Alan took a quick decision.

'Hist, lad,' he whispered as loudly as he dared. 'Will you do something to help save Robin Hood?'

The eyes which looked out of the boy's thin, sunken face were bright and intelligent.

'Try me and see,' was all he said.

'Then get this message to him,' said Alan. 'No matter what it costs you. Tell him that Alan-a-Dale has his horses at the gate, and if he can once make that point, we may yet see Sherwood again.'

Without another word the Weaver's boy slipped like a weasel through the crowd, while Alan uttered a fervent prayer to heaven that he might succeed in getting the message through. It was torture to listen to the fight from the outside and know that he could do nothing to help his leader.

All at once there were loud shouts and oaths from the centre of the square. There seemed to be some diversion: yes, it was the Sheriff himself, who had come post-haste from the castle to supervise, as he thought, the capture of the outlaw. The temporary distraction gave Robin and Will just the opportunity they needed. Emboldened by Alan's message, they feinted to the left, shook off Walter of Weybridge for a second, then ran like the wind through the back streets of the town. It was true that the Normans were only a couple of yards behind them: nevertheless, Robin knew Nottingham like the back of his hand and he was confident that he could shake them off.

'Follow me, Will,' he shouted. 'We'll show those Norman dogs a thing or two.' So saying, he dodged, ran, jumped, twisted and turned with such speed and agility that Will was panting to keep up with him. Would they ever reach the gate by this devious route? The Norman soldiers were now quite bemused, but Robin kept his head, and like an eel, slipped between two old houses, felt in the wall for a loose brick, and by some strange trick known only to himself, swung open a secret door which led them right out by the town gate.

Now it was only a few seconds before all three men were on their horses and belting for Sherwood as fast as they could go. The halloos and shouts of their pursuers grew fainter as the forest grew nearer. This time the Sheriff did not make the mistake of sending his men too far after them. He was beginning to think that no one could capture Robin within the forest itself – unless it was by treachery.

'Phew, that was a close shave!' panted Robin, as they plunged through the undergrowth which led to the hide-out.

'I must think of some way of rewarding the Weaver's boy,' murmured Alan. 'He is a brave lad, like his father.'

And in the Castle of Nottingham Oswald Montdragon tugged at his beard when he heard of the Sheriff's latest defeat at the hands of Robin Hood.

'Forsooth, Your Highness,' he said to the Prince. 'It will be interesting to see whether *my* plan for capturing this wily outlaw is more successful. Our dear Sheriff seems altogether baffled. Perhaps he finds his duties too *arduous* for him?' Oswald Montdragon smiled the quizzical smile which the Sheriff of Nottingham had begun to detest.

4

MAID MARIAN

SOME FOUR OR five days later, early one morning when the sun was high, and the birds in Sherwood were carolling their morning greeting to Robin Hood's band, a small procession could be seen winding its way through the forest. Ahead rode a soldier in armour with his visor down. Then came a litter drawn by two horses. Its velvet curtains were drawn; but from the richness of its trappings, it evidently contained some lady of high rank. Lastly came a rather humbler man-at-arms, who looked fearfully round him: none other than our old friend, Dickon Barleycorn.

This was the handsome cortège which Robin Hood spied from behind a tree as he rode through the forest, with his bow slung across his back, searching for a fat buck to shoot for his men's dinner. He drew rein at the sound of horses' hooves, and concealed himself and Troubadour behind a broad oak. It crossed his mind that here was some fat bird for the plucking – a merchant perhaps, on his way to the Fair, or a farmer on his road back from market, with his money-bags stuffed with gold. Robin's eyes glinted at the thought of a juicy piece of robbery, which, like the sheriff's gold, would benefit the poor of

Nottingham. But his arrow, poised in his bow, was stayed by the sound of a woman's voice.

''Tis mighty hot inside these velvet curtains,' said the voice plaintively. 'Good Sir Oswald, may I not draw them and enjoy the clear fresh air of the forest?'

'Hush, Maid Marian,' replied the leading soldier, 'Sherwood Forest is a dangerous place these days. It is not safe for your pretty face to be seen. Who knows what bandits may not spy you from behind these murky trees? Besides, the arch-brigand, Robin Hood, is always lurking to prey on innocent damsels.'

'Zounds!' muttered Robin angrily. 'You do me an injustice, my fine soldier. Robin Hood never yet hurt a hair of a lady's head.'

But Robin had no time to grumble further: for at that moment the bushes on the far side of the path parted, and four or five desperate looking rascals, brandishing daggers and swords, burst out. Oswald Montdragon's horse instantly reared up and, bucking spiritedly, cast off his rider. Montdragon fell heavily to the ground, where he lay without moving, apparently stunned and senseless. Dickon Barleycorn gave a shrill scream of terror, and springing from his horse, dashed wildly away into the woods, passing not an inch from Robin Hood's nose. Maid Marian flung open her velvet curtains and gazing wildly out, shrieked to the empty air:

'Help me! Help me! I am attacked by brigands!'

She did not have to shout long. Robin Hood soon heard her distraught cries and rushed to her assistance. First he launched two arrows at her attackers, and, in an instant, the foremost ruffians were lying groaning on the ground. Then he put his bugle to his lips and blew a loud blast, to summon assistance from his men. A mile away, in the valley, half a dozen brave fellows leapt up from the fire and flung themselves on to their horses. Soon the flower of Robin's band was thundering towards the scene of battle.

In the meantime, however, Robin was left to combat three ruffians single-handed, while Marian cowered in her litter and buried her head in her hands. With nimble thrust and cut, Robin held off his assailants, in spite of the fact that they were three to one.

'Fly, lady,' he shouted. 'There is still time to save yourself. I can hold these chickens off for another half an hour.'

Marian did not flee: however, there was no time for Robin to puzzle over the mystery. The fight was too fierce. He pinioned one of his attackers to the ground with his sword, then rushed at the other two with only his bare fists against their weapons. By sheer force, he wrested a dagger from the hand of the first, and slashed at him until the blood streamed from his jerkin and he collapsed on the ground. Then he whirled round, to meet the assault of one of the wounded men, who had struggled from the ground, despite the arrow in his breast, and flung himself towards him. For a moment the odds looked heavily weighted against Robin – with two men at his throat, and no sign of help. But Robin was not dismayed: like lightning he swung himself out of reach of their attacks, on to a low-lying branch of a tree, then proceeded to leap upon his last unwounded assailant and bear him down with a cry of triumph.

All this time Oswald Montdragon had lain senseless on the ground, but now his eyelids were beginning to flicker, and his body twitched slightly. Why did he not make any attempt to assist Robin against his attackers? Robin had no time to puzzle out the answer to this question either, for he was sore pressed, and his strength seemed to be failing. In the very nick of time, the sound of horses' hooves filled the forest, and a hail of arrows burst from the trees into the glade. With a cry of joy, Robin recognized Will Scarlett and Alan-a-Dale.

'You come in good time, my merry men,' he shouted. 'This little game is nearly over, but I doubt whether I could have finished it single-handed.'

'Well fought, brave Robin,' cried Will, as he neatly parried a blow and laid the last attacker low. 'Your bugle summoned us at the right moment.'

Breathlessly, Robin explained what had happened, as he helped Will and Alan to tie up the ruffians. Then he ran to the litter and tore open the curtains. But Maid Marian appeared to have fainted dead away. Robin chafed her wrists gently and was relieved to see the pink creep back into her white cheeks. Soon her eyelids were fluttering and she was asking weakly what had happened.

'There is nothing more to fear,' explained Robin, marvelling at her great beauty even as he spoke. 'We have beaten off your attackers, and you can go safely on your way.'

To his dismay Maid Marian only started to weep. 'Oh do not leave me,' she cried. 'I dare not go any farther in this forest. One of my men-at-arms has fled and the other lies senseless. Let me rest a while with you. I feel so weak and frightened. Supposing there were more brigands on the other side of Sherwood? Who would save me from them? Please, gentle sir, permit me to rest myself in your dwelling, and then help me on my road.'

Now, if Maid Marian had not been a maiden of more than usual loveliness, who gazed innocently and trustingly up at him, Robin Hood might have asked her how she knew that he dwelt in the forest. But he was so overcome by her beauty that he replied at once:

'Of course you shall rest with us, my lady, for you have been through a terrible ordeal.'

It was Will Scarlett, the ever-cautious Will, who said sharply to Robin:

'Do not forget that no stranger is allowed to set foot in our camp.'

'Peace, Will,' said Robin angrily. 'A truce on your discourtesy. This is no stranger, but a lady in distress.'

However, as a concession to Will, he agreed that Marian should be blindfolded, so that she should have no idea of the route which they took. The problem now remained of the wounded brigands, and also, of course, of Marian's escort, the soldier who still lay stunned upon the ground. Robin solved it in his usual lordly fashion. He bid the dozen of his followers who were clustered round bind all the wounded loosely, make rough stretchers, and convey them to the outskirts of the forest. There they were to be left until some charitable wayfarer appeared, some monk or pilgrim, who would escort them to the precincts of Nottingham. Oswald Montdragon's heavy inert body was hoisted on to his horse, and the mournful procession set off.

Robin Hood was in the highest spirits as he rode along beside Maid Marian's litter. He could not resist telling her, in answer to her apparently guileless questions, that he was in fact that Robin Hood on whose head Prince John had set such a price. He told her, boastfully, that it was the largest sum of money that Prince John had ever offered for anyone.

MARIAN TAKES HER COURAGE IN BOTH HANDS

Now all this time Maid Marian's heart was heavy. Never in her life had she met anyone so gallant and courteous as this outlaw. Marian's heart was won by his gentle and winning manners, as well as his handsome face. And this was the man she was sent to betray! Everything she said to him, every action, every gesture, was all part of the monstrous plot which Oswald Montdragon had outlined to her in the Castle of Nottingham. How different things had seemed then. Then it was a question of her mother's safety. Now it was a question of betraying the man whom already she felt that she loved. For Marian had sworn to Oswald Montdragon that she would discover the whereabouts of Robin Hood's secret hiding-place. She had agreed to take part in a false ambush, and had deliberately coaxed Robin into taking her back to his camp.

Oswald Montdragon had himself spurred his horse into the wild bucking and rearing with which he had seemed to fling off his rider, and during the whole of the fight he had lain in a sham faint. It was Oswald Montdragon himself who had hired the desperate ruffians who had lain in wait for Marian. Montdragon rightly guessed that Marian's screams of terror would bring forth the Lord of Sherwood to her assistance! Now it only remained for Marian to fulfil the last part of her bargain, and by discovering the position of the camp, enable Oswald Montdragon to capture the whole band. At that very moment, Oswald Montdragon was licking his lips in triumph as he roamed the forest waiting for Marian's return. Once he had taken Robin Hood, it would only be a matter of time before he persuaded Prince John to make him Sheriff of Nottingham. A further prize would be the hand in marriage of Marian of Whitby herself!

All this was mercifully hidden from Robin as he made his way down the winding track to the secret valley. He only knew that the sun seemed brighter, the grass greener, the bird-song sweeter, because Maid Marian was beside him.

Once within the valley, Robin immediately ordered the finest venison to be cooked in Marian's honour, while Alan-a-Dale was bidden to sing and strum his lute gently to please the lady's ear. Only Will Scarlett sat slightly apart from the rest, brooding: for, if Marian was the innocent damsel she seemed, why had she dropped a number of white pebbles from her litter, as she was carried along towards the camp, thus making it easy for anyone to trace the path again? Will had not said anything to Robin, whom he rightly judged to be dazzled by Marian's presence. But when his sharp eyes first detected the presence of the pebbles, he made it a point to go back along the route and pick them all up again.

'You may be innocent, my lady,' he thought. 'And again you may not. Either way, it is best that you should leave no trace of your visit to Robin Hood's camp.' And he threw all the pebbles away into the bushes.

By now the feast was in full swing. The fire leapt up, and Much the Miller turned the great haunch of meat on the spit. From the bottom of her heart Marian felt that there had never been such a merry life as the life of the men of Sherwood. How she would love to have shared it with

Robin! With every passing moment it was becoming more and more impossible to betray him and his band. As Alan-a-Dale's last song died away upon his lips, a sad and lovely ditty which he had composed to the memory of the Lady Lucy, Marian took a brave decision.

'Men of Sherwood,' she said in a loud voice, which made everyone turn their heads. 'Hearken to me now, and of your mercy, forgive me for the great wrong I was about to do you.'

Robin's band exchanged astonished looks: for what wrong could this beautiful maiden have planned? Robin himself turned pale, and said fervently:

'Lady Marian, do not speak, I pray you. You are feverish and unwell after your ordeal.'

Marian laid her hand on Robin's arm and quieted him. 'There was no danger to me,' she said gravely. 'Only to you, brave Robin Hood. For you must know, Robin, Will Scarlett, Alan, Tom – all you noble outlaws – that I was sent hither to betray you!' At this there was a great murmuring among the band, and an outbreak of confused protests. No one knew what to think, whether they should condemn Marian for a black-hearted wench, or praise her for her courage in confessing to them. With an imperious gesture, Marian bade them hear her further.

'It is true,' she said, with her head held high. 'Oswald Montdragon, the greatest villain at court, persuaded me to take part in his wicked plot. I do not ask you to understand – only to pardon a poor weak maid, who was terrified out of her wits by their threats and sought to save herself and her lady mother from harm.'

Marian's voice suddenly faltered and burying her face in her hands, she started to weep. Robin comforted her gently. Between sobs she finished her story, and confessed how Oswald Montdragon had used her mother as a weapon to terrify her into submission; piece by piece the pitiful tale was revealed – the false ambush, the hired brigands, the swoon of Oswald Montdragon, which was in fact no swoon at all, and the white pebbles dropped in the forest to mark the route to the camp. When all was revealed, Marian hung her head and murmured in a stifled voice:

'Forgive me, gentle sirs, for since I have been with you in Sherwood, I have been filled with such love for you and for your leader, that I can no longer betray you. I will go back to Oswald Montdragon and tell him that he must find some other tool to do his evil deeds, for Marian of Whitby will no longer serve him.'

'Bravely spoken!' cried Tom Turpin, and his shout was taken up by all the rest of the men. Only Will Scarlett was silent. Robin rounded on him angrily.

'Do you alone hold your peace, Will?' he cried. 'Will you punish a young maid for her weakness, and her great love for her mother?'

Will Scarlett flushed and retorted furiously:

'Never shall Will Scarlett bear such a reproach, Robin of Locksley. You insult my honour by speaking thus.' And leaping to his feet, he knelt down before Maid Marian and kissed the hem of her blue robe. 'As long as you live I will serve you, Marian of Whitby,' he said in a low voice, 'for I have seen many beautiful maids, but none so beautiful as you.' Then Will turned to Robin. 'I was but casting around in my mind how best we can fool Oswald Montdragon, without harming the Lady Hilda of Whitby,' he said coldly.

Robin had the grace to look ashamed. He begged Will's pardon for his words.

'It is my old fault,' he said sadly. 'Speaking first and thinking afterwards. What should I do without you, Will?'

Thus the two friends were reconciled. Then Will revealed to the whole camp that he had himself gathered up the white pebbles in the forest and cast them away. Many were the exclamations of admiration and wonder at Will's quick wits! Robin Hood felt even more ashamed of his harsh words to his friend, when Will unfolded a plan for getting Marian safely back to Nottingham, without arousing the suspicions of Oswald Montdragon. Will suggested that Marian should be sent back blindfolded as she had come, and should tell Montdragon that her white pebbles had been discovered by one of the band, who had thrown them away. It was after all no more than truth, Will pointed out. Marian was also to exaggerate the numbers of Robin's band so that the Sheriff would be even more reluctant to lead a second attack.

Gratefully, Marian agreed to do as Will said. And now the time had come for her to bid farewell to Robin's camp and return to the castle. So Marian drew a little apart with Robin.

'Have you truly forgiven me?' she asked him softly.

'Ah, Marian,' said Robin. 'If I were not a penniless outlaw, I would ask you to share my life in the forest. But what inheritance have I to offer you now except Sherwood? What roof over your head except a log hut? What food except the royal venison stolen from Prince John? What life indeed except the rough and dangerous life of an outlaw? Come back to me, Marian, when I am Robin of Locksley again: for you must have no more dealings with Robin Hood.'

'Do not speak thus,' exclaimed Marian. 'But let me share your life in the forest, Robin, for I can imagine nothing sweeter. What care I for castles and earldoms, when love is at stake?' And Marian pleaded with Robin to be allowed to stay. Gently Robin persuaded her that her duty lay with her mother, who would surely suffer if her daughter went to live in Sherwood with the outlaws. So, weeping and disconsolate, Marian entered her litter once more, allowed herself to be blindfolded, and set forth on her dangerous mission to trick Oswald Montdragon. Robin's band waved sadly good-bye, while Robin himself sat silently by the fire, feeling as if his heart had gone with her.

OSWALD MONTDRAGON SUSPECTS

Marian was a girl of spirit, and after a short while she staunched her tears on the white cloth which blindfolded her; she told herself that the best way to help Robin Hood was not to weep, but to fool Montdragon – no easy task, for he had eyes like a lynx and missed nothing. It seemed hours before her litter was roughly thrown off balance, and her horses checked by a strange hand.

'Is it you, Sir Oswald?' inquired Marian cautiously, for she could see nothing through the thick cloth, and had indeed allowed her palfreys to guide her wherever they wished, trusting to the animals' instinct to take her towards Nottingham.

''Tis I, Maid Marian,' said the hated voice, and the

cloth was torn from her eyes. Marian composed her face to a suitable expression of relief.

'Alas, good Knight,' she said, 'I have been so affrighted. Those brigands used me so roughly – I never thought I should see decent Christian folk again.'

Oswald Montdragon took her bridle and guided her horse to the clearing where he had been lying in wait. To her secret joy, Marian noticed that they were by now right on the edge of the forest, and many miles from Robin's camp. Pleased with her success, Marian was longing to pour out her false tale to Oswald Montdragon, but he, for some reason of his own, would not allow her to speak at all until they reached the castle. Marian's high spirits sank slightly when she discovered that she was to relate her story in front of a veritable jury, consisting of Prince John, the hostile Sheriff, and Guy of Gisborne, as well as Montdragon himself. But her love for Robin spurred her on, and she was able to spin a pretty tale of how the outlaws had ill-treated her, particularly when one of them – that ruffian they call Will Scarlett – had discovered that she was scattering white pebbles to mark her track.

'Then you mean that in spite of all my plans you have no idea where the camp is?' shouted Oswald Montdragon. His swarthy face blackened, and he grasped Marian's wrist so tightly that she cried out with pain. The Sheriff saw a good opportunity to score off his enemy, Montdragon.

'Do not bully the girl, Montdragon,' he said fussily. 'She is doing her best to tell us what happened. It was unfortunate that the outlaws discovered the pebbles, but of course,' the Sheriff sighed, 'I always did think your plan was over ambitious. Perhaps you were taking a little too much on yourself.' And he glanced at the Prince, hoping that the shaft had gone home. There was nothing Prince John disliked more than the suggestion that one of his servants was overreaching his position. But Prince John was tired of his barons squabbling round him: Montdragon was a tyrant and the Sheriff was an inefficient fool. There did not seem to be much to choose between them. As for the girl, she was obviously terrified out of her wits, and quite useless.

'Take the maid away,' he said testily, waving his hand. Two soldiers immediately stepped forward. But Marian was determined not to let the opportunity slip.

'Oh, Your Highness,' she said. 'Is my mother now safe? Can I leave the court and return to the convent where she dwells?'

'Alas, the poor Lady Hilda,' said Prince John, in a voice of assumed sadness. 'We have had news from York this very hour that some fever has carried her off. God rest her soul.' The Prince piously crossed himself, then added kindly, 'But of course have no fear, Marian, you shall remain here under our protection. It was your dying mother's last wish. We shall find some noble lord for you to wed.'

But Marian hardly heard what he was saying. Then her mother was dead! Had died, no doubt, before she set out for Sherwood! She had been duped, tricked, deceived, by these cold-hearted plotters.

'Thank God I did not betray them!' The words burst from her lips before she could stop herself. Then, realizing what she had said, Marian blushed red, and corrected it to: 'Thank God I did not betray her.' To her relief, no one seemed to have noticed the slip, and she was allowed to retire to her chamber with her grief. Her tears alarmed Prince John, and he was glad to have her out of his sight.

'It was a scurvy trick to play,' he muttered. 'Oswald Montdragon, I should never have listened to you. The poor girl loved her mother, and we should not have used her to decoy the outlaws, when the Lady Hilda was already dead. In any case the plot failed.'

'Yes,' chimed in the Sheriff. 'To threaten the poor maid with the death of her mother on the very day her mother actually died! You have no heart, Montdragon.' And the Sheriff, wiping away an imaginary tear, tried very hard to look as if he did have a heart. Oswald Montdragon said nothing, but, bowing deeply to the Prince, backed out of the room.

A moment later, he was climbing the steep stairs which led to the chamber of the maids of the court.

It was lucky that he could not hear the conversation in the maids' chamber, between Marian and her closest friend, the black-eyed Barbara Nevill. This damsel had acquired the nickname of Black Barbara at court – not only for her sparkling black eyes and jet black hair, which showed her French ancestry – but also for her love of stirring up trouble and her sharp tongue. Only the gentle Marian refused to believe any evil of her, and gave her her warmest friendship and her confidences. She little suspected the jealousy which seethed in Barbara's heart at the tale which she unfolded. Barbara could not bear to think that Marian, gentle, soft-hearted Marian, had won the love of this brave outlaw.

'Ah, if only I could meet with a man like that!' she thought. 'Someone worthy of my steel!' And forthwith she made a secret vow to win Robin Hood from Marian. But outwardly she only said:

'Oh, Marian! What good fortune! Was he indeed marvellously handsome?'

It was at this moment that Oswald Montdragon, ascending the stairs, pushed open the door slightly and overheard the last sentence.

'Aha!' thought Oswald Montdragon, 'so these rough brigands were not so ill-favoured as our demure Maid Marian would have us believe. I must hear more.' And he bent his ear to the crack in the door. His luck was out. Marian simply replied:

'Peace now, Barbara, and let me say my prayers for the repose of the soul of my mother. To think that they let her die without summoning her daughter to her side! Alack, poor lady.'

Oswald Montdragon knocked loudly on the door and entered. He found Marian on her knees, with Black Barbara spinning in the window.

'I have come to give you my condolences, Maid Marian,' he said smoothly. 'It is grievous news.'

Marin could not keep all the hatred which she felt for Montdragon out of her glance.

'It is indeed kind of you, Sir Oswald,' she replied, smoothing her gown. Then she turned her head away, and began to finger the leaves of her prayer book.

'Nevertheless,' thought Montdragon, as he bowed and left her, 'there is some mystery here. The Lady Marian could not altogether conceal some secret elation in the forest. Then there was that muffled cry, "Thank God I did not betray *them*", which she thought to cover up with tears and exclamations. Lastly, this reference to a marvellously handsome man. Methinks I shall have to keep a close watch on my Lady Marian – and perhaps

that way I shall at last secure the capture of this knave,
Robin Hood.'

5

LITTLE JOHN JOINS THE BAND

AFTER OSWALD MONTDRAGON's plot, Robin and his band kept a sharp look-out for any further tricks which the villians of Nottingham Castle might try to play upon them. From time to time bold youths would seek them out, and ask to join their band, but Robin made it a rule that they should prove their good faith by some deed of daring. In this way many fine adventures were had, and much rich booty was plucked from the wealthy wayfarers through the forest, all of which was distributed secretly among the poor of Nottingham.

The poor wretches who had been starving under the Sheriff's exactions came to bless the name of Robin Hood for his generosity. They never knew when they might not wake up to find a sack of gold, or a silver goblet, gleaming on their doorsteps with this message pinned to it:

'Greetings from Robin Hood, who robs the rich to pay the poor.'

Of all the escapades by which Robin Hood gained new recruits to his band, none was merrier than that which won the allegiance of Little John. It all began one sunny afternoon in spring, a month or so after Robin had said a sad farewell to Marian. Robin was lounging idly in the camp, while all around him his men busied themselves with their various duties – Much the Miller was preparing the meat for the evening meal, Will Scarlett was working out some complicated system for sounding an alarm when an enemy approached the camp, and Alan-a-Dale was strumming mournfully on his lute as usual, dreaming of his lady love. Robin Hood felt ripe for some adventure.

It came even sooner than he had expected: a great arrow whistled through the air, and landed in the ground at his feet. Robin examined the arrow, and instantly recognized it as the black-feathered arrow which the band had agreed to shoot when some stranger was approaching and danger threatened. A few minutes later Tom Turpin arrived panting and breathless, with the news that an enormous man, 'A giant, no less,' had been sighted a mile away and was coming nearer with huge strides.

'He seems to know his way,' gasped Tom. 'I fear me he comes from the Sheriff or that crew in Nottingham Castle who are after our blood.'

Robin seized his quiver of arrows and his bow, slung them across his back and ran nimbly up the slope which led to the secret exit. Will Scarlett shouted after him to be careful and take someone with him, but Robin retorted:

'One outlaw against one enemy. We don't use the Sheriff's methods here.'

The forest was still and quiet, and Robin sloped silently through the undergrowth for a mile or so without finding any sign of a visitor. Then, on the banks of one of the many streams which coursed through Sherwood, he came on some footprints in the moss. Robin was well skilled in wood lore. He saw at once that either the footprints belonged to a strange sort of animal, or else the man he was tracking had the largest pair of feet that ever a human being owned.

'This is a joyful quest,' thought Robin. 'Methinks I am likely to find a doughty fighter at the end of it.' A moment later he spied his victim on the opposite bank of the stream, standing beside a narrow plank which served as a bridge. Yes, Tom Turpin had not exaggerated! This was a giant of a man, with a giant of a bow to match, slung across his broad back.

'Ahoy there, stranger!' shouted Robin, cupping his hands.

The unknown turned and cast a silent, speculative gaze at the slim figure on the opposite bank.

'Greetings to you, my young friend,' he said in a slow deep voice.

Robin was rather annoyed by this form of address – for was he not Lord of Sherwood, and were not all visitors to Sherwood his subjects? To be called a 'young friend' hardly suited his new dignity.

'What is your business in Sherwood, giant?' he shouted.

The large man gazed at him again, that slow enigmatic look which seemed to take in everything around him. After a minute he replied in the same deep, ponderous tones:

'What is that to do with you, mannikin?'

Now this time Robin really was annoyed. It was bad enough to be called 'young', but 'mannikin'! He was devoutly thankful that none of his men had heard.

'Everything in Sherwood concerns me, fat one!' said Robin impudently. 'So answer up, and tell me what you are after.'

The giant surveyed Robin once more. 'At this very

moment, little man,' he said, 'I am wondering whether to cross the bridge and throw you into the river, or just tip you gently into the water from here with this stout staff of mine.' And the giant indicated the broad oak staff which he held in his other hand.

'That's good,' said Robin laughing, but taking care at the same time to step back out of range. 'That's good! Throw *me* into the river, indeed. I am the Lord of Sherwood Forest, and no one even crosses this bridge without first bowing to my authority. Come on, giant, bow that stiff neck of yours, or before you are much older you will find yourself in the very water with which you are threatening me.'

'Little man, little man,' said the giant, wagging one large finger. 'You are taking too much on yourself for your size. If I choose to cross this bridge, there is no man this side of the Scottish border who can stop me.'

'Come on then, giant, and see,' shouted Robin joyfully, cutting himself a staff from a nearby thorn bush. 'Let's put the matter to the test and see whether or no I am Lord of Sherwood.'

'Willing and ready, little man,' shouted the giant in return, with a smile which creased his huge face from ear to ear. 'Willing and ready.' The giant threw down his quiver and bow, and tested his staff, bending it and cutting the air this way and that, so that the nearby branches shook. Robin in his turn tested his newly-fashioned staff before taking up his position at one end of the bridge.

The two fighters smiled at one another. Neither moved.

'Ready, giant?' cried Robin.

'Ready enough, little man,' answered the giant, and he

started to lumber forward, his great weight shaking the frail plank which served as a bridge. Robin looked strangely slight beside him, but he was putting his trust in strong muscles and quick wits to defeat his adversary. He knew that he could dance rings round most of the Nottinghamshire yokels, whatever their weight and size, and he felt confident that he could do the same with this stranger.

The Fight on the Bridge

But the stranger's first blow of his staff, a mighty well-delivered blow which narrowly missed Robin and came down with a thwack upon the swaying plank, showed Robin that he was up against a more formidable opponent than a rustic farmer.

Crash! Robin retaliated with a blow which would have overbalanced a lesser man and toppled him into the stream. Not so the stranger: nimbly he leapt back, as if he were a mere stripling, and let the whole weight of Robin's staff fall upon the bridge. Then he rushed forward and placed his own weapon squarely across Robin's, so that the gallant Lord of Sherwood could do nothing but retreat a pace or two, and try to get his aim again.

'Ha, ha, mannikin,' panted the giant, 'you did not expect to find me so nimble, I'll be bound. Others have made that mistake ere now, and there is not one of them that has not regretted it.'

'You boast now, but I will make you eat your words,' cried Robin, and so saying, he sprang free from the giant's clutches and aimed a swift, deadly blow at his enemy. This time the giant did not quite succeed in avoiding all contact: he received a glancing blow on the shoulder, of which, however, he appeared to take as little notice as of a fly. Before Robin had quite recovered from the effort of launching his blow, he was being belaboured by a series of heavy thwacks on his own head, which made him dart quickly backwards to the safety of his end of the bridge.

'Frightened, eh?' shouted the giant, his great voice booming across the stream. 'Come forward again, little man, and see what I have in store for you.'

Robin's blood boiled at the suggestion that he was frightened.

'Take that!' he yelled. 'And that! And that!'

In a blind fury, Robin managed to direct four or five hard-hitting blows at his opponent, which made even this man of iron blench. Now the fight was fast and furious, with blows being given and received on both sides which would have quite finished off two lesser fighters. Neither side appeared to have the advantage for long. If Robin was pressed back to his side one moment, the giant was forced back the next. And still the champions had breath enough to taunt each other!

By this time, Tom Turpin and Will Scarlett, who had followed Robin at a discreet distance, had caught up with their friend and were watching the battle from behind two trees. Tom Turpin, full of loyalty to Robin, would have dashed forward and attacked the stranger. But Will, who knew Robin's nature better, restrained him.

'He would never forgive you,' he whispered, 'for this is a foeman worthy of his steel, and Robin had ever a liking for a good fight with quarter staves. See, Tom, what bulging muscles that great giant has! We could use those in our camp, to chop down trees.'

'And smite down sheriffs!' added Tom Turpin with a smile. But he respected Will's opinion and made no further move to help Robin.

Meanwhile the fight on the bridge had not abated in fierceness in the very least. Neither side showed any sign of tiring. It was Robin who showed the first sign of weakness when he faltered slightly, and seemed about to fall. Was his strength failing? The giant was quick to press home the advantage with a sudden lunge and half a dozen flailing blows of his staff. On the instant, Robin had wriggled sideways, eluded the giant's blows, and even as the big man sought to regain his balance, given him a mighty push which sent him flying into the stream!

It was a fine end to the battle, and Robin stood panting on his staff as he surveyed the struggling figure in the water.

'Well, now who is Lord of Sherwood?' he said triumphantly.

'Give me a hand out of this water,' was all the giant said. 'I am too heavy a burden to struggle out by myself.'

Robin bent down and stretched out a hand. The next thing he knew, he, too, was gasping and spitting out mouthfuls of icy water, while the giant was clambering out by the bank, giving great bellows of hearty laughter.

'Brains, my little man,' he cried. 'Brains – it often succeeds where brawn fails.'

Robin laughingly admitted that he had been outwitted.

'But I warrant that your brawn does not often fail,' he added.

'You are a fighter after my own heart, lad,' said the big man. 'I would as soon cross staffs with you as with anyone from this accursed county of Nottingham. And I freely avow that, but for that little trick of mine, you would have fairly had the best of me. Let us shake hands on it.'

So Robin Hood and the huge stranger, both dripping wet, but now quite reconciled, solemnly shook hands in the middle of the forest and swore a pact of friendship.

'Can you tell me something, lad?' asked the stranger after a while, just as Tom Turpin and Will Scarlett were thinking it was time to come out of hiding and join their leader. 'Can you tell me where dwells this famous Robin Hood they talk so much about in this part of the country? I have a mind to meet him.'

All at once Robin's suspicions returned. After all, who was this stranger? He was a stout fighter, and had a pretty wit. That was all he knew. Something of Robin's feelings must have shown on his face, for the stranger patted him on his damp shoulder – a pat which was more like a buffet because of the size of the hand and the muscular arm behind it.

'Nay, lad, don't be disquieted. If you are one of his band, you may say so straight out. For I have a strong desire to throw in my lot with this famous outlaw who robs the rich to pay the poor. He has the sort of spirit I admire. I have been in some trouble in my own county and must lie low for a while.'

'What sort of trouble?' asked Robin.

'I tell thee freely, lad, I was too outspoken in praising our good King Richard, and criticizing his brother, that poor-spirited Prince John, whom they dare to call Regent of our country.'

Robin sprang to his feet and stretched out his hand for the second time.

'Stranger,' he said, 'whoever you are, you are welcome

to Sherwood! All loyal subjects of King Richard can find a home with Robin Hood and his band.'

The stranger's jaw dropped open, and he gazed at Robin in amazement.

'You are not – you cannot be Robin Hood himself?' he stammered, gaping for all he was worth. 'I had thought Robin to be an old man well tried in years. Was it you who robbed the Sheriff of all his gold, and sent him back to the castle with a note to Prince John pinned on his breast? You see, the fame of your exploits has spread to foreign parts.'

'I am indeed he,' said Robin with a smile. 'I have an old head on young shoulders, or rather' – he pointed to Will Scarlett who was approaching – 'this is my head, who does my thinking for me. Will, Tom, this noble fighter wants to join our band. What say you?'

'Agreed!' cried Tom enthusiastically, throwing his cap in the air. 'What do they call you, fellow?'

'I am really called John the Smith,' said the stranger, modestly. 'But for my great size, men have christened me Little John.'

'Then Little John you shall be! Welcome to Sherwood, Little John! Come now to my camp, and meet the rest of my band.'

THE RIVAL BRIGANDS

Little John proved a most popular member of the camp. 'Willing and ready' was his motto: and his gigantic strength was always at their disposal to cut down trees and heave logs. It was Little John himself who pointed out that his membership of the band had never been tested by any feat of daring.

'What,' cried Robin Hood. 'Do you not call our fight a feat of daring? Shame on you, Little John. It was the hardest fight I have ever fought.'

Little John smiled but would not be persuaded.

'I would fain show my worth to you in some other way than pulling you into the stream,' he said with a smile. 'How say you if I set out by myself to hold up some rich merchant and pillage him?'

Now Robin Hood was always loath to see anyone set out on an adventure without accompanying them, but he understood that Little John was anxious to prove himself in the eyes of the rest of the merry men. So he watched the big man stalk off through the forest, with only his bow and a quiverful of arrows to protect him, and did not try to accompany him.

It seemed to Little John that he had walked at least a hundred leagues before ever he heard the sound of a human voice. He peered through the undergrowth and spied a plump gentleman in a fur-trimmed cloak, astride a fine white mule, finely caparisoned in velvet and gold. To Little John's observant eyes, one or two money-bags were clearly visible hanging from the richly adorned saddle.

'Booty!' said Little John to himself, smacking his lips.

He drew an arrow from his quiver, which he fitted carefully to his bow. He was just on the point of loosing it into the trees above the plump gentlemen's head, hoping to give him a good fright, which would make him fall from his horse, or at any rate panic, when to his amazement, from the opposite side of the path, an identical arrow whizzed out of the bushes and landed not an inch from Little John's face! The surprise was such that Little John stood quite still for a second, hardly knowing what to do.

Not so the plump merchant – he bellowed and bawled for help, then shrieked and shouted for mercy. Altogether he made such a noise that it was a wonder the whole of Nottingham did not hear him. There was not a moment to lose if Little John was to snatch his booty! He bared his dagger from the sheath at his belt, flung down his bow, and rushed out into the clearing.

Imagine his bewilderment when he was confronted by a ragged boy, not more than twelve years old, holding an enormous sword, so heavy that he could hardly lift it.

'Take another step and you die!' said the stripling bravely, trying to wave the sword in Little John's face. Little John hesitated in the face of this unexpected hazard. It was one thing to rush at a grown man with his dagger – quite another to attack a mere child. All this time the plump merchant was being quietly and efficiently robbed on the other side of the clearing by a fellow in a brown jerkin, with a hood over his head.

'Let me be, boy!' shouted Little John, enraged at the idea of being balked of his prey. He brushed the child aside, sword and all, and ran towards the merchant, who was praying loudly on his knees for mercy, while his attacker counted his gold coins on to the grass.

'Have at you!' cried Little John, circling round his opponent. The stranger leaped up and lunged at Little John with his dagger.

The merchant took advantage of their fight to gather up his rich robes, cram what money he could into his pockets, and run like a rabbit into the nearest undergrowth. Meanwhile all his jewels and riches lay in a gleaming heap between the two fighters. Little John soon realized that he was facing a practised swordsman.

'You would, would you?' he growled, neatly parrying a savage thrust which had all but slipped beneath his guard. His opponent said nothing, but occasionally emitted a slight grunt from between his closed lips when one of Little John's more weighty blows had scratched him. It was Little John who brought the fight to an unexpected end by exclaiming, under his breath, after one particularly savage exchange of thrusts:

'Well fought, my friend, we could do with you in Robin Hood's band!'

Instantly his opponent threw away his weapon and knelt down at Little John's feet. To Little John's utter astonishment, he clutched at his jerkin and begged his pardon for having attacked him.

'Never would I have raised my sword against you if I had known that you were one of Robin Hood's men,' cried the stranger. 'I am Dickon Barleycorn, and it is my fervent desire to join the merry band of Sherwood. Take me to Robin Hood, sir, and I will turn over all the gold which I have amassed these past months to Robin Hood's coffers.'

At this, the child came forward and piped up:

'Yes, take us to Robin Hood's camp and we will give him all our treasure!'

Little John felt that there was some mystery connecting this strange pair – the rough, bearded man, with a desperate hunted look in his face, who called himself Dickon Barleycorn, and the fair-faced young boy, lively and intelligent enough, but so thin that his arms and legs were like match-sticks. However, he agreed to conduct them to Robin's camp and allow them to seek admission.

Bob the Weaver's Boy tells his story

As the ill-assorted companions entered the valley the first mystery was solved. The boy flung down his sword and ran helter-skelter down the slope towards Nat the Weaver, who was dozing by the fire.

'Father!' he cried. 'Oh, Father! How long is it since I have set eyes on you!'

'Bob, my boy Bob!'

Nat the Weaver rubbed his eyes, fearing that he was dreaming. Could this really be his eldest son, holding out his arms to him in Sherwood?

Bob the Weaver's boy, between tears and laughter, explained how he had fled from Nottingham after the fatal night on which Robin Hood and Will Scarlett had nearly been captured outside the Weaver's house. Then for many days and weeks he had wandered quite alone in the Forest of Sherwood, drinking from the streams, and eating berries, or the occasional rabbit which he had managed to snare. His one thought had been to contact Robin Hood's band, where he felt instinctively that he would find his father. But fortune had not favoured him, and never once had he even heard the chink of a bridle, which might have meant that Robin's men were riding near. Twice he had had to hide from the Sheriff's men and the forest rangers, and once had narrowly escaped being trapped by Walter of Weybridge himself, travelling on one of his sinister errands for his master.

Then, one evening when the sun was sinking and the poor homeless lad was beginning to think that he must find somewhere to lay his head for the night – some empty tree-trunk, or grassy hollow – he had run right into the arms of a wild-eyed man, with an unkempt beard and ragged clothes. They stared into each other's faces: the starving man and the starving boy. Both had a sort of desperate courage in their expressions, as if they had suffered so much that the future could hold nothing worse.

'Are you from the Sheriff?' asked the boy at last.

He felt instinctively that this ragged maniac could hardly be one of the Sheriff's men, and yet at the back of his mind he dimly recollected having seen his face, plumper, more contented, among the Sheriff's retainers.

'I am Dickon Barleycorn,' said the man. 'Formerly one of the Sheriff's men-at-arms and, since a few weeks past, a common outlaw. Alas, young fellow, I was a cowardly sort of soldier, and always fled at the first sign of trouble.' The man sighed. 'Again and again I tried to overcome my failing,' he said. 'It is my ambition to join Robin Hood's band. Yet I did not even have the courage to save him from Oswald Montdragon's conspiracy; for when Robin fell into the trap of the false ambush, what did I do? Did I stand by his side? Alack, I fled into the undergrowth, where I have lurked ever since like the rat that I am. Robin Hood would never accept a coward such as me among his men.'

Young as Bob the Weaver's boy was, he was sensitive enough to realize the world of bitterness that lay behind Dickon Barleycorn's sad little tale. He put his hand into his, and asked Dickon trustingly if he would look after him, because he was afraid to be all alone by himself in the forest.

The lad's confidence raised Dickon's spirits a little, and as the days went by and Bob showed him how much he admired him and looked up to him, Dickon began to feel more of a man than he had felt since the fatal wave of blind panic he experienced in his first armed skirmish at the age of sixteen. He would instruct Bob in the arts of swordplay and archery, and teach him how to bring down the deer which raced through the forest, for their dinner. Caring for Bob, and thinking of the boy's safety rather than his own, Dickon's courage grew until, as we have seen, he had sufficient spirit to fight Little John himself, although formerly the very sight of the giant would have been enough to make him turn tail.

'And right well you fought,' said Little John, when Bob the Weaver's boy had finished his story. 'Dickon Barleycorn, I am proud to be your comrade, if Robin will admit you to our band.'

Robin smiled and clapped Dickon on his shoulder.

'You have indeed changed from that timid, cowering soldier who was so frightened by my magic on Christmas Eve,' he said with a laugh. 'Welcome to our band, Dickon Barleycorn – from now on you are one of us. Anyone who can hold his own with Little John needs no further testimonial as a fighter. As for you, young fellow-me-lad, we know that you are a trusty messenger, and you can be most useful to us here. Welcome to Sherwood, young Weaver, you, too, are one of us.'

So it was that Dickon Barleycorn and Bob the Weaver's boy joined the merry men. They added a goodly store of treasure to Robin's coffers, which they had gained by their own robberies while they had been together. All this was distributed in Nottingham secretly, and you may be sure that one particularly large sack found its way to the doorstep of the Weaver's wife. On the corner of the usual message of greetings from Robin Hood was a tiny sign, with the shakily pencilled words:

'Bob, his mark.'

Thus the Weaver's wife knew that her eldest son was safe, and rejoiced.

6

A TRAITOR IN THE CAMP

'THE SHERIFF has enough things to think about without concerning himself further with the merry men of Sherwood,' said Robin Hood to Will Scarlett one day, when they had heard nothing from their enemy for many weeks. 'I vow he has quite forgotten the existence of Robin Hood.'

Will Scarlett shook his head gloomily as he trimmed his arrows.

'Do not count on it, Robin,' he replied. 'The Sheriff will not sleep safe in his bed until he has you and all your band by the heels. As for Oswald Montdragon – that black heart of his conceals more evil than you know.'

Robin whistled a carefree air, to show what he thought of Will's caution.

'Nay, Will,' he said good-humouredly, 'it will not be long before King Richard returns to England. Prince John will be cast off the throne – and then, Will, then at last I shall see Maid Marian again.' So saying, Robin slung his bow over his back and set off to shoot something for the larder.

It was while Robin was away that Tom Turpin came in with the news that there was a fellow outside, seeking admittance to the band. Only Little John and Dickon Barleycorn were idling by the fire, keeping a watch on the camp, for the others were about their various errands in the forest.

'We may not decide while Robin is absent,' said Little John doubtfully. 'What sort of fellow is this?'

Tom Turpin sketched a very round outline with his hands.

'More than common well fed,' he said with a smile. 'Methinks he has never wanted for anything till he came to Sherwood. But he has gentle manners, and a pleasing way with him. It would not do for us to turn him away.'

Now, ever since Dickon Barleycorn had come to the camp, he had longed to show himself a useful member of the band.

'Bring him in, Tom,' he commanded. 'I know all the Sheriff's men by heart – for did I not serve with them these five years? I can smell a spy as a bear smells out honey. And if we *do* find this fellow is false . . .' Dickon traced his finger across his throat with a significant gesture. Tom Turpin was impressed with this display of bravado and summoned the stranger.

So it was that Harry Roundfellow – as the merry men soon nick-named him – joined Robin Hood's band, after being vouched for by Dickon Barleycorn. As Tom Turpin had said, his manners were agreeable and he was ever ready to help another in distress. He seemed almost too eager to be friendly – he was forever joining in conversation and asking questions. When Robin and Will drew apart to plan some piece of robbery in the forest, Harry Roundfellow was sure to sidle up to them and ask if he could be of any assistance. Even Robin, the happy-go-lucky Robin, who got on well with all the world, confessed to Will that Harry Roundfellow disquieted him in some way which he could not define.

' 'Tis not that he is discourteous,' burst out Robin. 'On the contrary, the fellow is so gentle and courteous to us all, his smile is so ready, his laughter and jests so frequent, that I feel a churl to dislike him. And yet . . .' For once Will Scarlett forebore to play the counsellor, having been twitted so often on his caution.

'Time alone will show whether our friend Harry Roundfellow is true to us,' replied Will. 'In any case one cannot do much harm against so many.' It was lucky for Will that he could not look into the future and see how false his rash prophecy was to prove.

It was lucky, too, for his peace of mind that he could not overhear a certain conversation between Prince John and the Sheriff, which took place late at night in a small chamber in the castle.

'Is the plan working?' inquired the Prince warily.

The Sheriff nodded.

'It is working, Your Highness. This very day Walter of Weybridge, my emissary, discovered a note from our friend under the white stone six paces north of the felled oak on the outskirts of Sherwood. It was here that we agreed to leave messages. Walter handed me this piece of paper.' And the Sheriff drew from the folds of his rich cloak a crumpled missive which he handed to the Prince.

'Tomorrow at dusk,' it read, 'a league from Guy of Gisborne's castle.'

Prince John smiled, well pleased.

'We must warn Guy of Gisborne that his treasure is in danger,' he said. 'And for the hatred which he bears Robin

Hood, I dare swear that he will be willing to join us in this enterprise. Harry has obeyed the instructions which I gave him well.'

It was the Sheriff who had the brilliant idea of persuading Guy of Gisborne to undertake all the fighting. He pointed out to the Prince that if Guy of Gisborne slew Robin Hood in a fair fight no one would be a whit the wiser that Prince John had had any hand in his death.

'You will be well rid of a troublesome outlaw, and if there is an outcry from the common people, who have an absurd love for this boy, well, it will be directed not against you, but against Sir Guy.'

This was exactly the sort of plan – cunning and cowardly – which commended itself to the Prince. An hour later a messenger was galloping post-haste to the castle of Guy of Gisborne, bearing a letter sealed with the royal seal.

The Great Robbery

Meanwhile the Sherwood hide-out was humming with activity as Robin and his band prepared for what was to be the greatest robbery yet – the capture of the string of mules bearing the gold with which Guy of Gisborne intended to pay his private army of retainers. The plans were well laid. The mule train was to be ambushed in a broad shady valley not far from the castle; the drivers and the men-at-arms guarding the treasure would be slackening their watch here, because safety was near. This hollow contained several boulders with shallow earthy caves at the back of them, where they had come away from the side of the valley. In these caves Robin and his men planned to lurk at dusk.

Although many dozen ambushes had been carried out with success since Robin first came to live in Sherwood, nevertheless there was always an atmosphere of tension as the picked band of archers filed silently from the camp. This time Harry Roundfellow, Little John, Will Scarlett, Dickon Barleycorn, Alan-a-Dale and six others, besides, of course, Robin himself, had been chosen to take part. The men had been selected for their skill in archery and their physical fitness – for a small posse of men always had to remain behind to guard the camp from surprise attack.

'Good luck go with you,' cried Nat the Weaver. Bob the Weaver's boy disconsolately echoed him, wishing with all his heart that he might be allowed to go with them.

In spite of the tension, the spirits of the band were high, and had it not been for the need for silence, they would have broken out into a rousing song. Little John indeed kept forgetting himself and singing snatches of ballads in his deep voice, until he was indignantly hushed by Will Scarlett. It was mid afternoon when they set out, but by the time they reached the Stone valley, as the country folk called it, the sun had gone. The mule train was expected at dusk, according to the information which Much the Miller had managed to glean from the kitchen wenches at Guy of Gisborne's castle. Much had managed to preserve the secret of his relations with Robin's band, and he still came and went freely among the various villages which surrounded Nottingham, plying his trade. In this way, he was of the greatest assistance to Robin in finding out details of rich baggage trains to be plundered.

Robin's men ensconced themselves in the caves – Little John and Harry Roundfellow together in the first, Will Scarlett and Alan-a-Dale in the second, the others in the third cave, which was deeper than the rest, with Robin himself crouching behind the first boulder, ready to give the signal for the attack.

About twenty minutes later, minutes which seemed like hours to the waiting men, their ears caught the welcome sounds of jingling bridles and neighing animals.

Robin raised one arrow in the air, which he was to fire when the moment was ripe for attack. No one spoke. Little John heard a faint rustling beside him and nudged Harry Roundfellow to go and investigate. To his surprise, his elbow met nothing. Slightly worried, Little John looked behind him to see where Harry had got to, only to find no trace of his companion. The cave was extremely shallow. There was no possibility of Harry Roundfellow concealing his stout form there.

Now thoroughly alarmed, Little John decided that he ought somehow to get word to Robin, and warn the rest of the band. But at that moment Robin's arrow sped like a bird into the heart of the leading man-at-arms, who had just appeared at the head of the valley, and the attack was on!

No time now to worry about absentees – all Little John's energies were concentrated on avoiding the hail of arrows which were coming from the other side, and returning them in good measure. Robin's men knelt behind the boulders and from this vantage point picked off the first four soldiers. The whole mule train was in complete disorder: the terrified animals kicked at their traces and tried to bolt. The heavy chests with which they had been loaded toppled to the ground and lay there, spilling forth their rich contents.

'All together, men!' shouted Robin, 'we'll rush them

now!' And running forward, he led a spirited foray on the few remaining soldiers, who were by now outnumbered and made haste to throw down their swords. It seemed as if the treasure was already theirs.

THE AMBUSH

Not so! As Robin's men were investigating the rich coffers of gold and silver, a storm of arrows plunged forth from the crest of the valley. For one moment Robin imagined that Nat the Weaver, Dan Shepheard, and the rest of the men who had been left behind, must have sent out a relief party. He was speedily undeceived.

'Surrender, Robin Hood!' shouted a familiar voice. 'Surrender, for you and your men are surrounded, and my archers have you covered on every side.' It was Guy of Gisborne.

Robin looked up. The situation looked desperate, but he had won his way out from other such desperate situations in the past. Courage!

'Come and get us, Guy of Gisborne,' he cried. 'Who will be the first to taste the edge of Robin Hood's sword?'

So saying, he loosed one of his green-feathered arrows straight at Guy of Gisborne's breast. At that distance it could not penetrate the baron's armour, and glanced off the steel: nevertheless, Guy of Gisborne drew his horse hastily backwards from the cliff edge. Robin's brave gesture had put new heart into his men. They were all prepared to stand by Robin, and die rather than surrender to the hated Baron of Gisborne.

Their courage only increased when Little John spied Harry Roundfellow skulking among Guy of Gisborne's retainers, trying not to show his face to his former comrades. Quickly, Little John explained to Robin how Harry had deserted them on the eve of the fight: it was not difficult then for Robin to guess who had betrayed them, and warned Guy of Gisborne where they were planning to ambush his treasure.

'Coward!' he yelled. 'Yes, I mean you, Harry Round-fellow! Do you not even have spirit enough to show your miserable face to the men whom you have betrayed? Come out and fight us, for my sword is itching to get at you!'

The men of Sherwood hurled every insult they could think of at Harry Roundfellow until he looked ready to spring down from the valley crest and attack them, but still Guy of Gisborne did not give the word for the charge. The truth was that at that distance Guy could not be sure of picking off Robin's band by archery alone. These men were doughty fighters, skilled in forest lore, and he was frightened to engage them on an equal level. So, for some time, Guy's men contented themselves with releasing an occasional volley of arrows, which were returned with good measure by Robin and his band. By now it was quite dark.

'Our supply of arrows is getting low,' murmured Dickon Barleycorn in Will's ear. 'Think you that we might rush the valley head, and see how many of us can get through?'

'A rash plan,' commmented Will. 'It will cost us too much in lives. No, I have a better idea, Dickon, but mind that you say nothing to Robin.'

'You can trust me, Will Scarlett,' said Dickon. 'I am your man for any hazardous enterprise.'

'Then how say you if we two draw off their fire at the rocky end of the valley and let the rest escape the other way? Guy of Gisborne is a cunning fighter, but it is now dark, and unless he has eyes like a cat, I think we can fool him.'

Dickon Barleycorn swallowed hard. It was one thing to volunteer for action, and quite another to be asked to undertake a particularly dangerous mission, with only one companion, while the rest of the band escaped. For a moment he experienced blind panic. What did he care if they all perished, so long as he escaped? Then courage reasserted itself – and shame also. Had he not introduced the traitor, Harry Roundfellow, into the camp? And how would he ever look Bob in the eyes again if he failed at this test? So Dickon Barleycorn nodded bravely and said, in as steady a voice as he could muster:

'I am your man, Will Scarlett.'

Nothing was said to Robin or Little John. Will simply told Alan-a-Dale to be ready to take advantage of the slightest opportunity to escape. Then silently Will and Dickon stole from the side of their companions, taking with them the remaining store of arrows.

No more was heard of them until all at once, half a mile away from where Robin stood, where the Stone Valley broke into slag heaps of boulders and gravel, and a horse would have to pick its way carefully not to fall, a great noise of banging and shouting broke out. Robin and Guy of Gisborne were equally taken aback – but Guy of Gisborne at least had no time to ponder on the surprise, for he found himself harried with a storm of arrows, which seemed to be coming from at least a dozen archers, perched up among the rocks.

'There they are, the impudent scoundrels!' he yelled. 'Trying to escape among the rocks. We'll show them! Forward, men, and a hundred crowns to anyone who takes Robin Hood alive!'

At these imperious words, practically the entire force of Gisborne soldiers deserted their allotted posts and charged along the edge of the valley, concentrating all their attention on what seemed to be a powerful nest of archers.

THE PRICE OF THE ESCAPE

At first Robin Hood had been so astonished by this development that he had not the wits to take advantage of it. Alan-a-Dale stung him to action.

'Quick, Robin,' he whispered. 'This is our chance. Out by the other end. The Gisborne crew have left it quite open, save for one or two puny guards whom we can soon overwhelm.'

Robin rallied his wits and beckoned the band forward. Very soon they were falling on the outlying Gisborne archers, who had stuck to their places, and silencing them ruthlessly. The way out of the valley, the way to freedom, was open!

The men of Sherwood needed no further encouragement to scurry for the cave where they had left their horses, and set off pell-mell through the forest for home. They were half-way there, when Robin suddenly checked Troubadour in mid gallop, causing commotion among his followers.

'Will Scarlett!' he shouted. 'Where are you, Will?'

Some terrible presentiment about Will's safety had suddenly struck Robin, and he cried aloud in the forest, regardless of the danger. There was no answer. The men looked from one to another in dismay. Who had last seen Will? No one recollected having seen him during the mad flight from the valley. The last person who remembered having had any words with him was Alan-a-Dale, who recalled that Will had warned him to be ready to take advantage of any opportunity to escape. Robin felt as if a cold hand had clutched his heart.

'An opportunity to escape,' he repeated slowly. 'And Guy of Gisborne directed his men to the other end of the valley, where those rough rocks make the path almost impassable. Oh God, protect him – for I fear that Will is in mortal danger, and has sacrificed himself for our sake.'

It was at this moment that someone discovered that Dickon Barleycorn was also missing.

'Only two against so many,' cried Robin. 'What chance have they got? We must go back at once and help them – if it is not too late.'

The ride back to the valley seemed long and fearful: each man was in agony lest they come upon the scene too late to assist their gallant comrades. Robin felt such a weight of apprehension for his friend that he could scarcely control his trembling hands, and it was Troubadour who had to guide him through the forest. Would the path never end? At last – and how arduous, how protracted, the journey now seemed, which they had ridden so fast and joyfully only an hour since – at last they reached the valley head.

No sound met their ears, no clash of swords, no cries of battle. The rocks were plunged in utter darkness, and for all the life the scene showed, there might never have been a fight at all. Robin wheeled his horse.

'I shall not rest until we find them,' he cried. 'Will Scarlett, where are you? Where are you, my old friend?'

The rest of the band took up the mournful cry:

'Will, Dickon, where are you? Will, Dickon, where are you? Where are you? Where are you?' The rocks echoed their cries.

Suddenly, from about six feet below them, came a faint groan. It was so gentle that at first Robin thought it was no more than the sighing of the wind. Then it came again – that soft unearthly noise. With one bound, Robin had leapt down the rocks and was searching desperately in the darkness for whoever, or whatever, had made the noise. All at once his hand touched something wet. He felt further, and came on leather, then cloth, last of all flesh and something which from its outline was a human face.

'Bring a torch,' he cried. 'Quick, for I fear me there is a gravely wounded man here.' He was right. In the flaring light of the torch he gazed into the ashen face of Dickon Barleycorn.

Robin saw that his hands were sticky with blood where he had touched him in the dark. It was not difficult to see where the blood had come from. A great wound laid open Dickon Barleycorn's side, from his shoulder to his hip. Robin felt his pulse. It was scarcely discernible, and only the faintest heart beats were still keeping him from death.

'He has not long to live,' said Robin gently, folding Dickon's arms over his chest, and making the sign of the cross over him. 'He could not survive a wound like that, if the greatest leeches in the kingdom were to attend him. Alas, he has nearly bled to death.'

The men of Sherwood doffed their caps and stood in silence over the prostrate body. Suddenly Dickon's eyelids fluttered; a moment later he opened his eyes wide and he stared straight at Robin Hood.

'Will Scarlett,' he whispered hoarsely. 'They have taken him to Gisborne Castle.' His voice weakened and became so low that even Robin, kneeling beside him, could scarcely hear what he said.

'Am I still a coward?' he asked feebly.

'Before God,' said Robin Hood in a loud, firm voice, 'before God, I swear you are the bravest man in my band.'

At this, a radiant smile lit up Dickon Barleycorn's homely features. He started to sit up, gasped out something which sounded like 'Tell Bob . . .', then choked, and fell back dead upon the ground.

'God rest his soul!' said Little John. 'For if ever a man died a good death it was he. See there, a dozen gashes upon his poor body. He must have sold his life dearly.'

'Let us take his body back to Sherwood and bury it by the flowering cherry,' said Robin sadly. 'As long as we dwell in Sherwood, his grave shall be tended and his memory honoured.'

So the melancholy procession wound its way back to the camp. To the deep sorrow of Dickon Barleycorn's death was added the grief of Will Scarlett's imprisonment – imprisonment, moreover, in the most impregnable fortress in the north, the Castle of Gisborne. As Robin watched Dickon's body being lowered into its grave, he wondered whether even now Will Scarlett was not enduring torments which would make death seem preferable.

'Will Scarlett shall be rescued,' said Robin aloud. 'If we all die in the attempt.' Then he put his arm round the shoulders of the weeping Bob, and consoled him gently.

'Do not mourn Dickon too bitterly, Bob,' said Robin. 'It was the death he would have wished for himself – defending his friends in battle. His last thought was of you. He had found true courage at last.'

7

THE CASTLE OF
GISBORNE

THE DEATH OF Dickon Barleycorn and the capture of Will Scarlett cast a deep gloom over the men of Sherwood. Robin Hood would sit every evening in the shadows away from the fire, brooding over ways and means to rescue Will.

'How can we hope to storm the castle?' he said despairingly to Little John. 'No prisoner has ever yet left Guy of Gisborne's stronghold alive.'

'There must be a way,' cried Alan-a-Dale. 'If not by fair means, then by foul – for we need not be over squeamish about our methods when dealing with a villain like the Baron of Gisborne.'

But it was Much the Miller who eventually hit on a plan. He had been able to pay two visits to the castle kitchens, on the pretext of bringing flour, and there he had struck up a friendship with Kate, the pretty kitchen maid. From Kate, Much learnt that Will Scarlett had not been wounded: he had been surrounded by Guy of Gisborne and six soldiers, and thus captured without suffering a scratch.

Then one day, to his horror, Kate mentioned to him in conversation that the 'outlaw' was to be hanged upon the morrow!

' 'Tis not true!' gasped Much. Then he added, in order to allay Kate's suspicions:

'My heart rejoices at the thought of the outlaw's death. These heinous outlaws who make trouble for honest folk should all be hanged as quickly as possible.'

'Oh, Master Much,' cried Kate. 'This outlaw is well-favoured and right manly to gaze upon. Can he really be so very wicked?'

Much's eyes narrowed, and he caught his breath. So this pretty nitwit had actually managed to get a glimpse of Will Scarlett! He had to know more about this.

'No doubt you saw him when they brought him into the courtyard after his capture,' said Much carelessly.

Kate giggled. 'Nay, lad,' she said. 'It was pitch dark when the men came back from the fight. 'Tis I who serve the prisoner. I take his food to him – and a right damp dungeon they have put him into, too,' she added with a sniff. 'My skirts are mildewed by brushing on those wet stones.'

Much tried not to let his excitement appear. He blessed the impulse which had first led him to chuck pretty Kate under the chin. For a plan to save Will had suddenly occurred to him.

'Is he well guarded?' he asked carelessly.

Kate nodded.

'Five men night and day,' she said, with round eyes. 'He must be mighty fierce to need so many guards. Yet he does not look over strong.'

Five men, thought Much. That is bad. But there is one weak link in your chain, my lord Baron of Gisborne, and that is your pretty kitchen maid. He stole an arm round Kate's trim waist and murmured a few soft words in her ear. Kate responded with yet another giggle, but Much could see that she was not averse to his attentions.

'Kate,' he said ardently, 'thou art the prettiest maiden for a hundred miles round Nottingham. I would that thou wert mine,' and Much sighed artistically.

He continued for some time in the same vein, until Kate was sighing too, and pressing his hand in hers. Much took advantage of her softened mood to suggest that she should walk out with him into the Forest of Sherwood, and spend the afternoon in the fresh afternoon sunlight. Kate made only a faint demur. Soon she was strolling happily through Sherwood, exclaiming gaily at every passing flower and bird.

When they had reached a mossy dell, the most romantic spot which Much knew of within walking distance of Gisborne, Much fell on his knees before Kate.

'Kate,' he said, gazing straight into her eyes. 'You seem to be a good-hearted girl, a girl who would help someone who was in trouble.'

Kate looked rather surprised – after all, this was not quite what she had expected to hear! But she nodded.

'I would do anything for you, Much,' she said softly.

Before she had time to regret her words, Much explained exactly what it was that he wanted her to do.

'Kate,' he said, taking both her hands in his, 'that prisoner, that "heinous outlaw", is none other than my dear friend, Will Scarlett, lieutenant of Robin Hood's band, to which I also belong.' Kate gave an exclamation of horror, but Much held fast. 'Kate,' he continued, 'Will Scarlett is no criminal, but an honest man who hates the Norman tyrants and Prince John. His only crime was loving justice and liberty too well. Would you condemn that man to death? You, who have Saxon blood in your veins?'

'Oh, oh, oh,' gasped Kate, overwhelmed by the situation. 'What shall I do? Oh, Much, say that you are jesting, say that you are not one of those rough outlaws? Oh, save me, someone save me, save me!' And Kate started to give a series of short hysterical shrieks.

A KITCHEN MAID IS KIDNAPPED

'Oh God, grant me patience!' thought Much. 'Patience to din some sense into this silly head. For upon this foolish wench depends the life of Will Scarlett.' Whereupon he efficiently silenced Kate by placing one hand firmly over her mouth. Kate stared at him with eyes as round as saucers. 'She evidently thinks I shall murder her,' thought Much. 'There is nothing to be done with such a brainless fool.' So he tied Kate's hands and ankles together, and slung her over his back. Then he started to trudge through the forest until he reached the camp.

At first the rest of the men thought that Much had lost his wits when they saw him appear with a kitchen maid all bundled up in rope. But when he explained exactly how important this particular kitchen maid was, they applauded his bold kidnapping heartily. Endless plans and ways of rescuing Will were discussed, while Kate lay in a heap on the ground.

But Kate was not wasting her time. She looked all round her, at first in fear and apprehension, and then with interest. So this was the famous robber's camp! And she, Kate, had penetrated the very stronghold. It was more romantic than any of the old ballads which the minstrels sang in the great hall in the evenings! What a tale to tell Sukey and Nell when she returned. Then Kate noticed another thing – how good-looking all the robbers were! Robin Hood himself was the handsomest man she had ever seen, and all the others were more than passing fair. Could they really be so wicked? It was then that it first occurred to Kate that perhaps after all she had behaved rather foolishly in the forest by screaming at poor Much. Kate blushed. What a ninny he must have thought me, she reflected, and she pulled gently at his sleeve.

'Master Much, good Master Much,' said Kate gently, 'I would fain say that I am sorry for my fright in the forest.'

Kate's humble words touched Much.

'Why, Kate,' he replied, 'have you changed your mind about us? Are we not so very wicked after all?' Kate blushed again.

'Pardon me, I pray,' she said. 'And tell me how I can help save Will Scarlett.'

Much's face changed.

'Will you indeed help?' he asked. 'Robin, Little John, Alan, Tom, listen, all of you. Our fair Kate has consented to help us.'

All this sudden attention confused Kate, and reduced her to silence. Eventually, however, with Much's encouragement, she found her voice and stammered out:

'Good masters, I am but a poor maid, but if I can help you, I will.' Then she added in a louder voice, 'On condition that I may stay here with all of you in the forest. For life here seems mighty pleasant to me. I can help prepare your food,' added Kate hopefully.

'Excellent,' said Much, graciously. 'You may assist me.'

Now Kate had taken the decision, she was all smiles and dimples, and coquettish looks. Farewell to greasy pots and pans, she thought, farewell to turning the spit in the smoky hall of Gisborne. Farewell to a bed of rushes shared with six other kitchen wenches. Henceforth, I shall sleep on the turf, and cook on an open fire. Kate felt delighted with her lot. Her one regret was that Sukey and Nell would never hear of it. Minions, she thought, tossing her head. Slaves of the Normans. I am working for honest Saxons, who love King Richard. In one breath Kate had shaken off all her old loyalties, and was prepared to devote herself to the cause of Robin Hood.

Now the time had come to plan the exact method of rescuing Will. For, in the excitement of Kate's change of mind, they had all forgotten that many dangers and hazards were ahead of them. And it was only twelve hours before Will was due to be hanged on the battlements of the castle! Robin Hood turned cold at the thought.

'To work, men!' he cried. 'We have all too short a time.' He discovered from Kate at what hour she was wont to give Will his evening meal.

'Nine o'clock,' she said, anxiously. 'Am I to go back to the castle, then? You promised me I should stay here if I helped you.'

'Do not fear,' said Robin gently. 'Kate the kitchen maid will give Will Scarlett his food as usual, but Kate of Sherwood will be safe in the forest.' Then, as Kate still gaped at him, he explained:

'You, Much, will dress up in Kate's clothes, moble your face well in her cap and veil, and take her place.'

Much swallowed hard.

'Yes, Robin,' he said in a doubtful voice.

The more Much heard of Robin's plan that he should impersonate Kate, the less he liked it. But it was no time for arguing – the situation was desperate. In any case, of all the band, Much had far the best knowledge of the inside of the Castle of Gisborne. Much concentrated on getting as full a description as possible from Kate of her duties, which way she went, and who she spoke to. For Much would not be able to speak to anyone – his deep voice would give away the whole situation. At the end of it all, Much was far from convinced that he would be able to carry it through. Still, for Will's sake, he was prepared to try.

MUCH THE KITCHEN MAID

Towards nine o'clock, in the Castle of Gisborne, a kitchen maid could be seen slinking, rather than walking, towards the great kitchens where the food for the many inmates of the castle – from Baron to prisoners – was being prepared. Kate had been a fine buxom wench, but this maiden was if anything more buxom, and her waist was definitely less trim. Nor could you see if her face was pretty, for it was muffled and veiled as if against some illness. But in spite of all these oddities not one man-at-arms, not one serving man, not even the dogs who lay sleeping by the fire, paid the slightest attention.

Who did not know Kate with her giggles and foolish laughter? And who was willingly going to engage her in conversation on a peaceful evening? No, the men-at-arms felt no particular inclination to say anything to the kitchen maid as she went on her way. Nor did Sukey and Nell have any desire to talk to their companion. They were busy in one corner, discussing the latest recruit to the Baron's retainers – a fair-faced youth known as Handsome Jack, who was rumoured to have a great way with the ladies. As they giggled and shrieked in a way that reminded Much forcibly of Kate, for the first time the Miller's son was grateful for the garrulity of all kitchen maids. He even managed to bob a curtsey to the Lady Alice, Guy of Gisborne's mother, although his first instinct had been to bow like a man, and doff his cap. What a commotion if Much had doffed his veils! He dreaded to think how the dozing soldiers would have leaped to their feet with drawn swords; even Sukey and Nell would have ceased their endless prattling to give one of those high-pitched screams. Devoutly thankful for his escape, Much took the platter of food from the table, and started on his journey back through the hall to the dungeons.

This time he was not so lucky. Scarcely had he entered, when he heard a loud hail from the fire.

'Hey, Kate, hey there, my pretty Kate, bring us a flagon of ale, like a good maid.' It was Handsome Jack, the new man-at-arms; Much had no difficulty in recognizing him from Sukey's enthusiastic description. How Much hated that fair and smiling face! He stood rooted to the spot, not knowing whether he could safely ignore the summons, or whether he would have to risk coming within a foot of Handsome Jack's keen glance, in order to hand him the ale. Much's presence of mind deserted him completely, and he felt the terrible numbness of fear cripple his brain.

Then it came again:

'Hey, *Kate!*' This time the voice sounded angry. 'Art made of stone, lass? Why do you stand there gaping at me?'

Any moment now the soldier would peer closer, see Much's homely features, Much's round figure, instead of Kate's pretty face and buxom curves. Then the game would be up! Much bobbed a trembling curtsey, and turned back to the kitchen, as if to fetch the ale as fast as possible. But he was called back by a furious shout.

'Numskull! The ale is in the cellar, as you well know. Are you sick, girl, that you behave like a witless calf?'

As Much stood there, not daring to move, like a terrified rabbit fascinated by a snake, Handsome Jack rose to his feet and began to walk towards his victim. . . .

'Why, Master Jack,' said a loud, cheerful voice – and never in all his life had Much been so pleased to hear anything as he was to hear the fluting tones of Sukey behind him – 'I will fetch your ale, right gladly.' Sukey pushed the false Kate out of the way.

Much dropped a clumsy curtsey, clutched his platter of food tightly, and backed gratefully out of the hall. He would find his way to the dungeons without risking any further requests from that dangerous line of soldiers at the fire! So he plunged down a narrow stone passage, climbed a flight of stairs, descended another, and looking out of an arrow slit, saw the courtyard, with the oak-studded prison door in the corner, below him.

The second part of his dangerous mission was about to begin. He prayed that it would be less alarming than the first. But as he tripped down the stairs, trying hard to bear himself in a maidenly fashion on the narrow winding steps, to his horror he heard the clash of mailed feet on the stone. Much froze into an embrasure in the wall. The next minute he was face to face with the Baron of Gisborne, Guy the Terrible, himself! Scarcely knowing what he did,

Much sank into something between a curtsey and a bow. All the time his terrified eyes held the Baron's, and gazed mutely, imploringly, into their cruel depths.

'This is the end of all our plans,' thought Much. 'How can he fail to recognize me? Will Scarlett, I have failed you.'

But, as it happened, Guy of Gisborne's mind was far away from thoughts of outlaws and executions. He was turning over the question of Oswald Montdragon in his mind, wondering whether that ambitious rival of his was not gaining too much influence over the Prince. In the absence of King Richard, the Norman barons were always worrying and intriguing thus among themselves. He noticed that one of the castle wenches was singularly ill-favoured, and seemed extremely frightened of him: but he dismissed the ugliness as a misfortune, and took the terror as a tribute to his own importance. Guy of Gisborne clanked majestically up the stairs, leaving Much to mop his damp brow with Kate's kerchief.

The Dungeons of Gisborne

When Much finally reached the dungeon head, he was still trembling so much that he could scarcely nerve himself to knock three times on the door. His raps sounded feeble enough for any weak female, and apparently they convinced the guards, who swung the door open and silently pointed the way down the steps. As Much scrambled down the steep staircase, he heard one say to the other:

'Poor wretch, that is the last food he will eat in this world.'

'Aye,' rejoined another. 'He dies at dawn tomorrow, hanging high from our battlements.'

'Fit punishment for an outlaw,' commented a third. 'I only wish that scoundrel Robin Hood were there to swing beside him.'

'Norman dogs!' thought Much. 'We'll show you a trick or two before you're much older!'

He scurried on. A moment later he found himself in a narrow dungeon, lit only by a tiny grating; it was quite empty, except for a heap of straw in the corner, upon which a sleeping figure was just discernible. His heart pumping with excitement at the sight of Will, Much put the platter down loudly on the floor, hoping to attract Will's attention. He did not dare say anything, for fear that a strange masculine voice would awake the suspicions of the soldiers. But Will did not stir. He was evidently too accustomed to Kate's ministrations to be much interested in them. Who knows what sad thoughts were passing through his mind – thoughts of Sherwood in the early morning when the dew was still on the grass, and the sun was just beginning to peep through the trees, thoughts of Robin and their old friendship, thoughts of all the gay, reckless deeds they had planned together, and now would never accomplish.

So eventually Much had to tip-toe across and touch him gently on the shoulder. Will Scarlett turned over slowly and apathetically. Evidently, thought Much, the good Kate tried her wiles on him without success.

'Do not move,' he whispered. 'Try not to show any surprise. It is I, Much the Miller!'

In spite of Much's instructions, Will Scarlett could not help letting out a startled exclamation, which made one of the soldiers prick up his ears.

'Hurry up down there, Kate,' he shouted. 'You are for ever lingering with the prisoners.'

'Yes,' agreed another. 'Our Kate should not waste her time on those Saxon curs when there are good Normans about.'

But when the supposed Kate did not answer, the soldiers lost interest and went back to their own conversation.

'Much, dear Much!' whispered Will. 'Can it really be you? Oh, Much, I knew that somehow Robin would contrive to rescue me.'

'We have got inside the dungeon,' said Much wryly. 'It remains to be seen whether we can get you out of it. However, we must soon make the attempt. I cannot dally here much longer without arousing suspicion. Listen to my plan: I shall stumble up the stairs, carrying my platter, masking as far as possible the mouth of the dungeon. You will lurk behind me in the entrance. When I drop my platter, you and I will both rush them with these weapons.'

Much handed Will two daggers from under his clothes and stuck two for himself within the folds of his bodice.

'I shall have to give the signal when I am fairly near the top of the stairs, so that the soldiers will have had time to open the door for me,' he added. Then Much grasped Will's hand, and the two men smiled wanly at one another, each trying to pretend he felt more confidence than he actually did.

Each step of the staircase seemed like a cliff to the Miller, as he dragged himself unwillingly nearer and nearer to the top. With his heart in his mouth, he saw one of the soldiers get up, and with a cursory glance towards him, begin to unbolt the dungeon door again. Much climbed another three steps. He noted that the other three soldiers had not moved. Where was the fifth? Much looked wildly round. There was no sign of him. Then Much remembered that Kate had told him that the soldiers sometimes stole off to the cellar to try and while away the long hours of duty with a pleasant carousal. Evidently this was one of those occasions.

Much climbed another two steps. It was now or never. Desperately hoping that Will, behind him, was on the alert, he missed his footing on purpose, stumbled, and dropped the earthenware platter with a heavy crash on the stone. It broke immediately into a thousand fragments, and, as Much had hoped, the soldier instinctively stooped down to try to save the pieces. This was Much's chance. He whipped out his dagger, and before the soldier even knew what was happening, plunged it straight into his heart. The soldier tottered and collapsed on the step. He was quite dead!

There was no sound from the guard room, and the door lay open. It seemed almost too easy to escape, as Will stepped lightly up the stairs behind Much; and indeed the two Saxons were within a yard of the door when one of the soldiers within, hearing perhaps the sound of two people, not one, ascending the stairs, and no sound of iron rings on the stone, became suspicious. He glanced out, just in time to see Will Scarlett stepping lightly over the threshold!

'Stop him! Stop the Saxon!' shouted the soldier, springing up and drawing his sword. He rushed after Will, shouting for help, closely followed by his two companions. At this moment the fifth soldier came round the corner, carrying a large jug of ale. In the split second of hesitation before he realized what was happening, Will managed to push the jug into his face and run swiftly on. The soldier spluttered in the thick stream of ale which poured all over him, and clutched at the nearest support. This proved to be one of his comrades, and they grappled angrily together for a moment, giving Much and Will one more precious moment in which to race across the courtyard towards the gate.

The Escape from the Fortress

All this time, Robin Hood and his men had been lying below the hill on which the Castle of Gisborne stood, waiting for the sound of disturbance within the castle itself, which would mean that Much and Will had succeeded in getting out of the dungeon. The castle looked dark and menacing above them. On the battlements they could make out the outline of the scaffold, already hoisted for the hanging on the morrow. No one spoke of it, but it was there all the same, to remind them all of what would happen to Will Scarlett at dawn if they failed in their mission.

Time passed slowly. It seemed hours since Much had left them. Robin looked at the moon, and decided they could risk creeping a little nearer the castle walls without being detected. The band darted from shadow to shadow, wriggled on their stomachs through the patches of moonlight, and eventually clustered together again beneath the very walls of the fortress of Gisborne. But still there came no sound from the castle. Robin knelt in the grass, a prey to a thousand fears. Suppose Much had been discovered long ago, and was now languishing with Will in the same dungeon? Suppose Will had been secretly executed at dead of night? Suppose the girl Kate had played them false? The possibilities of failure were endless, and Robin went over them all in his mind.

He groaned aloud.

At that moment came the first shouts from the castle, the first cries of wrath and the first sounds of men running. Undoubtedly something untoward was happening within Gisborne, and from the faint snatches of words which reached the eager listeners outside, it was indeed connected with Much and Will Scarlett! Now was the time for every man to bare his weapon, and hold himself in readiness for the great assault.

A second later there was a great outcry – a burst of shouting and a thunder of battering. The next moment the gates of Gisborne – those fearful portals of the dark fortress – were flung open, and clearly outlined against the lighted courtyard, Robin saw a figure in a woman's dress. Even in the confusion, he had no difficulty in recognizing Much!

Yes, the faithful Much had managed to make the gates and fling back the great iron bar which held them closed. Thankfully, he fled out into the darkness and fell, panting, half weeping with exhaustion, upon the cool, free turf outside. Yet where was Will Scarlett? Robin heard the sound of swords clashing within, and he waved wildly to his men to rush the castle.

'On, on!' he shouted. 'Better we all perish together, than that we leave Will Scarlett within this cruel fortress.'

All together, twenty sturdy fighters rushed madly through the gates, shouting their Saxon war-cries, prepard to sell their lives dearly for the sake of their comrade. They were just in time: Will, bleeding and weary, was still desperately holding off his attackers, but his blows, once so skilful and energetic, became feebler each moment. It would only have been a matter of seconds before he finally succumbed beneath the savage Norman battery.

'Courage, Will!' yelled Robin, fearful lest he should finally sink to the ground in the very hour of rescue. Guy of Gisborne, who had been leading the attack, whipped round and found himself facing the Lord of Sherwood.

'Ah, bandit,' he growled, 'have you come to die, too?'

'On guard, Guy of Gisborne!' was all Robin said, aiming a fierce blow at his face with his sword. From that moment on, the Norman baron had no more breath to taunt his opponent, for he was pitting himself against no less a combatant than Robin of Locksley, the flower of the Saxons!

Despair lends fresh strength: although Robin's men were far fewer than the Norman retainers, they acquitted themselves so well that the Normans were driven back into their gate-house. Now was the time to flee, and shake the dust of Gisborne for ever from their feet. Little John and Alan helped the fainting Will through the gates; then Little John lifted him gently in his mighty arms and carried him, half running, half walking, to where their horses had been tethered. The other men followed, casting fearful glances backwards, to see if the Normans were still confined to their gate-house. But the storm of arrows which pursued them from the arrow slits did not encourage them to linger. The departure of Robin's band from Gisborne was more of a rout than a triumphant procession; and yet, because they had rescued Will Scarlett, each man in his heart felt triumphant.

Only Robin Hood did not flee. He remained behind until he was sure that every one of his men was safely out of Gisborne. Then, standing squarely in the middle of the courtyard, he waved his sword round his head, and shouted defiantly up at the gate-house:

'Long Live King Richard! Death to Prince John and his treacherous minion, Guy of Gisborne!'

Already the Gisborne soldiers were preparing to rush from the gate-house, now that they saw that the Saxons had departed. But Robin Hood almost sauntered from the castle. After mounting his horse, he turned and looked up at the mighty stronghold frowning down at him. He saw the white face of the Baron of Gisborne regarding him with baffled rage from the battlements. Robin Hood made a low mocking bow, and galloped away into Sherwood.

8

FRIAR TUCK

IT WAS HIGH SUMMER before Will Scarlett recovered altogether from the effects of his imprisonment, and his escape from the Castle of Gisborne. Patiently Robin would sit with him beside the fire, as he lay, wan and exhausted, and plan with him the many gay adventures which they would have once Will had recovered. Much of Robin's zest for brigandage abated when Will was sick. He vowed that once Will rode beside him again, he would harry every fat merchant from Nottingham to London town – in the meantime, he busied himself directing plans for strengthening the camp, and building more huts.

For, as summer drew on, more bold youths sought out Robin Hood and sought admission to his band, and his numbers were rapidly increasing. But because Robin no longer rode abroad so often, the farther confines of Sherwood gradually became as wild and lawless as they had been before Robin arrived and made himself Lord of Sherwood. Little John, whose adventurous spirit was not dimmed, would ride into the northern thickets and marches and find that other bandits were establishing themselves there. All this he would duly report to Robin, only to receive an impatient nod of the head, and the hasty remark:

'Very good, very good. I'll see about it one of these days.'

But eventually there did come a day when Will Scarlett was fit to ride his faithful Polly once again. Then Robin's spirits rose, and he became once more the alert and energetic Master of the Forest. It was at this moment in Robin's fortunes that Little John chose to come to him with a long face and report that there was a troublesome hermit friar dwelling on the outskirts of the forest, who refused point blank to acknowledge the lordship of Robin Hood.

Robin frowned.

'Either he bows to Robin Hood, or he leaves the Forest of Sherwood,' he cried, 'for I can tolerate no rebels here. Root and branch, they must be cleared from my path. The time has come to have a thorough destruction of all those rebellious characters who have grown up like weeds during my absence.' Then he bade Little John command the seditious friar to send some token of his obeisance to the Lord of Sherwood.

Little John look doubtful, but he said nothing, and departed on his errand with a shrug of his mighty shoulders.

An hour later he was back again.

'Well?' demanded Robin. 'Show me the token.'

Little John looked rather embarrassed and mumbled something about 'not being quite suitable'. When Robin pressed him further, he produced an arrow.

'Zounds,' said Robin in a voice of thunder. 'That is a clear enough message. Bring me my horse, Little John, for I must rid Sherwood of this troublesome friar, if he cannot be brought to heel.' So saying, Robin rammed the arrow angrily into his quiver and galloped forth from the camp with a face of fury. Much the Miller and Kate the kitchen maid, who had been cooking by the fire, sprang aside from his path in terror, when they saw his black expression.

But in the course of his journey to the lonely hermitage, Robin's wrath somewhat abated, and his spirits began to rise at the thought of a gay adventure.

'I have become a thought serious of late,' he reflected, 'and Sherwood has not been the merry place it used to be. There must be songs and mirth once more – ah, Marian,' he sighed, 'if only you were with us! How different things would seem then.' For it was now many months since Robin had set eyes on the fair Maid of Whitby.

The first inkling Robin had that he was anywhere near the domain of the rebellious churchman was the hiss of wood, and the sound of an arrow burying itself in the tree behind him. Robin automatically reined in Troubadour and looked round for cover. He was on the banks of a stream, and there was nothing but sparse bushes and young trees around him. He was at the mercy of this friar, and by the looks of things he was dangerous!

'Show yourself, friar!' shouted Robin. 'Show yourself for the scurvy knave you are, who must now bow to the true Lord of Sherwood Forest.'

There was a rich laugh from the opposite bank of the stream, and a rubicund smiling friar, dressed in a coarse brown robe, stepped out from behind a tree. To show that he meant no ill will, he cast aside his bow, and unhitched his quiver from his back.

'Well met, my fine young fellow,' said he. 'I have had a great desire to clap eyes on the so-called Lord of Sherwood, and now he has done poor Friar Tuck the honour of paying him a call.' The friar swept a mock curtsey.

Robin laughed back at him.

'I see you are fond of a jest, Friar Tuck,' he cried, 'and you have a right merry tongue. Come over to this side of the river and let us settle once for all who is the Lord of Sherwood.'

Friar Tuck chuckled, but did not budge.

'Nay, Robin,' he said. 'I am too wily a bird to be caught like that. Come over to *my* side of the river.'

Now, although the river was shallow, and there was a kind of ford, there was no actual bridge over it. So without more ado, Robin plunged into the water up to his calves and waded over to the friar's side. Friar Tuck kindly helped him up the bank. But, instead of letting go his hand when he was safely on dry land, Robin only grasped it the firmer and, whipping out his dagger, pointed it at the friar's throat.

'Aha, good friar,' he cried. 'I have you now. Carry me back to the other side of the river, I pray you, for I have the greatest reluctance to getting my feet wet again!'

The friar said nothing. With a broad, good-tempered laugh, he simply hoisted Robin on to his back, and plunged bravely into the water. Soon they were on the other side of the stream, with Robin congratulating himself on having mastered the friar so easily. But . . .

'Not so fast, my fine young cockerel!' cried the friar, once they had reached the other bank, and Robin was preparing to depart. This time it was the friar who held Robin firm in his grip of iron and propelled him remorselessly towards the stream once more.

'Now it is my turn for a ride, good Master Robin, and I fear you will find good living has made my weight a little more than yours!' It was too true! Robin had indeed got the worst of the bargain. He groaned and sweated under Friar Tuck's great weight, as he struggled through the water to the opposite bank, slipping on the treacherous stones, so that once or twice it looked as if he would fall and precipitate Friar Tuck over his head.

'Take care, good donkey,' cried the friar anxiously, drubbing Robin's sides as if he really were an animal. 'I would fain not fall into the stream.'

'It would be the fate you deserve,' muttered Robin between his teeth, but he took care that the friar did not hear him, for fear of further beatings. So the ill-assorted couple – the portly friar on the back of the slight young man bending beneath his weight – reached the farther bank once more. This time Robin did not waste a moment in getting his revenge. He was determined not to leave the impertinent friar master of the situation. Before ever Friar Tuck had time to ward him off, Robin had his weapon pointed meaningly at the friar's heart, with the friar's arms twisted behind his back so that he could not struggle.

'Into the water again, friar!' said Robin grimly, deter-mined to turn the tables on his enemy. How he belaboured Friar Tuck's sides! The poor friar cried for mercy.

'Is the water cold?' inquired Robin mockingly.

'Why don't you go in and see for yourself?' shouted Friar Tuck. With a mighty heave of his shoulders, he unseated Robin Hood, and managed to plunge him head first into the water. Then he stood, arms akimbo, laughing loudly at his victory. When Robin emerged, he, too, had the grace to laugh at his discomfiture. By the time both men had struggled out of the water and dried themselves, they were firm friends.

'I like your spirit, Robin Hood,' said the friar frankly,

stetching out his hand in friendship. 'And I confess that I am growing weary of the hermit's life. What say you that I join your band, and come and act as chaplain to your men?' The friar gave a prodigious wink.

'I can draw a bow like the best of them,' he said, 'and am not averse to killing a royal stag or two myself. As for robbery . . .' he winked again. 'The Normans are an ungodly crew, and it is no more than they deserve, in my humble opinion.'

'Willingly do I admit you to my band,' said Robin. 'Let us go now to the camp, and we shall have a feast in honour of our new chaplain.'

So that night there was a right merry feast in Sherwood, with a roasted sheep which had been poached from the pastures of Guy of Gisborne, and some good Malmsey wine, which had been part of the baggage of a royal messenger, unwarily travelling alone through Sherwood. Robin pledged a toast to Friar Tuck on behalf of all the band, and received in return from the friar a handsome compliment on his ability to carry heavy burdens!

THE ADVENTURE OF THE FALSE PILGRIMS

For some weeks all went well in Sherwood, and never had there been a jollier companion than the friar, who could indeed, as he had boasted, draw a bow with skill, bring down a buck at a fine distance, and transfix a target with his arrow with the best of them. But one fateful day Friar Tuck found that he was not to be the only churchman in the forest. On his return to the camp, after a hard day's hunting, what should he find but a band of pilgrim friars, feasting by the fire, and telling the men of Sherwood the stories of their travels and adventures in foreign countries. Robin's band were listening with open mouths. No one had any time to spare for Friar Tuck, and the story of his day's hunting. When Friar Tuck attempted to join in the conversation with an anecdote of his own pilgrimage to Canterbury, and how he had walked the whole way with peas in his shoes, he was rudely ignored. Meanwhile the pilgrim friars spun more and more wondrous tales of Saracens and magicians, Eastern enchantment and the strange sights which were to be seen in the Holy Land.

Deeply affronted, and secretly extremely jealous, Friar Tuck withdrew from the happy circle round the fire, and brooded by himself. He learnt that the pilgrims had been found by the band marching through the forest singing, and had inquired where they might spend the night (taking Little John and Tom Turpin for woodcutters or rangers). It had been Tom Turpin's idea to offer them hospitality for the night in the camp.

'They are holy men,' he reasoned, 'and can do no harm.'

Little John agreed that it would be a kind and charitable action to provide the pilgrims with shelter: besides, they might bring some news of King Richard and the progress of the crusade.

It was true that the pilgrims turned out not to know much, if anything, about the crusade: but they sang some good songs, and told some good stories, even if one or two of them were scarcely what the band would have expected from men of God. However, in the general laughter, and genial atmosphere of the evening meal, this small detail passed unnoticed. As for Friar Tuck's behaviour – that was dismissed as the veriest pettiness.

So the feast continued well into the night, with such carousals and songs and jests and merry tales, that you would have thought Guy of Gisborne and Prince John would have heard the noise of it in their castles. Eventually, long after midnight, the fire died down, the last song was sung, the last beaker of ale quaffed, and the men of Sherwood began to think of sleeping. The air was fine and mild, and the sky clear and starry. Robin offered to give up his couch to the leader of the pilgrims and himself sleep in the open. Whereupon the rest of the band also courteously offered up their couches to their reverend guests.

To their surprise this offer was firmly refused. The leader of the pilgrims, a red-faced monk, with a bottle nose which might have signified a too great love of ale had he not been a holy man, explained that the rules of their order forbade them to lie on anything but the earth itself. Straightway he laid himself down by the fire, and signed to his monks to do likewise. The men of Sherwood had no option but to withdraw into their own huts and there sleep off the effects of their evening's merry-making.

Only Friar Tuck did not immediately sink into a deep sleep. He lay for over half an hour tossing and turning, grumbling to himself about the unhappy evening which he had spent.

'Ungrateful knaves,' he thought. 'One day they will find that faithful Friar Tuck is more use to them than they think. I do not trust some pilgrims. Methinks there is something afoot, some treachery which we know not of.' On this gloomy note, Friar Tuck eventually sank into an uneasy sleep. As he slept he was troubled by a curious and extremely vivid dream. He dreamt that he saw the leader of the pilgrims rise, throw off his pilgrim's garb, revealing the arms of the Sheriff of Nottingham emblazoned on a soldier's tunic. Then the false pilgrim beckoned to all his men to rise also, and they in turn threw off their robes, revealing the hated mark of the Sheriff.

So vivid was the friar's dream that he awoke, sat up on his couch of rushes and stared wildly round him in the darkness. The sky had clouded over, and he could barely discern the sleeping forms of the pilgrims by the dead fire, whose ashes were now only a faint spot of red in the middle of the clearing.

FRIAR TUCK SAVES THE SITUATION

There was no movement at all from the huddled figures. Friar Tuck cursed himself for an over-imaginative fool, and decided to go back to sleep again. But once again sleep eluded him. This time not even an uneasy doze came to him. As every minute passed, Friar Tuck felt more and more wakeful. Berating himself soundly for his foolishness, Friar Tuck decided to abandon the struggle and go for a stroll. Perhaps the cool air of the forest would calm him. He stepped quietly out into the clearing and felt his way among the huts towards the dim red glow of the fire. There was absolutely no movement among the pilgrims.

'They sleep soundly indeed after their ale,' reflected Friar Tuck sourly, 'while honest folk remain awake and sleepless.'

He tiptoed past the first pilgrim. As he was passing the fire itself, he tripped on a root which had remained unburnt and, before he had time to save himself, fell headlong on top of the sleeping form of the prior. To his amazement he found himself falling on nothing more than a soft bundle of clothing! Desperately, Friar Tuck felt the heap next to him. Another dummy! And the next, and the next, and the next! Those motionless heaps, so still and tranquil beside the fire, were all dummies. Then where in heaven's name were the pilgrims?

Friar Tuck opened his mouth to let out a yell of warning to the band. The next thing he knew, he was grappling in the iron grasp of two muscular arms which had seized him from behind and pinioned him. A series of guttural squeaks was all the friar could manage to get out. But they were enough to awaken Robin Hood, who slept in the nearest hut, and alert the watchman at the top of the valley, who blew the bugle signifying danger. Instantly every man in the camp was on his feet and searching for his sword or his bow in the dark. Friar Tuck's split-second warning had just managed to save Robin Hood and his men from complete annihilation at the hands of their false guests. Friar Tuck suddenly felt his attacker release his grip, as cold steel in his back felled him to the ground.

Now the valley was like a battle-ground as outlaws and Sheriff's men engaged each other in a deadly combat (for Friar Tuck's dream had been prophetic – it was indeed the Sheriff's crest which these traitors bore emblazoned on their breasts). The prior of the pilgrims was felled by the hand of Little John, and two others of the false friars went to the score of Alan-a-Dale. In all five false friars died, and one of Robin's men – Nat the Weaver – sustained a serious wound. The Sheriff's men had relied upon surprise, rather than large numbers, to win the day. Their plan had been to fall upon Robin Hood and his men while they slept, and murder them in their beds. Friar Tuck's warning had nearly foiled this plan, and the Sheriff's men were not adroit enough with the sword or bow to win in a fair fight. So it was not long before Robin Hood was surveying a line of pinioned soldiers with grim, if exhausted, satisfaction.

'So you would have tricked us,' he said. 'You would have used our reverence for the holy garb of the pilgrim to kill us all. It would be no more than you deserved if we strung you up on a gallows and let your corpses be picked to the bones by the ravens.'

'Mercy, lord, mercy,' prayed the former prior. 'We did no more than carry out the Sheriff's orders. We had no wish to harm you.'

Tom Turpin, who was standing by, spat eloquently to show what he thought of this excuse.

'Enough of your prating, Master Prior,' growled Robin. 'Suffice it to say that we shall not, after all, hang you, because we Saxons have not yet descended to hangings and murders. We shall simply send you back to the Castle of Nottingham to bear a message for us to your master!'

The prior's face showed his relief.

'The Sheriff of Nottingham is no master of ours now,' he said hastily. 'Why, we would never have served him at all if we had not been obliged to. His very livery is odious to us.' The prior smirked self-righteously as he twitched at his crested tunic.

Robin smiled. An excellent revenge on the false monks had just occurred to him.

'In that case,' he said softly, 'if the Sheriff's livery is distasteful to you, and you have no right to wear the habit of a monk, it looks as if we shall have to send you back to Nottingham in your shifts. Come on, men, strip these false pilgrims!'

The men of Sherwood needed no further urging. They

fell upon the soldiers and tore off the hated uniform of the Sheriff. Soon the false friars were shivering in nothing but their thin shifts.

In this fashion they were compelled to set out into the forest. Blindfolded and shivering in the night air, they were conducted to the outskirts of Sherwood by a gleeful Little John, who marched them briskly through briers and thickets, streams and marshes, without heeding their cries for mercy.

'You would have murdered us without mercy,' he reminded them. 'Why do you cavil at a few thorns?'

It was a very sorry band of men who finally arrived at Nottingham Castle. Around the neck of each one hung a placard bearing the mark of Robin Hood and the message:

'Greetings to the Sheriff of Nottingham. Robin Hood of Sherwood Forest herewith returns to him for punishment a dozen unworthy varlets.'

Nor was the ordeal of the wretched monks over when they confronted their master: his wrath was terrible to behold, and as he raged and ranted at what he called their stupidity and bungling, one or two of the soldiers wished that they had thrown themselves upon Robin's mercy and remained within the confines of the forest.

'Fools! Nitwits!' shouted the Sheriff. 'You have failed me, and you shall pay the penalty for your failure! Into the dungeon with you, the lot of you. Guards, take these men away!' The wretched erstwhile monks then found themselves hustled down the steep steps which led to the dank, unwholesome dungeons beneath the Castle of Nottingham. Their plaintive cries for mercy were soon drowned by the clanging of heavy oak doors and the turning of keys. So ended the adventure of the false friars.

Meanwhile, in his chamber, the Sheriff paced up and down, still scarlet with rage and baffled fury. Once again he had been outwitted by the impudent outlaw of Sherwood – once again Oswald Montdragon would be able to point to him as a muddling nincompoop who could not even direct one successful expedition.

'Just let me meet Robin Hood face to face!' muttered the Sheriff. 'Just let me get my hands round his slippery neck!'

9

ROBIN DINES WITH THE SHERIFF

'To Nottingham!' cried Robin Hood, flinging his cap in the air. 'The fancy takes me to visit the town again and see what sport there is to be had there. Are you with me, Will?'

'I'm with you, Robin,' replied Will, 'for that hot head of yours needs a sober one to prevent you getting into serious trouble. Let us ride forth together.'

The comrades mounted their faithful steeds, Troubadour and Polly, and set out for the town which they had once known so well, but which they had not visited for a six-month.

'I wonder if I shall catch a glimpse of my Lady Marian,' thought Robin.

Of course, Robin and Will were taking a risk by thus riding openly into the town where they were both named as dangerous outlaws, with a heavy price upon their heads. But they were counting on two things – in the first place, the loyalty of the Saxon people to the man who had robbed the rich to help them in their poverty; and secondly, the royal feast which the Sheriff was holding to mark the anniversary of the Prince's Regency. They estimated that the preparations for the banquet would keep their enemies safely within the castle.

Fearlessly – because assumed carelessness is the best remedy for anxiety – Robin and Will tethered their horses in the market place and mingled with the people. It was market day, and there was a great crowd in the square. Will picked up several pieces of interesting gossip, including news of one or two rich caravans which were due to pass through the forest in the future. He noted them down in his memory for future reference. He also learnt a piece of news which pleased him much less well. He discovered that it was common talk at the castle that Oswald Montdragon was paying court to Maid Marian.

'And does she return his affection?' inquired Will nonchalantly, trying to cover up his interest.

' 'Tis said she cannot abide the sight of him, master,' replied the countryman, 'but that is not a very likely tale, methinks. Oswald Montdragon is one of the most powerful barons at court: a maid would be wise to accept his favours.'

'A maiden's heart is difficult to fathom,' said Will Scarlett diplomatically, and allowed the subject to drop. Under his pretended indifference he was thinking hard. So Oswald Montdragon was pressing his suit on Marian! He must pass that piece of news to Robin.

But where was the Lord of Sherwood? Will looked quickly round. Robin was apt to run into trouble if he was left alone for too long. The mischievous vein in his nature would surely lead him into some mad venture. Will gazed anxiously at the market stalls, and searched the seething, busy crowd for sight of his leader in his striped jerkin. To his horror, when he eventually saw him, Robin was deep in conversation with a very familiar figure – none other than the Sheriff's own steward, the man who was responsible for the feast at the castle in the evening. What could that ill-assorted pair have to say to one another? Was Robin's face really not known to the steward? Or was he in fact luring Robin on to his doom, knowing perfectly well all the time who this well-spoken stranger was?

Will recalled that Raynald the steward was reported to be a stupid fellow, with no more brains in his head than were needed to order oxen for dinner, and see that the Prince's cup was filled. He hoped devoutly that he was stupid enough to be fooled by whatever story Robin was spinning to him.

' 'Tis monstrous hard, Master Raynald,' Robin was saying, with a wise shake of his head. 'Monstrous hard. No venison *at all* left for the Prince's feast? I can scarcely believe that villain Robin Hood has bared the forest of Sherwood completely.'

Raynald the steward nodded sagely.

'Every single beast,' he said. 'Or so my rangers tell me. The huntsmen will not even penetrate deeper into the forest. They assure me that the woods have been stripped, and that it would be a waste of time.'

'The cowards!' thought Robin Hood. 'There are plenty of good bucks left in the forest. They fear our arrows. I could show them glades and thickets bursting with fine fat bucks all ready for the royal table – if I wanted to.' Then a mad, mischievous scheme crossed his mind. Why should he not show this dumbwit of a steward where to find as much meat as ever he could want for his feast? Robin Hood would do Prince John a service for a change. He composed his features into an expression of great seriousness.

'It happens,' said Robin, 'that I am a butcher.' He allowed the words to sink in.

'And it grieves me to think of our beloved Prince John suffering at the hands of that knavish outlaw. Perhaps I can help you out of your difficulty?'

A wonderful look of relief and gratitude crossed Raynald's face.

'Oh, Master Butcher,' he breathed. 'If only you could. I fear that if I do not somehow provide enough meat for the banquet this evening, I shall be cast into prison by the Sheriff. For he is a cruel, hard master.'

'Well, it may hap that I can do something,' said Robin slowly. 'But I must warn you that the meat is a long way off; you would have to come and inspect it yourself, and of course. . . .' Robin's voice trailed delicately away. 'Of course, I should have to see your money first.' He wanted to make sure that the pigeon was worth plucking!

The steward nearly fell over himself in his eagerness to accept Robin's offer. He told Robin that he was carrying sufficient gold on him to pay for a veritable herd of animals. Robin's eyes glinted at the sight of the bursting money-bags.

' 'Tis enough, methinks,' he said carelessly. 'Let us forthwith ride out, for we have a long way to go. I must summon my servant, and tell him of our intention.' Robin beckoned grandly to Will Scarlett, who had been regarding him with amazement all this time.

'Hither, knave,' cried Robin, 'and listen to your master's commands!'

Will fell into the part as best he could, and bowed before his 'master'.

'I have been telling Master Raynald, the Sheriff's *steward*, here, that I am a *butcher*,' said Robin meaningly. Will still could not quite understand what was afoot, but he did all he could to show that he was ready to fall in with Robin's plan.

'Aye, the best butcher in Nottingham,' said Will, tugging at his forelock and making a rough bow to Master Raynald. Robin nodded.

'We are off to look at that meat of mine,' he continued. 'You know the meat I mean. It is so good, that it might almost be *royal* meat.' This time Will did have a faint inkling of what was going on.

'Aye, the best meat you ever tasted,' he agreed, imitating the voice of a countryman.

'Now, Peter, be off and tell my family that we are coming to inspect my wares,' said Robin carelessly. 'Tell Dame Tuck and my little brother John, and Sister Kate and all the rest of them. We want to give the Sheriff's steward a right hearty welcome, do we not?'

'We do indeed,' said Will fervently, making haste to depart.

He thought he saw now what part he was required to play. He would make sure that the Sheriff's steward had no cause to complain of inhospitality in the Forest of Sherwood! A moment later Will Scarlett and Polly were no more than a cloud of dust as they galloped at top speed along the road to the forest.

The Butcher of Sherwood

Robin Hood and Raynald followed slowly. Robin wanted to give Will time to warn the band, and he made the excuse that Troubadour was slightly lame. The good horse pricked up its ears, and pressed forward as if it understood what Robin was saying and wanted to show that it was not true. But Robin kept it back. It was some time before the first shades of the Forest of Sherwood began to close around them.

The steward shivered as he recognized the surroundings.

'Is it wise to penetrate the depths of the forest?' he asked fearfully, as Robin took the path which pointed farther and farther into the gloom. 'Is there not some other road that we can take? If the huntsmen who have known Sherwood all their lives will not ride abroad there, are we not rather rash in venturing farther?'

Robin shook his head, and firmly took yet another path which would bring them deeper into the thickets and the undergrowth.

'I know this forest passing well,' he said carelessly, 'and I care not a whit for Robin Hood and his band. I should be very surprised if any of these outlaws laid a finger on *me*.' Robin smiled to himself at the secret irony of his words!

But the steward's fears were only temporarily allayed. He kept looking nervously around him, and urging his horse on. Robin's leisurely pace maddened him. Once he actually thought he saw someone peeping out at them from behind a tree. Trembling with apprehension, Master Raynald plucked an arrow from his quiver and loosed it wildly into the distance.

Robin pretended great surprise.

'Are you really frightened, dear Master Raynald?' he inquired solicitously. 'Shall we turn back? But I thought you were anxious to have the meat as soon as possible, and I am taking the quickest road.'

The unfortunate steward groaned.

'You are somewhat rash, Master Butcher,' he cried, 'for

you are leading me where no other honest Norman in Nottingham dares to come – into the heart of Sherwood itself!'

In a panic, Raynald loosed off several more arrows. Robin prayed that his men were having the good sense to avoid these crazy missiles. By now they were experts in dodging through the undergrowth. So cunning indeed was their tracking that only once or twice throughout the whole journey did Robin even catch the rustle of a twig breaking behind him. He suspected that the mysterious figure which Raynald had seen flitting through the forest was in fact Bob the Weaver's boy.

'A dwarf!' said the steward. 'A malignant dwarf, I swear it! The country folk say that there are pixies and fairies in this forest still, and I dare swear that there are dwarfs as well!'

Robin thought it best to encourage the steward to think that he had seen a dwarf.

'If it was a dwarf,' he pointed out, 'there is no avail in firing arrows into the trees, for no mortal arrow can harm a fairy. Indeed, they just rebound upon the person who fired at them.' At this the steward turned pale, and hastily abandoned his shooting.

Now Robin considered that he had frightened the steward enough – for after all he had no quarrel with him. He was no more than a foolish fellow who had the stupidity to be in the service of the Sheriff of Nottingham. So he quickened his pace and directed Troubadour's steps to that part of the forest where he knew the herd of royal deer would be lying.

'We are now very near my butcher's shop,' said Robin seriously to Raynald. Raynald gaped at him.

'Here!' he cried, incredulously. 'Here, in Sherwood Forest?'

'Why not?' said Robin blandly. Then he suddenly caught Raynald's arm.

'Why, look, here we are,' he said triumphantly. 'Behold in front of you, Steward, the finest array of meat you are ever likely to see. And all of it for you, Steward; all of it yours to take back to your master with the compliments of ... ROBIN HOOD!' With these words, Robin Hood brandished his sword wide in the air, and placed its point against the steward's breast!

Raynald the steward knew not where to look for amazement and terror and confusion and rage. Before him he saw the royal herd of deer, in all its splendour, fleeing from their approach. In front of him stood the Bandit of Sherwood Forest himself, laughing into his face, with a bared sword in his hand. All around him he saw the men of Sherwood, their bows fitted with arrows and already drawn to fire if he so much as moved a muscle.

Gritting his teeth, he flung down his bow and arrows, and divested himself of his sword.

'You have fooled me neatly,' said he. 'Never before was I so bamboozled by an impudent outlaw.'

'No outlaw, Steward,' said Robin gaily, 'but the Lord of Sherwood Forest. I rule over Sherwood as the Prince rules over England – except that I rule with a good deal more justice and equity than he does. Now kneel to me, Steward, and swear your allegiance to your new master.'

Daring not to refuse, Raynald clambered from his horse and knelt on the floor of the forest before Robin Hood. Oh, shame and humiliation! That one of the Sheriff's servants should have to kneel before a common criminal!

When he was allowed to remount, he vowed to himself that he would have his revenge for this insult. But he was not allowed to depart until he had given Robin every detail of the royal banquet which was to take place that evening. Unknown to the others, another hare-brained scheme was already forming itself in Robin's mind, and for that he needed information which only Raynald could give him. When he was satisfied that he knew as much about the banquet as the steward himself, he permitted the unhappy steward to depart.

The Uninvited Guest

Sorrowfully Raynald wound his way back to the Castle of Nottingham, there, as he well knew, to face the wrath of his master. He could not decide whether it was better to desert the Sheriff's service altogether and flee to the south, with the risk of being hunted down like a dog by the Sheriff's men, or face up to the punishment which awaited him.

With these gloomy thoughts to occupy him, Raynald took no account of the cloaked figure, with a cap pulled well over the eyes, which rode behind him.

Together, the two riders arrived at the gates of the Castle of Nottingham. The steward was immediately admitted, with a good deal of deferential bowing from the men-at-arms. They took it for granted that the insignificant-looking person at the steward's heels was some unknown minion. No one thought of questioning the stranger's right to enter the castle: for Master Raynald was in charge of the Sheriff's household, and therefore above suspicion.

So the unknown gained admission to the castle. Once there, he took care to melt away from the steward's presence. The steward made his way immediately to the Sheriff's chamber, there to confess his failure and receive whatever treatment the Sheriff thought suitable for this dire offence. The stranger merged discreetly with a crowd of scullions, potboys and kitchen maids who were scurrying about, preparing for the feast. They were all far too harassed to spare time to question anyone: besides, the stranger did no harm. He simply settled himself down beside the fire, pulled his cap still further over his eyes, and appeared to fall asleep. There were a number of royal guests in the castle who had ridden up from the south at the bidding of the Prince. It was generally assumed that the weary stranger was one of these.

So the hours passed, and soon it was time for the banquet to begin. The frightened underlings bowed low as Prince John swept into the hall. They noted that although the Prince's face was smiling and genial, the Sheriff looked both unhappy and frightened. Oswald Montdragon, however, had a saturnine smile on his cruel features. Something seemed to have pleased him.

But where was the steward? Where was Master Raynald himself, who should have been there to receive the credit and the royal thanks for having prepared the banquet? It was customary for Prince John to express his gracious gratitude by the gift of a silver goblet. Surely Master Raynald would not be absent when there was a silver goblet in the offing? The soldiers and servers looked at each other in surprise. Yes, Master Raynald's chair was definitely empty!

Now the Sheriff was rising to his feet and whispering in

the Prince's ear. What could the Sheriff be saying that brought such an expression of annoyance and disgust across His Highness's face? In front of the fascinated gaze of the whole court, the Prince stood to his feet and banged his fist on the table.

'No venison!' he shouted. 'Not a single haunch of venison to be had from the whole forest of Sherwood! All because of that dastardly Saxon cur, Robin of Locksley! And you say that you have thrown the *steward* into prison for his failure. It seems to me, Sir Sheriff, that a taste of one of your own dungeons may be what *you* need to bring you to your senses and make you see that Normans do not eschew a whole forest because a few wretched outlaws dwell in one corner of it.'

Prince John banged the table again, so that the beakers and platters rattled, and glared at the Sheriff.

'Is it venison you want?' came a cry from the doorway.

The whole court looked round in surprise to see who dared to speak out thus boldly in front of the Prince himself. They saw a lithe young man spring on to the bottom of the long dining-table and, with a grand gesture, throw open his cloak to reveal the head of a magnificent twelve-point deer, which had been roughly hacked from its body!

'Take that!' shouted the stranger. 'Take that, John Plantagenet, for it is one of your own deer. I, Robin Hood, have brought it to your banquet to do you honour.'

With these dramatic words, Robin Hood hurled the head down the table, so that it landed with a huge crash in front of the Prince himself. The next moment he was gone, before anyone could even rally their wits enough to alarm the guards; his flying figure was seen galloping like the wind across the castle drawbridge and along the good road to the forest.

To say that the company was thunderstruck would be no adequate description of the consternation which Robin left behind! Everyone shouted at once. Some cried vainly to the castle sentries to shoot him down. Others tried to scramble out into the courtyard and mount their horses. They became hopelessly involved with those who were trying to ascend the stairs to the battlements and draw their bows after the outlaw. Meanwhile the Prince shouted orders at the Sheriff, and the Sheriff yelled orders at his men. The men yelled at each other, and Oswald Montdragon tried to countermand the Sheriff's orders with commands of his own. The royal banqueting-hall had never in all its history seen such confusion and dismay.

Only one person in all this hurly-burly sat calmly with a secret look of happiness on her face. Most of the maids at court had screamed or fainted or burst into tears when the notorious outlaw suddenly materialized in front of their very eyes. Marian of Whitby alone gazed with love and joyful excitement at the figure of Robin Hood. How hard she prayed that he might escape safely from his pursuers and return safely to Sherwood after his daring adventure! No words had passed between them, but one long, straight look had been exchanged in the second in which he held the great antlered head poised before the horrified eyes of the whole court of England. That look was enough to tell Marian that Robin Hood loved her still in spite of the castle walls which lay between them.

'Robin,' she murmured, 'today you have done a deed whose fame will ring in every Saxon home. Every true

Saxon will rejoice to hear the tale of the uninvited guest at the royal banquet!'

10

ALAN-A-DALE TO
THE RESCUE

ALAN-A-DALE sat sorrowfully by himself in a far corner
of the camp, strumming some melancholy lament on his
lute. He was ever playing gently to himself thus, as if
his thoughts were far away from Sherwood and everyone who dwelt in the forest. Robin's band knew that his
far-away look betokened that his thoughts had strayed
to his lady love, Lucy. It was now many months since
Alan had set eyes upon the fair Lucy – for as a rich
heiress she was sturdily guarded by her father, Count
Robert de Passy. Many times did Alan send messages
to her by her maid Matilda, assuring her of his devo-
tion: but never once was the Lady Lucy able to smuggle
out a single token of her regard. Her father, who had
strongly disapproved of Alan-a-Dale as a penniless
Saxon, even before he had joined Robin Hood's band
and been outlawed, watched his daughter carefully, and
scrutinized her least action. Thus Lucy languished
alone in her remote stronghold.

Alan-a-Dale's musings were interrupted by a breathless shout from Much. The plump miller panted up to
him, evidently bearing some important news.

'Hearken, Alan,' he breathed. 'Not an hour ago I was

speaking with Matilda, own maid to the Lady Lucy.' Alan sprang up.

'What news of my lady?' he cried. ' 'Tis a full sennight since I have had a message from Matilda to say that she was safe and well. I found no note under the stone of our usual trysting-place last time I visited it.'

Much shook his head and looked grave.

'Matilda was indeed downcast,' he confessed. 'It was the purest chance that I encountered her as I was delivering flour to the Castle of Passy. She looked pale as if she had not seen the daylight for some days. I questioned her as quickly as I could, fearing lest I should incur suspicion by talking to her, and she unfolded this sad tale to me.'

MATILDA'S STORY

One evening, when Matilda and Lady Lucy were sitting in the lady's chamber, the lady embroidering an altar cloth, and the maid spinning, their door was roughly flung open by two soldiers, and Lucy's father, Count Robert, strode in. Lucy saw at once from his black expression that he was in one of his fearsome rages. She was frightened that he had discovered one of Matilda's missives to Alan-a-Dale, and the Count's first words showed her that she was right.

'Well, mistress,' he said in a furious tone, flinging a crumpled piece of paper down on the rushes. 'What story have you to tell that will explain *that* away?'

Lucy signed to Matilda to pick up the piece of paper. With perfect composure the maid unfolded it and examined it with an expression of great interest.

'Why, my lady,' exclaimed Matilda in a voice of great indignation, ' tis my mark that is writ here. What can it mean? For sure, I never wrote this note.'

Lucy looked suitably surprised. She gave an exaggerated start of astonishment as she perused the note. Then she gazed in wonder at her father.

'I know not what it may mean, my lord,' she said, 'unless we have some enemy who seeks to harm us by incurring your wrath with this false message.'

The fatal note in fact said:

'My lady is in good health and bids me tell that she loves you still. She vows she will never wed another.'

'Zounds!' shouted the Count, banging his fist on the table and upsetting two spinning wheels in his rage. 'Do not play the innocent to me, daughter mine.' He wheeled round and fixed Matilda with his angry glare. 'Nor you, wench, for let me tell you that my man Sebald followed you on your evil errand, and with his own eyes saw you place this missive below a white stone in the forest. Now can you deny that you wrote it?'

Matilda turned pale, but Lucy was quick-witted enough to give another start of indignation and surprise. She rounded on Sebald, who was standing behind the Count.

'Why, Father,' cried Lucy, 'all the castle knows that Sebald has been sick with love for Matilda this past three months, and she will have none of him. This is his way of taking revenge. My poor Matilda feared all along that his love would turn to hatred, for he has a sour and jealous disposition.'

Matilda was quick to enter into the spirit of the plot. She nodded her head emphatically.

'Ah, the base varlet,' said she. 'Sebald, you should blush for very shame to have perpetrated such a deed.'

So convincing was Lucy's indignation and Matilda's reproaches, and Sebald looked so utterly taken aback and confounded, a dull blush spreading across his cheek, that for a moment Count Robert was almost tempted to believe them. Then he remembered how obstinate his daughter had been in clinging to her love for the outlaw, Alan-a-Dale. No, for all Sebald's confusion, women were the devil when it came to deception, and he would sooner take the word of one of his men-at-arms than all the promises of a couple of scheming wenches.

'A pretty story,' he said grimly, 'and false enough too, I trow. No, my mind is made up, daughter. This hankering for a common outlaw has gone on long enough, and I will have no more of it. In a week's time you are to wed Guy of Gisborne!'

The blow was so unexpected, the news so terrible, that for a moment Lucy's composure quite deserted her. She turned deathly white, swayed backwards, and would have fallen if the faithful Matilda had not rushed to her assistance.

'Oh, no,' she cried. 'Father, spare me, spare me, spare me! Guy of Gisborne has been thrice married, and each of his wives has died of sorrow and ill-treatment. He is old and cruel and ugly. Surely, Father, you would not wish such a fate upon your daughter.'

But the Count refused to let himself be moved by Lucy's pleading. The Baron of Gisborne was one of the most powerful barons at court, and the match would bring her father position and influence. It would teach his rebellious daughter a good lesson to be forced to fall in with her father's wishes for once.

'Say no more,' said the Count. 'Your tears and pleas will not avail you. Seven days hence you are to wed the baron in the castle chapel.'

By now Lucy had recovered from her temporary outbreak. She was pale and the traces of tears still showed on her cheeks, but she held herself right nobly as she answered:

'Robert of Passy! Although you are my father, you are a cruel and unnatural man. One day you will reap the reward of your brutality. As for Guy of Gisborne, I swear before God that never will I address one single word to him, either during my betrothal or after my marriage – if you can term such a mockery of a holy ceremony a marriage. You may force me to wed, my lord, but you cannot force me to love or honour a man whom I hate. Not one word or smile or mark of respect shall Guy of Gisborne have from me, unless he chooses to wring it from me by torture.'

So saying, the Lady Lucy swept from the room, leaving her father speechless behind her. When he had recovered from his indignation at this new display of rebellion from his child, he shouted after her:

'Say what you will, my proud lady. You will not alter my decision. And until you consent to address your future husband with the courtesy which is his due, you will not leave your apartments.'

But the Lady Lucy made no answer.

All this the maid Matilda had unfolded to Much the next day, in the courtyard of the castle, where she was about some errand on behalf of her imprisoned mistress. She related to Much how the two maidens had wept and prayed in secret all that night, and tried to devise some method of getting a message to Alan-a-Dale. Matilda was no longer allowed to walk in the forest, and Lucy was not even allowed to go down to the chapel, for fear that she might try to escape.

'The Baron of Gisborne comes hither today,' cried poor Matilda. She was near to tears on behalf of her beloved mistress. 'They are slaughtering the oxen and the sheep for the wedding feast, and the guests are being bidden from far and wide. There seems no way of escape.'

Much tried to comfort her. He was uneasily conscious that Matilda was attracting too much attention by her distress: and his position as a harmless, not very intelligent miller, who could come and go as he pleased in the great castles round Nottingham, was too valuable to be jeopardized. So he assumed a witless air and said loud enough for anyone to hear:

'You must ask the Count Robert yourself for flour, mistress. For my orders are to supply it direct to him, and I cannot give you any.' Then he added quickly, under his beath, 'Courage, Matilda, and bid your lady keep her spirits up. I will get word of all to Alan-a-Dale and my master, Robin Hood.' He pressed Matilda's hand and scurried away.

ALAN-A-DALE LAYS HIS PLANS

'We must haste and rescue them!' cried Alan, when Much had acquainted him with the whole grievous story. 'We must storm the castle and burn it to the ground. We must batter Count Robert until he pleads for mercy. We must. . . .' He was interrupted by Will Scarlett, who had been listening to the latter half of Much's tale.

'What avail to burn the castle if the Lady Lucy is inside it?' he said sensibly. 'No, Alan, our hearts grieve with you, and you can count on us all to help you. But we must plan this carefully, and not lose our heads. Robert de Passy is a wily fighter, and we know that Guy of Gisborne is longing to revenge himself on Robin Hood. Together they make a formidable combination. Let us use all our brains as well as our strength in trying to outwit them.'

So Alan and Robin and Will Scarlett put their heads together to devise some plan which would snatch the Lady Lucy from the grasp of her father and the evil husband whom he had chosen for her.

'There is bound to be a great bustle and disturbance at such a famous wedding,' said Will Scarlett. 'Our best hope is to attire ourselves as wedding guests, or at least some folk connected with the wedding, and thus pass ourselves off as harmless onlookers. For it will be useless for one of us alone to penetrate the castle: there is need for a score of men at least to carry off a bride from her father's own castle – especially when that father is Count Robert de Passy himself.'

'A score of men,' murmured Alan-a-Dale. 'There will be a score of choristers from Tyndale at the wedding for sure, for the Count is the protector of Tyndale Abbey, and the Tyndale choristers are famous for the sweetness of their voices.'

Will Scarlett clapped his hands.

''Tis the very thing,' he exclaimed. 'Tyndale lies five miles north of the forest and to reach the Castle of Passy the choristers must surely pass through Sherwood. Nor will they scruple to use the forest road, since they carry no gold nor jewels with them. We can waylay them.'

The plan commended itself to them – although it would need the greatest boldness to snatch the bride from the altar itself, in front of her father, her groom, and all their retainers! But the very boldness of the scheme seemed to make it their surest chance of success. By the time the ceremony was actually beginning, the Count would surely have relaxed his watch on his daughter.

Unfortunately there was no way to warn Lucy of their plan, for Much was not due to visit the castle again before the wedding.

'She will believe that I have deserted her!' cried Alan in torment. 'She will come to her wedding believing that I have deserted her in the hour of her need. Somehow, we *must* get a message through.'

Will Scarlett persuaded him that it was more important to preserve absolute secrecy about their plan than to warn Lucy. After all, if she knew she was on the point of being rescued her triumphant mien might give away something to her father. Whereas if she was indeed distraught, she would be able to give a most convincing display of despair.

Will Scarlett's logic was sound, although Alan-a-Dale's romantic nature still rebelled at the thought of the agonies of mind which his lady would endure. He seized his lute and poured out his feelings into a wild song of longing and despair.

Meanwhile at Passy the days seemed to flash by to the unfortunate maiden immured in her chamber. She spent hours gazing out of her window, as if hoping against hope to see Alan-a-Dale coming at the head of a great army to rescue her. Three times a day a page would arrive with a message from Guy of Gisborne.

'Guy, Lord of Gisborne, kisses the hand of the Lady Lucy de Passy, and craves the honour of an audience with her.' Each time Lucy told the page that she had nothing to say to the Baron of Gisborne.

Three times a day also her father visited her in her tower and raged up and down the room, calling her an ungrateful hussy who wished to ruin her father's position by her churlish behaviour. To all his insults, Lucy replied firmly that she had vowed herself to silence before God, and she would not break her vow. Seeing that she was obdurate, eventually the Count lost his temper completely and told her she would be given neither food nor water until she had given her affianced husband a civil greeting. Lucy was not moved.

'Then I shall be a starveling bride indeed,' she observed. 'But still will I not break my vow.'

The Count stormed from the room.

Inwardly, Lucy was not nearly so composed as she appeared. Would Alan-a-Dale never come? It was now only two days to the wedding, and still there was no sign, no message. She dispatched Matilda to search the castle and see if she could find Much the Miller. But Matilda came back with the news that Much had not been seen since that day, and was not expected to return until the castle stores of flour needed replenishing by his father – and that would not be for some time, since Count Robert was served by many other millers around and about Nottingham.

For the first time Lucy felt a pang of despair.

'Perchance he will not come, then,' she said dully to Matilda. Two tears coursed slowly down her cheeks. 'If he has indeed deserted me, perhaps it is best that I should wed the Baron of Gisborne. For they say his wives do not survive his cruelty more than a twelvemonth, and that way my life without Alan-a-Dale will at least be short.'

The forty-eight hours which still divided her from her wedding passed quickly. In all that time neither she nor Matilda heard anything to make them believe that Alan was intending to effect their rescue. It was a hard time for them both. Matilda tried to keep up a pretence that help was near at hand, in order to cheer her mistress, but even her cheerfulness wore thin as the night before the wedding wore on, and the maidens were left strictly alone and undisturbed in their chamber.

Lucy was weak from want of food, although Matilda had managed to smuggle her a crust or two from her own portion. She was pale from weeping and faint from her long vigil when her mother's tiring maids came to dress her in her long and gorgeous wedding-robe. Listlessly, and now almost entirely without hope, she allowed herself to be decked in her finery and led to the chapel.

As she gazed at the rich array of guests, and armed soldiers all round her, the burning candles at the altar, the priests in their golden vestments, and her father standing implacably at her side to lead her up to her bridegroom, the last ray of hope vanished from the heart of the Lady Lucy, and at the very moment she reached the altar rail on the arm of the Count, with a small despairing cry, she fainted dead away.

THE SINGING OUTLAWS

What had been happening to Alan-a-Dale while the Lady Lucy kept her lonely vigil in the Castle of Passy? Neither he nor anyone else in Robin Hood's band had been idle. Since dawn there had been a bustle and a stir in the camp, and when the sun was turning from the pink of the sunrise to the pale yellow brightness of the early morning, a score of sturdy fighters, armed to the teeth, marched out of the clearing in single file. At their head went Alan-a-Dale; for everyone recognized that this was a project which touched him so deeply that none but he must be the leader.

The first inkling they had of the approach of the choristers – whose route Much the Miller had managed to discover – was the sound of voices floating through the forest towards them. It sounded almost unearthly, this disembodied chant which pervaded the air with its sweetness.

'See yonder,' exclaimed Little John, pointing through the trees.

Following his finger, Alan saw a band of young men in the white robes of choristers, led by an old man with a harp. Their mouths were open and they were singing lustily and happily. They were evidently quite unaware that they were being followed, and continued blithely on their way for about a mile, while the outlaws trailed along behind them.

As the path narrowed, before descending a steep incline, Alan gave the signal; the outlaws ran lightly forward and stealthily encompassed the choristers; then, at a second signal, each outlaw marked one chorister, and fell upon him. The poor innocent youths were checked in mid-song. Their mouths were still gaping with the effort of producing a particularly high note, when they found themselves grasped from behind, and their trilling stifled by firm hands.

'Make no noise and we will not harm you,' said Alan-a-Dale, stripping off the white robe of the chorister he had captured and putting it over his head. He pinioned the man's hands and feet with a length of rope and deposited him gently on the floor of the forest.

'You shall have your garments back within the hour if all goes well,' Robin told the old harpist.

The old man trembled with fear at the sight of the mighty band of outlaws, and he could hardly speak at all. Eventually he managed to speak out the words:

'Have mercy on us, good masters, for we have no gold! I implore you to let us go free, for we are commanded to sing at the wedding of the Lady Lucy de Passy, and we must be there in half an hour's time, else my Lord de Passy will be sorely angry with us.'

Alan-a-Dale pretended to look very surprised at this news.

'Verily, verily,' he said. 'But never fear, good sir, we would not spoil a lady's nuptials, would we, Men of Sherwood?' The men all shook their heads. 'I promise you there will be right merry music at the wedding, for we will take upon ourselves to replace you.'

With this grim jest on his lips, Alan summoned the men to follow him forward on the road to Passy. Robin Hood brought up the rear, attired in the clothes of the old harpist, and carrying his instrument.

Alan felt that the new choristers should emulate the old ones in singing, in case some passing man-at-arms on his way to the wedding should see them and become suspicious at their silence. So he commanded the men to break out into song. Unfortunately, with the exception of Alan himself, and Friar Tuck, who could sing passably well, none of the outlaws had the faintest idea how to keep in tune, let alone sing the sort of holy song which they had heard issuing from the pious lips of the previous songsters. Little John's deep voice, accustomed to bawling out hearty hunting songs and ballads, sounded oddly incongruous, and indeed he kept forgetting himself and breaking out into snatches of them. Tom Turpin dutifully tried to follow Alan's lead; but alas, poor fellow, he had not the remotest sense of tune and his well-meant efforts were more trouble than they were worth. As for Robin's strummings on the harp – they did nothing to keep the men in tune.

In spite of the ordeal that lay ahead of them, the whole proceeding reduced the outlaws to such helpless laughter that in the end Alan-a-Dale had to order them to cease singing altogether and concentrate on marching. He alone never forgot for a moment the grim errand upon which they were bent. Henceforward Alan's voice alone was heard, and as he was at the head of the column, it seemed not unconvincing that he should be singing a solo.

In this fashion they reached the gates of the castle of Passy and gazed up in awe at the mighty battlements which extended high above their heads, seeming to touch the sky itself. The wedding was to be celebrated at midday; it was then five minutes to the hour.

The outlaws cast down their eyes in a most holy fashion at the approach of the sentries. Friar Tuck, who naturally had the most ecclesiastical bearing, was deputed to speak with the guards and explain who they were and what their errand was. To their relief, they were not questioned further: the name of the Tyndale choristers was sufficiently well known for them to be ushered immediately towards the chapel. Piously, with small shuffling steps, and folded hands, the twenty most notorious outlaws in England were led into the very heart of Count Robert de Passy's castle, by one of his lordship's own retainers! It was a situation which the men of Sherwood would have found plainly humorous, but for the great stakes involved.

Once inside the gilded chapel, the outlaws still did not dare raise their eyes for fear some observant soldier might recognize them and give the alarm. Robin Hood in particular took care to station himself in the deepest corner of the choir stalls, and let the shadows fall on his face. He was afraid his features had become somewhat too well known!

Thus the stage was set for the wedding: with only the bride needed to complete the gorgeous picture.

'Ah, my proud beauty,' thought Guy of Gisborne, 'you cannot escape me now. No power on earth can save you.' Little did he know that even as the thought formed in his evil mind, Little John, his eyes demurely cast down, had taken his place not a yard from the Baron of Gisborne!

The Bride of Gisborne is snatched away

And now the moment had arrived for the bride herself, pale and trembling, to walk down the aisle. As we have already seen, the Lady Lucy's thoughts were a tumult of unhappiness. Did no premonition of her lover's presence cross her mind? With all his heart Alan-a-Dale prayed that some inkling of his plan would reach her, and prevent her experiencing the ultimate despair. To his horror, he saw her reach the altar rail, saw her sway on the arm of her father, and witnessed her swoon upon the floor of the chapel.

Flesh and blood could stand it no longer! Profiting by the confusion of the moment, in which servants, soldiers, maids and priests scurried hither and thither, some calling for water, others crying out that the lady needed air, Alan-a-Dale leapt from his post in the choir.

With one bound he had reached the side of the Lady Lucy, and gathered her into his arms. The next moment he was brandishing his sword in the air, a strange wild sight, with his white robe still half covering his jerkin. The men of Sherwood were quick to follow his lead. Tom Turpin, with great presence of mind, seizing the terrified Matilda, and carrying her off too. Before the amazed eyes of the congregation, the twenty choristers transformed themselves in a second into twenty fully armed outlaws. Guy of Gisborne's men were completely unprepared. As Alan-a-Dale made for the door of the chapel, with Lucy in his arms, a few soldiers made an attempt to draw their swords and bar his way. But they speedily found themselves pinioned by the stalwart choristers, and their weapons rudely torn from them. Alan and Lucy, with two of the men were out of the castle gates before ever Count Robert de Passy had fully realized what was happening.

With a mighty roar, Guy of Gisborne urged on his retainers to take charge of the situation, and flout the dastardly kidnappers. But as he spoke, he found himself seized from behind, in the surprisingly muscular grasp of an elderly harpist, and flung to the floor. The harpist then ran nimbly for the door, leaving his harp to encumber his pursuers. The momentary glimpse which Guy of Gisborne got of the harpist's face was sufficient to enable him to recognize his old enemy.

' 'Tis Robin Hood!' he shouted. 'After him, seize the

impudent knave!' His words were scarcely noticed in the general hubbub which filled the chapel. By now the majority of the choristers had hacked their way free, and were fleeing through the gates, on horses stolen from the castle. When the Passy and Gisborne retainers came to pursue them in earnest, they found that their own mounts had been stolen! The armed band which finally pelted forth from the castle gates looked a sorry spectacle, on their old hacks and gentle palfreys, little accustomed to galloping pell-mell through Sherwood.

Guy of Gisborne himself was forced to mount on an old grey mare, which was used to draw wood, and had not ridden faster than a trot in twelve months. It added to his rage and exasperation to discover that he could not even pursue his stolen bride at full tilt, but must hobble along on a wretched nag. However, they had not been riding long in the forest when one of his men actually spied the glint of a white robe through the trees.

'Ha ha,' thought the Baron of Gisborne, 'our birds have not flown far. Now for my revenge on these daring outlaws.' He spurred on the old mare in the direction of the white flutter. Soon the men of Gisborne were riding down upon the band of choristers – for it was indeed the fatal troop whom they had spied, cowering among the trees – with whoops of triumph and delight.

'Spare us, spare us!' wept their leader, kneeling in his flowing harpist's robes, on the turf. Guy of Gisborne pointed his sword at his throat and laughed evilly.

'These are poor words from Robin Hood!' said he. 'Come now, outlaw, strip off that disguise of yours, and tell us where you have hidden my bride. Off with their chorister's robes, men, and show them up for the impudent scoundrels they are. There is an outlaw's jerkin beneath every one of those holy robes.'

But the choristers only shrieked for mercy. Indeed, their behaviour was so amazingly poor spirited, their cries so womanish and piteous, that Guy of Gisborne began to suspect that he had made some hideous mistake. He looked closer at the harpist's face. Were these verily the well-known and hated features of Robin Hood? On the contrary, this face was truly gnarled and lined with age, such lines as no disguise could possibly effect.

With a cry of horror, he ordered his men to desist from their attacks.

'We have been trapped!' he exclaimed. 'Once more that wily Robin Hood has had the better of us. These poor wretches are indeed the choristers of Tyndale. See their pale and terrified faces! These are no outlaws!'

The harpist fell on his knees of Guy of Gisborne's feet and kissed his hand.

' 'Tis true, 'tis true,' he cried, sobbing with relief at his narrow escape. 'Oh, good Baron, have pity on our misery. An hour ago the dreadful outlaws ambushed us and forced us to surrender our robes. We shivered in the forest, not daring to proceed to the wedding in our shifts. Then, as we knelt and prayed in the forest, lo and behold, those scoundrels were upon us once more, casting down our clothes and ordering us to dress as fast as possible. Good Baron, I do assure you that we were so much afeard that we dared not disobey. With all dispatch we re-attired ourselves, and started off for the castle, to explain our absence.' At the end of ths recital, the aged harpist and his choristers all began to weep and pray for mercy.

Guy of Gisborne brushed them impatiently aside.

'Go back to Tyndale,' he said curtly. 'There will be no wedding now at the Castle of Passy.'

With these words, which left a multitude of questions in the dazed minds of the singers still unanswered, Guy of Gisborne wheeled his horse and rode angrily back to his own castle at the fastest pace of which its exhausted frame was capable. He knew that by now Robin Hood, Alan-a-Dale and the rest of the band would have profited by their good start, to get clean away with his bride.

It was one more score to add to the list which he would one day settle with Robin Hood.

While Guy of Gisborne ranted in his castle, and Count Robert de Passy bit his nails with fury to think that all his schemes had been foiled – with Guy of Gisborne mortally affronted to boot – in the Forest of Sherwood all was happiness and rejoicing. The very next day the Lady Lucy pledged her troth to Alan-a-Dale before Robin and all the merry men. Friar Tuck married them there and then, under the greenwood tree, with bird song for music and wild flowers to decorate the altar. Never had there been a happier wedding: throughout the length and breadth of the land you would not have found a handsomer groom than Alan-a-Dale, nor a prettier bride than the Lady Lucy de Passy.

11

THE TREACHERY OF
BLACK BARBARA

EVER SINCE MAID MARIAN had paid her visit to the camp of the merry men in Sherwood, she had pined to see Robin Hood again. But the weary months passed, and still no opportunity came of escaping the watchful vigilance of Oswald Montdragon and the Sheriff. Her sole confidante in her sorrow was Black Barbara – alas, an unfortunate choice. For Black Barbara was eaten up with jealousy of Marian. She was determined to win the love of Robin Hood for herself.

'Why do we two not visit the Forest of Sherwood?' suggested Black Barbara to her friend one day, as they were spinning in their tower. Marian's gaze was fixed dreamily on the distant forest as usual. 'You cannot forever be pining for this outlaw of yours and never make some attempt to see him,' said Barbara, the temptress.

Marian sighed. She, too, was beginning to wonder whether the time would ever come when Robin would send for her. Perhaps Barbara was right; she ought to venture to seek Robin out, instead of waiting for him to send a message to her.

The next morning, very early, two cloaked figures could be seen stealing forth from the castle by a postern gate.

They mounted two palfreys, and proceeded towards the Forest of Sherwood at a fast pace. As they penetrated deeper and deeper into the forest, both maidens kept a watch for any signs of Robin or his men: in fact, it was Little John, out shooting in the forest, who first spied the wayfarers and gave the alarm.

'I mistrust these veiled visitors,' said Little John to Alan-a-Dale. 'Methinks Robin had better be told of this. Let us steal up behind them, and see if we can overhear their conversation.'

The two men concealed themselves behind a broad oak tree and watched the muffled figures go by them. To their surprise they heard one say to the other:

'How shall we ever find the outlaw camp, Barbara? We might wander about in this forest until nightfall and see nothing but the deer.'

Little John tugged Alan's arm. 'That confirms my suspicions,' he said. 'These ladies mean some harm to Robin. We must take action.'

Silently, the two outlaws stole up behind the unknown visitors, and before either of them had even time to cry out a warning, they found themselves pinioned from behind, with hoods neatly slipped over their heads so that they could see nothing of their attackers.

Both maidens struggled violently and tried to shake themselves free, but in vain – only muffled sounds issued from inside the thick hoods, sounding something like 'Let us go, let us go, let us go!' In this fashion they were conducted by the two outlaws to the camp itself. Imagine Little John's surprise and horror when he threw off the hood from the head of his first captive, to reveal the fair and innocent face of Marian of Whitby! His confusion and distress were quickly forgotten in Robin's joy.

'Marian,' he cried, his voice echoing round Sherwood with the warmth of his welcome. 'This camp becomes a castle when you grace it with your presence! Much, Friar Tuck, Little John, all you men, get ready a feast such as has never before seen in Sherwood, for Marian, our queen, has returned to us.'

All this time Black Barbara had been standing, still enshrouded in folds, boiling with fury at the fact that no attention was being paid to her. It was only her violent jerks up and down inside the hood which eventually drew the notice of Little John to her. Hastily and shamedly, he unloosed his second captive and revealed the proud features and haughty gaze of Black Barbara to the outlaws' inspection. Because this haughty maid had come to Sherwood as Marian's friend, she had to be welcomed as an honoured guest. So Robin stepped forward courteously and bade her welcome to the Forest of Sherwood on behalf of his band.

Black Barbara smiled demurely and cast down her eyes. She was sufficiently skilled in deception to conceal her evil intentions from all save Will Scarlett, who felt an indefinable pang of foreboding when he saw her. She toyed with the rich venison which was set before her, and sipped the good ale, listening with a tight smile on her lips to Alan-a-Dale's roundelays of love, which he sang gazing at his bride. When Friar Tuck started to tell one of his celebrated stories of merry days gone by, Black Barbara forced herself to laugh and applaud with the rest. However, as soon as darkness fell, she rose to her feet and smoothing her kirtle, said commandingly to Marian:

'Methinks we should be starting on our way

homewards, for the road is long and the night is getting dark.'

Marian looked regretfully at Robin, but she rose obediently to her feet at Barbara's command, and re-mounted her palfrey. Once more she exchanged vows with Robin and swore to return to him when the evil days of Prince John were over. Then sadly, the little procession wound its way through the forest back to the Castle of Nottingham. Robin escorted them to the outskirts of the forest, but farther than that he dared not to go, for fear of running Marian into danger.

BLACK BARBARA BETRAYS MARIAN

With a hevy heart Marian heard the castle gates clang behind her.

'Alas, Barbara,' said she, 'this visit has increased my love for Robin a hundredfold.' Wearily she mounted the steep stairs to her chamber. Barbara said nothing. Her heart, too, was a tumult of love for the bold outlaw.

As soon as Marian was safely within her turret, Black Barbara slipped away and went in search of Oswald Montdragon. It was as well for Marian, sleeping peace-fully in a shaft of moonlight, that she could not overhear the conversation which followed.

'Here is proof!' Black Barbara was saying, and forth-with from beneath her cloak she drew one of Robin's own green tipped arrows, which she had stolen from the camp when no one was looking. Montdragon's eyes narrowed. Up till the present he had taken Barbara's revelations for the false tale of a jealous wench: but now she had offered him proof indeed. His face darkened. So Marian of

Whitby was enamoured of the outlaw! That made one more count to which Robin Hood would have to answer one day: for it was the intention of Oswald Montdragon to wed Marian himself, and thus inherit all her rich lands and possessions.

'The Prince shall know of this,' said Oswald Montdragon. 'And straightway Marian of Whitby shall have a taste of the royal dungeons to teach her who is master here in Nottingham.'

'We could use this information to our advantage,' said Barbara meaningly.

'*Our* advantage?' Oswald Montdragon looked surprised. He was still inclined to think that Barbara had betrayed Marian out of jealousy for her beauty and fortune. Barbara hastened to repair her mistake, for she did not want Oswald Montdragon to know of her own interest in the outlaw.

'I mean that we may use this knowledge to trap the rascally outlaw of Sherwood,' said Barbara, and swiftly she outlined a plan which had long been maturing in her brain, by which she intended to lure Robin into her power.

'You have courage,' commented Oswald Montdragon when she had finished. 'It requires a stout heart for a maiden to do what you have suggested. I will see that you are well rewarded, Barbara Nevill.'

'I do not require gold,' replied Barbara. 'Only promise to grant me one wish, Oswald Montdragon.'

'Name it,' said the knight, carelessly. These wenches were ever desirous of jewels or some gewgaws. He felt sure that Barbara's wish would be something of that nature.

'Nay,' said Barbara cunningly. 'The time has not yet

come. But promise me that it shall be granted when I do name it.'

Oswald Montdragon had no choice but to shrug his shoulders and agree.

An hour later Marian of Whitby found herself roughly awakened by six of the prince's retainers. In harsh tones they ordered her to attire herself and follow them. In vain Marian pleaded with them to tell her what wrong she had done. All they would say was that she had offended Prince John and the Sheriff mightily, and was to be cast into a dungeon as a punishment. With a sinking heart, Maid Marian guessed that some inkling of her expedition to the forest must have reached the Sheriff's ears. She looked wildly round for Barbara, to warn her of the danger. To her surprise, there was no sign of her. Before Marian had time to ponder what this might mean, she was hauled away and pitched into the darkest dungeon in the castle. There the poor maiden was left without bread or water or light, to pine alone the whole night through.

While Marian mourned in her dungeon, Black Barbara wasted no time in putting her evil plan into effect. As dawn was breaking, she was to be seen mounting once more upon her palfrey, and heading back for Sherwood. This time she made no effort to conceal the manner of her going: for what need was there for concealment, when she had the protection of Oswald Montdragon himself?

Secure in the knowledge that the most powerful baron at court was watching over her, Black Barbara wended her way purposefully towards Robin Hood's camp. Although the exact route was still unknown to her (for Robin had thought it safer to leave both ladies in ignorance of this dangerous piece of knowledge, lest at some future date it should be wrung out of them by torture) she was confident that she would meet with one of the band before she had got very far.

Fortune favoured her. In one of the clearings near the outskirts of the forest she spied Will Scarlett, evidently on his way home to the camp, for a fine stag was slung over his back. Joyfully Black Barbara hailed her unsuspecting victim.

'Will Scarlett, oh, thank heavens I have found you!' she cried.

Will Scarlett looked up in surprise and saw Black Barbara, apparently all alone, in a state of the greatest agitation.

'Why, my Lady Barbara,' said he in great surprise, 'what brings you here to the forest in the first light of dawn?'

'Alas, alas, grievous news!' sighed Barbara, wringing her hands and making great play with her false sorrow. 'I hardly know how to break it to you. The Sheriff and the Prince have discovered the secret of Maid Marian's love for Robin Hood, and have cast her into a dungeon! She only just had time to scribble this note for Robin, before they took her away.' Barbara showed Will a crumpled piece of parchment.

'Robin must see this forthwith,' said Will, knitting his brows. 'He will surely have some plan for rescuing his lady love.'

Forthwith he conducted Barbara towards the camp. Even in his distress, however, he did not forget to blindfold her, so that she should not remember the way. In the course of his life as an outlaw, Will Scarlett had learned to trust no one.

When the news of Marian's imprisonment was broken to Robin Hood, he became so distraught that it was with difficulty Will restrained him from setting forth at once to burn down the whole Castle of Nottingham. Alternately he raged against the Prince and wept for the hurt which had been done to Marian, until the men feared for his reason.

All this time, Barbara sat demurely upon a fallen log, and offered no comment at all upon what happened, except to murmur her sympathy from time to time. The note she had handed to Robin bore the simple message: 'Robin, help me, Marian.'

When she saw that Robin was calmer and that the time had come to put the second part of her evil plan into effect, Black Barbara said in a small clear voice:

'Good masters, in all your plans to storm the Castle of Nottingham, do not forget that you have one friend inside the walls. Although I am only a helpless maid, perchance I can assist you to free Marian of Whitby.' Barbara cast up her eyes to heaven. 'I would do anything inside my power to help her,' said she with all the conviction she could muster.

To Will Scarlett's critical ear, however, there was something about her words which did not quite ring true. But before he had time to analyse it, Robin Hood had leapt to his feet and kissed Barbara's hand.

'God bless you, Barbara Nevill!' he cried. 'May He reward you for your goodness. Let us not forget, men, that this innocent maid has come alone through the forest in the misty dawn, entirely to help her friend.'

Carried away by their emotion, the men of Sherwood gave Black Barbara a lusty cheer. When she suggested to

Robin that she should leave open a postern-gate at the side of the castle, he vowed that she was the fairest and truest maid that ever walked the earth – saving only Marian of Whitby.

Will Scarlett alone sat apart and brooded on the ominous instinct which told him that Black Barbara's presence threatened the men of Sherwood with evil. Yet of what avail would it be to warn Robin? Had he not plucked the bold outlaw's sleeve a hundred times and urged caution – only to be scoffed at for his pains? Now Marian was in danger, it was even less likely that Robin would act prudently. So Will held his peace.

After Black Barbara had rested and partaken of some home-baked bread and an egg from one of the hens which Bob the Weaver's boy tended in the forest, she rose to her feet and, with a convincing show of reluctance, said that she must return to the castle if she was to carry out her plan.

'Have no fear. The gate will be left open at dusk,' said Barbara. Did a sly smile curl round her lips at these words? In the thin light it was hardly possible to tell, but Will Scarlett, who was by now in a considerable state of nervous apprehension, could have sworn that for an instant an expression of malicious triumph crossed her fair face. Once again – alas for Robin Hood – he did not have the courage to voice his suspicions.

ROBIN HOOD FALLS INTO THE TRAP

At dusk when the shadows were lengthening in Sherwood, Robin Hood, Will Scarlett and Little John set out for the Castle of Nottingham. It was decided that the three of them alone should attempt the dangerous enterprise of rescuing Marian, since it would be difficult for more than one to slip through the castle unobserved, and impossible for more than three. When they reached the walls of the castle, however, Robin motioned his two men to stand back.

'Alone I will enter the castle,' he said. 'Methinks the three of us will create too much disturbance. Will and John, do you stand back amid those trees, and let me go forward alone.' At this, both Will Scarlett and Little John protested violently, and Will in particular was loth to let his leader face the perils of the royal castle entirely unsupported. But with an imperious gesture, Robin motioned them back. He was determined that he, and he alone, should rescue his lady love.

Apprehensively, Will Scarlett and Little John watched their leader tiptoe forward and gently, very gently, try the latch of the postern-gate. It lifted! They saw Robin let himself through the gate with infinite care, and disappear from their sight into the depths of the castle.

It was the last they were to see of him for a long time.

Once within the castle, Robin found himself standing in a narrow passage. The dim light of dusk did not penetrate here, and Robin was blinded by the sudden blackness. All at once, standing there in the dark, he sensed that he was not alone. Someone or something was waiting for him at the end of the passage. Could it be Black Barbara? He dared not risk making any sound to attract her attention. The faintest whisper would be enough to give away his whereabouts. In any case, if it was Barbara, why did she give no signal?

The very faintest sound, no more than a sleeve brushing

against a wall, from the opposite end of the passage warned him that his unseen companion was coming nearer. Friend or foe, the unknown was certainly behaving very suspiciously: and Robin decided rapidly that since he was all alone in a hostile castle, discretion was the better part of valour. This was no place to face an enemy – a narrow, lightless passage, scarcely more than a tunnel, in the bowels of a hostile castle.

Stealthily, Robin moved backwards, and felt with his hands for the latch of the little gate by which he entered. Yes, here it was. As noiselessly as he could, he started to lift it. To his horror, it would not move! Desperately now, for every instinct warned him that there was danger all around him, desperately he struggled with the latch. The thing at the other end of the passage was coming nearer every minute, and still he could not get free!

Throwing caution to the winds, Robin began to hammer on the gate.

'Little John, Will Scarlett!' he shouted. 'Break down the gate! I am caught like a rat in a trap!' Even as the words left his mouth, he felt the icy chill of steel against his throat.

'That will avail you nought, Robin of Locksley, or should I say Robin of Sherwood?' said a low, menacing voice in his ear. At the same time he felt himself grasped in a grip of iron, which seemed to crush the very strength from his bones. In vain Robin tried to wrest himself free and batter down the gate which stood between him and liberty. No sound came from the other side of the gate: it was evidently too thick for his frantic cries to be heard. There was no escape from the remorseless grip of his enemy.

Struggling, wriggling, doing everything he could to wrench himself free, Robin was half dragged, half carried up the passage, then roughly pushed out into the courtyard. He found himself in the midst of a circle of flaring torches, held by a dozen men-at-arms. For the first time he saw the face of his captors. They were Oswald Montdragon and the Sheriff.

'At last, outlaw, I have you in my power,' said the knight with a cruel smile, and so saying, he buffeted Robin Hood in the face, as he stood there helpless. 'Into the dungeon with him, men, and let him have a taste of the royal hospitality.'

With these words, Robin was hustled away, and before the gloating eyes of Oswald Montdragon hurled down the steps which led to the deepest dungeon of all in the whole castle of Nottingham.

He heard the door clang to above his head, the bolts slide in, and then he was alone in darkness.

12

THE CONSPIRATORS

'Now FOR my reward, Sir Oswald Montdragon!' said Black Barbara complacently to the knight. 'My plan was successful, and we have both triumphed.'

'Name whatever you wish,' replied Oswald Montdragon generously: for had not the Prince rewarded him with the lordship of two rich abbeys, so delighted was he with the news of Robin's capture? Montdragon was quite prepared to pass on a little of his good fortune to Black Barbara.

'First tell me when the hated outlaw dies,' said Barbara.

'In three days' time,' replied Montdragon. 'He will be strung up on the battlements, or perhaps publicly executed in the market square at Nottingham as an example to the Saxon oafs. The details of his death have not yet been decided.'

'Then on the eve of his death,' said Barbara slowly, 'I should like to be admitted to his cell, alone. That is the favour I would ask of you.'

Oswald Montdragon looked at her in amazement. What a strange, cold-blooded wench was this, who first betrayed her friend out of jealousy, and then asked for an audience with the very man whom she had lured to his doom! What other evil thoughts did the serene face of this young maid conceal? In spite of himself, he shivered, and drew back a pace.

'You cannot refuse me,' said Barbara, ruthlessly. 'You have given your word, Oswald Montdragon, and you must honour it.'

'It shall be as you ask,' said the knight slowly. 'But may the day be far distant when you cross my path in hatred, Barbara Nevill.' And he crossed himself as if she had been a witch.

Black Barbara paid no attention. The important thing was that she had gained her way. She retired, well satisfied with the day's deeds, to her apartments.

Meanwhile in Sherwood Forest the little band of outlaws were in despair at the fate of their leader. Little John and Will Scarlett had waited for half an hour outside the postern-gate, waiting for some sign from Robin that he wanted them to follow him. In all this time no sound had reached them of the terrible struggle raging hardly ten yards away: for the walls of Nottingham had been built thick enough to stifle the most desperate cries. Yet both men had been uneasy, and Will in particular had hardly been able to contain his restlessness as the minutes ticked by and still Robin did not appear, either alone or with Marian. Robin's horse, Troubadour, pawed the ground and snorted and refused to be restrained, as if the faithful beast realized that some danger threatened its master. Eventually Troubadour made so much noise that the attention of the castle guards was attracted to the patient watchers by the gate.

'Who are you and what's your business?' cried one of the sentries. Then, as there was no answer, he loosed off a warning arrow into the darkness.

Will Scarlett and Little John held a brief consultation. Little John was for trying the postern-gate and if possible forcing an entry. Will pointed out that this would only attract the attention of the sentries to the gate and perhaps endanger Robin still further. Alas, he did not know that at that very moment Robin was beating in vain against the walls of his prison!

'Do you stay here and keep watch,' said Will. 'I will scout round the front and see if I can glean some news of what is going on inside the castle.'

The first thing Will Scarlett discovered at the great gate of the castle was that something of extreme importance had occurred within its depths. The guards were scurrying hither and thither, and to Will's amazement, there appeared to be a great amount of ale flowing. Plucking up his courage, he pulled the sleeve of one fellow and asked him what was afoot.

'Have you not heard?' said the soldier jovially, pressing a goblet upon him. Will surmised that he was already half drunk. 'Why, 'tis great news, master. Oswald Montdragon has captured the outlaw, Robin Hood!'

All the self-possession in the world could not prevent Will from starting backwards and turning pale at this dreadful news. Robin in the hands of Montdragon! Alas for all their hopes, alas for the merry band of Sherwood, now deprived of its leader, perhaps for ever!

Licking his dry lips, and trying to make his voice sound normal, Will inquired how it had happened. The soldier was willing enough to tell him. Oh yes, the scoundrelly outlaw had been trapped: one of the castle maids, a cool wench if ever there was one, had lured him from the forest with some tale or other. He did not know the details, but that seemed about the sense of it.

'One of the castle maids,' repeated Will bitterly. 'Yes, a cool wench indeed. . . . Oh, Robin, Robin, why did I not speak my mind? I might have saved you.'

'What's that?' asked the soldier stupidly, grabbing back the mug of ale and taking another great swig. 'What's that you say?'

'Nothing,' said Will dully, backing away. He had to get the news back to the camp as soon as possible. No time now to reflect on its disastrous consequences!

To Little John he only said very briefly that Robin had been captured, and the big outlaw was tactful enough not to question him further. Together they wheeled their horses and rode at full gallop in silence towards Sherwood.

'Black Barbara betrayed him!' announced Will Scarlett when they arrived. 'May God curse her for her wickedness. Men of Sherwood, we will not rest until we have avenged our leader!'

'Agreed!' cried all the men together.

Gathering round Will, they spent the whole night planning mad schemes and plots. Will Scarlett was convinced that as Robin had been captured by cunning and treachery, it was only cunning and treachery which would free him. Therefore he decided that once again they must make use of Much the Miller's special position in the royal castle.

'Much, are you brave enough to undertake yet another deception for the sake of our leader?' said Will.

The Miller swallowed. 'For Robin Hood's sake I will,' said he.

So Will Scarlett unravelled his plan, which involved,

indeed, much courage upon the part of the Miller. He was to spirit Robin out of the mouth of the royal castle in one of his own sacks, as if the outlaw leader had been no more than another cargo of flour! It was by this daring, if rash and foolhardy plan, that Will Scarlett aimed to pluck Robin from the jaws of death.

None of the other outlaws shared Will's hopes: for surely Much could not repeat his success twice. Yet, rack their brains as they might, they could think of no other way of saving him.

So two days later, the allotted day for Much's visit to the castle with his tithe of flour, the Miller set forth to accomplish this daring plan. Little did the Sherwood band know that this very day was the eve of Robin's death. But Robin himself realized it as he gazed hopelessly around him in the darkness and sought in vain for some way to escape.

MARIAN OUTWITS OSWALD MONTDRAGON

Marian of Whitby had heard the news also, because Oswald Montdragon had taken the trouble to come and inform her of the approaching death of her lover.

'You yourself will die on the next day, unless you give way, and consent to wed me,' said the knight with a gloating smile.

'Never, let me die in peace,' said Marian faintly, shrinking from her cruel persecutor.

'What good will it do your lover if you die too?' inquired Montdragon, angry at her continuous obstinacy. 'Surely even he would prefer you to be at liberty, when he is dead.'

It was at that moment that an idea sprang into

Marian's head. Suppose she gained her liberty – would she not be able to help Robin better, than by languishing in prison? For the first time since her imprisonment, she forced herself to smile wanly at her tormentor and say in a gentle voice:

'Perchance my lord is right,' said Maid Marian. 'Yes, what avail is it now to mourn for Robin Hood; I have been grievously wrong in my love for him.'

Oswald Montdragon was delighted at her change of heart. 'The wench is seeing reason at last,' he thought. Eagerly he raised her to her feet, and ordered her guards to set her free. In a short time the news was spreading rapidly through the castle that Maid Marian had at last given way and agreed to wed Oswald Montdragon. Prince John, as the Maid's guardian, was delighted to give his consent.

'We shall celebrate the wedding of the maid and the hanging of the man on the same day,' he said jovially. 'Let preparations be made for a double feast on the morrow.'

With difficulty, Maid Marian concealed the horror with which these words filled her. She tugged at Oswald Montdragon's arm.

'Suppose the outlaw escapes!' she said timidly.

Oswald Montdragon gave a deep guffaw.

'He will find it hard to do that,' said he, patting his belt, 'for the only key to his jail hangs here at my belt, and you may be sure I shall not give it up in a hurry!'

Marian's eyes riveted on the fatal key. Here at last was the chance for which she had been waiting! Oh, for just one opportunity to steal that key!

So the last day of Robin's life passed – slowly for Prince John and the Sheriff and Oswald Montdragon, who could scarcely believe that the dreaded outlaw was helpless at last in their power, and all too quickly for Marian and the men of Sherwood, who were scattered round the town, waiting for Much the Miller to emerge when darkness came, with some news of their leader.

But before all the dramatic conclusion of Robin's imprisonment could be reached, two important meetings had to take place. The first of these was a lucky accident. Crossing the courtyard with a sack of flour on his back, Much suddenly spied Maid Marian, walking with bowed head and a prayer book in her hand. He was amazed to see her at liberty, and drew back into an alcove to ponder what this development might mean. Could Marian have betrayed Robin? Impossible. Yet how otherwise would she have gained her liberty? However, the situation was too desperate to ignore any chance of success. Much seized his opportunity as Marian passed slowly by him, and plucked at her arm. Before she could cry out with surprise, he put his hand across her mouth and hissed in her ear:

'Are you for us or against us? Tell the truth, else you will surely die.'

'I am for Robin Hood!' gasped Maid Marian, wrenching herself free. 'Ah, Much, how thankful I am to see you. Tell me what I can do to save him.'

She explained to the Miller how she had promised to wed Oswald Montdragon in order to gain her liberty and so help Robin in some way. In return, Much related to her Barbara's treachery. Then Marian told him of the key which dangled temptingly at Montdragon's belt.

'That is your chance,' exclaimed the Miller excitedly. 'If you can free Robin from his dungeon, then I can spirit him from this devilish castle.'

Black Barbara visits Robin Hood
in his Dungeon

While Marian and Much were plotting, Black Barbara also was forwarding her fell schemes. For now it was the eve of Robin's execution, she claimed from Oswald Montdragon his promise that she should visit the prisoner.

'Who's there?' cried Robin, when a chink of light at the head of the steep dungeon stairs warned him that he had a visitor.

''Tis I, Barbara,' replied the black-hearted maiden.

'False wench!' exclaimed Robin. 'Get you away from me. What have you to say to the man you have betrayed?'

'Ah, Robin, do not speak to me in that harsh voice,' said Black Barbara in honeyed tones. Then she knelt down on the rough straw before him, and stretched out her hands in a suppliant gesture.

But Robin Hood turned angrily from her, and only repeated:

'Begone, false witch.'

'Poor Robin,' sighed Black Barbara. 'You have indeed been wronged, although not by me. Who would have thought that such a fair-spoken maid as Marian would have been capable of such treachery?'

In spite of his disgust at the very presence of the traitress, Robin could not keep silent at this taunt.

'It is not true!' he cried. 'Marian of Whitby would never betray me. 'Tis you, Black Barbara Nevill, who have brought me to my present pass. Accursed be the day on which I ever saw you!'

Black Barbara shook her head as if Robin's words pained her.

'Indeed, my lord, you do me grievous wrong. For from the very first my heart was filled with such love for you, that I would never, never do you harm. No, Robin of Locksley, I fear it was the false Maid Marian who schemed against you. I myself only discovered this recently. I would never have suggested that you rescued her if I had known the truth.'

'Prove it, Black Barbara,' said Robin scornfully. 'Prove that Marian betrayed me, and I will listen to you.'

Barbara's eyes gleamed with triumph, for Robin had played into her hands!

'Suppose I proved that Marian's reward for her services to the Prince was the hand in marriage of his favourite courtier – no less a knight than Oswald Montdragon himself?' she said softly.

'Never, never,' shouted Robin, in agony.

'Then follow me up these stairs,' said Barbara, and taking the prisoner's arm she led him forward to the narrow grille in the heavy door, which provided the sole crack of light in his dismal dungeon.

'Look there, Robin of Sherwood!' said the temptress.

Robin gazed in horror through the grating – for there in the courtyard not five yards from his gaze stood Maid Marian, with her hand in the hand of Oswald Montdragon. On her finger gleamed a great ring bearing the Montdragon crest! Robin gave a strangled cry. Oh no, it was not possible, not possible, that Marian should have fallen into the clutches of Oswald Montdragon! And yet what other explanation could there be for her presence there, free as air, smiling docilely into the face of the Norman knight?

He buried his face in his hands, and stumbled down the

steps into the darkness, caring not that Black Barbara witnessed his anguish. The false wench tiptoed after him and said softly in his ear, as he lay groaning on his straw palliasse:

'She has played you false, Robin, but I will not forsake you. I will help you to escape – on condition that you will promise to wed me.'

Robin rolled over on his side and glared at her in anguish, his face ashy pale.

'Begone, Black Barbara,' he said. 'And do not torment me in my terrible grief. Be she as false as hell itself, still shall I love her till I die.' With these words he buried his face once more in his hands, and began to groan aloud in agony.

'Then perish through your own stupidity and obstinacy!' exclaimed Barbara, furious that all her wiles had not persuaded Robin to reject Marian. 'At dawn tomorrow you shall die, and I will rejoice to see it.'

With these bitter words, revealing herself in her true colours, Barbara turned angrily from the outlaw and rushed from the dungeon.

THE KEY

'Will my lord partake of this goblet of wine?'

With these soft words, Marian tempted Oswald Montdragon to drink from the golden cup which she offered him. It was a hot summer's night, and Montdragon felt in need of some soothing refreshment, so he gulped down the long cool drink gladly.

Marian watched him eagerly: with all her heart she prayed that the desperate plan she had concocted with

Much the Miller would succeed. For a few minutes she said nothing at all. Then to her delight, she saw the knight's head begin to nod.

'Sleepy . . . very sleepy,' he muttered. They were the last words he managed to speak before his head sank on to his breast, and he began to snore as if he was drunk.

With beating heart Marian approached her victim and fumbled at his belt for the key. Here it was, the precious key to her hopes. In terror all the time lest the knight should awake and apprehend her, she detached it from his belt, and then with one last backward look of mingled dread and triumph, she tiptoed from the room.

Much was waiting for her outside. At his side he had a large sack, one of the empty sacks whose contents now resided in the castle granaries. Marian did not speak, but simply nodded to indicate that she had succeeded. Together the conspirators stole towards the dungeon.

A dangerous moment faced them when they passed the guards. Marian had to endure this alone. Holding her head high, she swept past the first soldier, and managed an excellent imitation of surprise when she was challenged by the second.

'Do you not recognize me?' she demanded haughtily.

The man looked abashed, for the news of Marian's impending marriage had spread swiftly through the castle, and he knew that he must treat Oswald Montdragon's bride with all honour and deference.

'Why, madam, yes I do,' he stammered. 'But my lord gave orders that only the Lady Barbara was to be admitted to the outlaw's cell, and she has been and gone some time. Besides, my lord himself keeps the key to the dungeon.'

Marian thought swiftly. What business had Barbara with the man she had betrayed? This boded no good. But she did not show her surprise.

'Do you imagine that Maid Marian is denied a privilege which is granted to Barbara Nevill? See, here is the key of the dungeon.' With these words, Marian proudly exhibited the heavy black key. The soldiers were impressed and conferred hastily among themselves. They dared not risk offending Maid Marian; on the other hand, they were loth to incur Montdragon's wrath by disobeying orders. Seeing their indecision, Marian stamped her foot and said haughtily:

'Very well, churlish knaves that you are, I shall return to my lord and tell him how his soldiers treat his affianced bride.'

These bold words – for what would Marian have done if her bluff had been called? – these words carried the day. The soldiers bowed clumsily and let her pass. With a muttered word of apology, they retired to their guard room.

Marian realized that she had not a moment to lose. She did not know how long the drug she had administered to Montdragon would hold him in slumber. Besides, it would only take one tiny incident to arouse the soldiers' suspicions. Like a bird she sped down the dungeon stairs and cried eagerly:

'Robin, Robin Hood. Here am I, Marian, come to save you!'

For a moment Robin thought he must have taken leave of his sense. This was some nightmare come to plague his last hours.

'Marian!' he said wonderingly.

'Yes, indeed, it is I, Marian.' And in a hasty whisper the maid explained all that had happened since she had left Robin in the forest.

'Ah, Marian, why did I ever doubt you?' exclaimed the outlaw. 'Now I feel a man again. I could fight a thousand Montdragons.'

'There is no time to lose,' said Marian. 'Follow me.'

Together they clambered back up the stairs, and Marian swung open the door, then locked it carefully behind Robin. They were fortunate: none of the soldiers was in sight, and there was Much, seated on top of his cart, piled high with the empty sacks, waiting only for the appearance of his fellow conspirators to set off at full speed for Sherwood.

'Hist, Much,' whispered Robin.

The Miller simply nodded his head in the direction of the sacks, and Marian and Robin burrowed their way down and concealed themselves as best they could among the floury sacking. Much cracked his whip across the back of his beast, and the cart started to roll towards the entrance. A hundred yards to go. Fifty yards to go. Twenty-five, twenty, ten, five, four, three, two, one. Now they were rolling slowly across the drawbridge itself. The free winds blew around them.

Suddenly, from the interior of the castle, came a mighty shout, rending the silence of the night. Its import was unmistakable.

'The outlaw! The outlaw! The outlaw has escaped!'

'Close the gates!' shouted someone.

'Bar the castle!' shouted someone else.

And all this time, Much's little cart was bowling across the drawbridge, while his passengers hoped against hope that their departure would pass unnoticed. They were nearing the very end of the drawbridge when the guard spied them and gave the alarm. Much dared not even parley with the guards. He whipped up his horse, thus giving away his guilt. Immediately the heavy drawbridge began to creak into motion. Would Much's weary horse make the end before the drawbridge rose?

Alas! Before the horse had quite reached the end, the fugitives saw the end of the drawbridge begin to rise.

'Go back, Much,' shouted Robin. 'Go back, else we shall perish in the moat below, Maid Marian with us.'

'Go on, Much,' shouted Marian. 'Go on. Better death in the moat than death at the hands of Oswald Montdragon!'

The Miller gritted his teeth and lashed his horse to one last effort. The gallant nag strained every muscle, seeming to sense the peril which threatened them. A final spurt – a bound – a stumble on the rapidly rising bridge, one last great leap, and the frail cart landed in a heap on the far side of the moat. Horse, men and maiden tumbled together, for a moment too shaken by the fall to be able to move. The next moment the willing hands of the men of Sherwood were helping them to their feet, and on to fresh horses. The drawbridge was by now high in the sky, but Robin, Marian and Much were safe and sound the other side.

Within the castle, Oswald Montdragon's rage was terrible to witness. Not only had the outlaw escaped, but his bride had been snatched from him!

'Pursue them, capture them, or I'll have you all hanged!' he screamed. In vain. By the time the drawbridge was lowered again and a posse of retainers had galloped towards Sherwood, the merry men were far away. Once more Robin Hood had outwitted the Normans.

13

THE PRINCE GROWS DESPERATE

AFTER HE had been rescued by Much, Robin Hood spent a
merry summer in Sherwood with Maid Marian and his
band, hunting the royal deer, and making good sport
among the trees and glades.

'If King Richard never returns, at least we shall have
made the best of our lot as outlaws,' said Robin, looking
round at his faithful followers – Will Scarlett, Little John,
Alan-a-Dale, with his Lucy, Tom Turpin now wedded to
Matilda, Nat the Weaver and his boy, Friar Tuck, Much
the Miller, and last but not least, Maid Marian. They
were all attired in forest green, and even Marian wore a
green kirtle, so that she should be less conspicuous among
the trees.

'Agreed, good Master Robin,' answered Alan-a-Dale.
'I for one care not if I never see the inside of a castle again –
and as for riches and lands, what are they compared to
loyal friends and a loving wife in the greenwood?'
Whereupon all the merry men together drank a toast to
life in Sherwood Forest.

While the outlaws congratulated themselves on their
good fortune, the atmosphere in Nottingham Castle was
not one whit so cheerful. Prince John blamed the Sheriff

and Oswald Montdragon alternately for their failure to capture and hang the outlaw. Even Black Barbara came in for her share of the blame, so that the evil maid was torn between fear for herself and hatred of Robin Hood who had rejected her advances. Oswald Montdragon treated her with scant courtesy when he passed her in the courtyard, and once it was known that Black Barbara was out of favour, the rest of the court lost no opportunity to demonstrate their hatred for her.

All this did not make Black Barbara resolve to mend her evil ways. Instead, she grew more bitter and more jealous as each day passed. Even her remarkable beauty began to wither with the fire of her hatred. She was eaten up with thoughts of revenge.

One day the fancy seized her to visit again the Forest of Sherwood, and see if she might not pick up some information which would help her outwit Robin Hood. She donned a thick cloak, veiled her face, poured grey powder on her hair and etched wrinkles on her white brow. Then she ensconced herself in her litter, and ordered one of the royal men-at-arms to escort her on a journey to an abbey which lay beyond the confines of the forest.

The fellow demurred at this command.

''Tis not meet that you should travel through Sherwood, my Lady,' he said, 'for since the bold outlaw escaped through our fingers, his robberies have increased tenfold. Only seven days ago he robbed my Lord Abbot of Yardsdale of ten bags of gold and departed laughing, with my Lord's own white horse, leaving him to walk home through the forest. When the abbot reproached him for his irreverence, the rascally outlaw retorted that an abbot had no right to ride such a fine horse, being wedded to holy poverty.'

'He has done worse things still,' another soldier chimed in. 'He stole all her jewels from the Countess of Ware. Then he distributed them lavishly among the poor people of Nottingham, so that the Countess was obliged to instruct her steward to buy them back again for much gold, in order that her collection of emeralds might be complete. Methinks Robin Hood was highly delighted at the success of his plan, whereby the poor were much enriched, and my Lady Countess, who is a proud hard woman, much impoverished.'

But Black Barbara would not allow herself to be dissuaded from her plan. She commanded the soldier to accompany her and set out immediately. She felt convinced that she could somehow discover the whereabouts of the outlaw camp, and at one stroke revenge herself on Robin Hood and restore herself to the royal favour.

In spite of the evident fear of her escort, Barbara ruthlessly ordered him to take the most direct route towards the centre of the forest. After an hour's journey, she spied a young boy in a clearing, trying to tame a little fawn which had evidently been abandoned by its mother. Barbara's sharp eyes identified him as the child whom she had seen shyly hiding behind one of the men in the Sherwood camp. What a piece of good fortune!

'Hither, boy!' she called imperiously. Bob started up and saw a stranger who was beckoning for him from the interior of a darkened litter. Life with the outlaw band had taught him to be suspicious of strangers, but outwardly he showed no sign of fear. He stared into the interior of the litter. At first sight this appeared to be some elderly lady confronting him. Then he noticed something which made him catch his breath.

'Good morrow, lady,' he said courteously, letting nothing of his suspicions appear.

Black Barbara assumed an expression of aristocratic disdain.

'I desire that you should do me a service, boy,' she said. 'I have some very important news to communicate to Robin of Locksley concerning his father, the Earl, and I should be grateful if you could indicate to me where I can talk to the noble gentleman.'

Bob thought quickly. Did Black Barbara know that he was a member of the outlaw band? Or could he fool her into thinking that he was just a stray lad, out playing by himself in the forest?

'I should like to help, my Lady,' said Bob slowly. 'But of course—'

'Tush, boy,' said Barbara impatiently, 'do not trifle with me. I know that you are a member of the outlaw band. My maid hath described you all to me. I believe that your father is one of their number, is he not?' Bob bowed his head.

'If so much is known to my Lady,' he said submissively, 'then I will not conceal from her where we dwell. Let the lady follow me, and I will take her to my master, Robin Hood.'

Black Barbara was delighted at the success of her plan. Forthwith she pressed a bag of gold into the boy's hand, and promised him still more if he would lead her to the outlaw's camp.

Bob leads Black Barbara a Merry Dance

So the ill-assorted procession set out, with Bob tramping ahead, and Barbara following behind in her litter. They wound their way through thick thickets and closely knitted shrubs; across fords where the horses drawing Barbara's litter had to go knee deep in water; down steep cliffs of whose very existence Barbara had never previously dreamt; and up hills which seemed like mountains to the exhausted travellers. All this time Bob refused to exchange a word with his strange companions. He met all Barbara's queries and petulant questions with a steady silence.

Once or twice they heard the chink of armour in the distance as if some soldiers were passing. Barbara's man-at-arms was all for meeting up with the strangers and making a joint expedition, but Barbara refused to allow him to give the alarm: she wanted all the credit for the discovery of the camp for herself.

At length Bob led them into a deserted valley, where none of the usual luxuriant green of the forest grew. Here were only stones and boulders and a sluggish stream trickling through the centre of the deserted spot. For the first time Black Barbara's suspicions were aroused.

'Is this indeed the way to the camp, boy?' she demanded imperiously. 'For I assure you that your master will be right angry with you if you do not conduct me thither.'

'My master will be right angry if I let you anywhere near our camp,' muttered Bob.

'What's that?' demanded Barbara.

'Fair mistress,' explained Bob, 'the road gets narrower

now, and I must fain ask you to dismount from your litter and continue on foot.'

At this, Black Barbara was greatly surprised. For surely it was possible to reach the outlaws' camp on horseback. Yet she dared not reveal her secret knowledge, and so she was obliged perforce to dismount and follow Bob on foot. The soldier, by now extremely surly and short-tempered, tramped after her. They travelled on for what seemed many weary miles to the footsore Barbara. At long last, Bob called a halt, and ordered Barbara and the soldier to sit down and rest while he went on ahead and scouted to see if any enemies were about.

'I must go forward alone,' said he. 'Do you wait here, until I give the signal of three long whistles. Then plunge forward down yonder cliff and you will find me waiting at the bottom.'

Black Barbara looked with distaste at the tangled nettles, and brambles which faced her. But she had sworn to revenge herself on Robin Hood, and she was determined not to let a few brambles stand in her way.

'So be it,' said she. 'But mind you are not over long, boy. For I am impatient to see your master.'

Barbara's plan was to penetrate the camp, and then dispatch her escort back to the Castle of Nottingham, to summon a great expedition of soldiery after them. She seemed to be on the verge of succeeding!

Bob vanished quickly from their sight down the slope; Barbara and the soldier were left in peace. The minutes passed. Nothing stirred in the forest, except the birds flitting above their heads in the trees, and the deer which bounded gracefully past them, looking as if they had not a care in the world.

The soldier began to grumble.

'The lad is an unconscionable long time, my Lady,' he said, crossly. 'Methinks we have come on a fool's errand. Besides, you instructed me to escort you to the Abbey of Yardsdale. There was no talk of visiting Robin Hood then, besides which I am greatly afeard to be left alone in this forest.'

'Peace, fool,' said Barbara angrily. 'Who gave you leave to speak? Together you and I are about to uncover the secret which has plagued the court nigh on six months. Yet you, weak poltroon, complain of a little delay.'

The soldier was abashed at the lady's rebuke, and held his peace although the minutes ticked on remorselessly until one hour had passed since their last sight of Bob the Weaver's boy.

'He cannot have played us false,' muttered Barbara. 'Why, he was friendly towards us, and all eagerness to guide us to the camp. He could not have recognized me, for I have greyed my hair, and etched wrinkles on my brow.'

It was fortunate for Barbara, sitting angrily in the forest, that she could not hear the report which Bob was making at that very moment to Robin Hood.

'Her hair was grey; her brow was wrinkled – but Master Robin, her voice was young and eager! So I looked down at her hands, and Master, by the rood I swear that they were the hands of a young girl!'

'Well spied, young Bob!' cried Robin, patting him on the shoulder. 'I have a long score to settle with my Lady Barbara, and you have helped me to settle some of it. You say that the lady sits there still, waiting for you to return?'

'That she does. And when she hears three long whistles,

she will straightaway plunge down a slope into the stickiest marsh in Sherwood! For she imagines that our camp lies at the bottom of this slope, whereas in fact she is sitting a mile or so away.'

The thought of Black Barbara's fate caused the merry band much delight and laughter. But Robin's soft heart and sense of chivalry refused to tolerate the idea of any lady, even such an evil-hearted damsel as Barbara Nevill, being subjected to rough treatment in one of the Sherwood mires. Frowning, he forbade Bob to carry his wicked plan further. Maid Marian added her gentle pleas to Robin's commands.

'For many years she was my old friend at court,' she said. 'And I cannot wish to see her humiliated. Let her be, Bob; the thorns of jealousy in her own breast are sufficient punishment.'

Bob reluctantly abandoned the idea of giving three whistles, and agreed to allow Barbara to keep her vigil as long as she cared to sit there, without interfering with her in any way. He could not resist, however, stealing out of the camp, in company with Tom Turpin, and taking away the horses which had been tethered at some distance away.

When Black Barbara eventually realized that she had been tricked, and cursing to herself in a most unmaidenly fashion, retraced her footsteps, she discovered that her horses had gone, and only her litter remained.

Then Barbara stamped her foot in fury.

'Dolt! Find my horses for me!' she screamed at the unfortunate soldier, who stood looking miserably around him as if he expected to see the horses in the midst of a bush.

'How can I, lady,' he stammered. 'Perchance some fairy or some witch has spirited them away.'

'Fairies! Witches!' shouted Barbara in her wrath, her face purpling with indignation. 'Outlaws more likely. We have been fooled, man, in the most dastardly fashion. Back to Nottingham at full speed, and if you say a word of this venture to your master, I swear that I will have you whipped.'

'Are we not to go to Yardsdale?' began the poor soldier, very timidly. He was quite confused by the events of the day.

'To Yardsdale!' exclaimed Barbara. 'What point in going to Yardsdale, idiot? No, back to Nottingham Castle, and let there be no more prattling on this subject.'

The dejected soldier and the angry damsel then set forth on foot to make the long journey back to the castle. Barbara's thoughts were a tumult of hatred for the outlaw who had fooled her and the boy who had thus cleverly outwitted her: moreover she had the unpleasant prospect of explaining to the Sheriff how she had allowed herself to be tricked once more.

To her surprise, when she arrived at the castle, no one paid the slightest attention to her arrival. A few dogs barked desultorily and a few kitchen maids curtsied to her, but there was not a soldier to be seen, and as for the Sheriff and Oswald Montdragon, there was not a sign of them anywhere.

Black Barbara was greatly puzzled. She questioned one of the beggars sitting idly in the courtyard.

'Why, mistress,' said he in surprise, 'have you not heard? A wandering minstrel has come hither, and they say he has news of King Richard. Yet he refuses to give it to anyone except the Prince himself, and the Prince has gone hunting. Methinks the minstrel will give his news to him at dinner.'

News of King Richard! No news of King Richard could be good news for the followers of Prince John, unless indeed the minstrel brought news of his death. Ever since Prince John had learned that the King had been imprisoned in a foreign country on his way back from the Crusade, his heart had been considerably lighter. The Prince had felt that there was a good chance the King would never return, and he had begun to act with even more tyranny towards the poor people of England, oppressing the Saxons and favouring the Normans. The exactions of the Sheriff – the taxes and tithes which he levied – had doubled since the rumour of the King's imprisonment.

'Perhaps the Prince's star is about to wane,' thought Black Barbara meditatively. 'Have I made a mistake in allying myself with the Normans? Yet I cannot find it in my heart to change at this late hour. I stand or fall with Prince John.'

'THE LION HAS ESCAPED'

That evening, when the candles were guttering in the great hall and the roasted oxen had been consumed, Prince John summoned his barons around him, and bade the minstrel relate the news which he brought. The minstrel was a pale and melancholy youth, who seemed to pour all his energies into his songs, long sad ballads of love and death. His white face suggested that he had suffered long imprisonment in some deep dungeon.

'My news is for the Prince's ear alone,' said the minstrel sullenly. He looked askance at the barons around him, particularly at Oswald Montdragon and the Sheriff.

'Speak up, fellow, speak up!' said the Prince angrily. 'We are all good Normans here, are we not, united in hatred of the Saxon race?'

'United in hatred of King Richard,' muttered Oswald Montdragon, but he said the words low, for he did not want to incur the further disfavour of the Prince.

The minstrel stared around at the faces which he saw about him – faces where fear and greed and distrust shone out.

'Alas, poor England,' he thought, 'to lie in the hands of such men as these.' But he kept these thoughts to himself, and only repeated aloud that his message was for the Prince's ear alone. Perforce, the Prince had to withdraw with him behind an arras and listen to his message.

'Your Highness,' said the minstrel, once they were alone. 'I insisted on giving this message to you alone, because I knew that you would not wish your barons to hear it. Sire,' the minsrel bent his head close to the Prince's ear, '*the Lion has escaped!*'

With these words, uttered in a low sibilant whisper, the minstrel flung back the arras, sprinted across the hall, and was away out of the castle before anyone could stop him. He left Prince John behind him in a dead faint. For this was the very message which had been prearranged to warn the Prince of King Richard's escape from prison.

'Water, water,' gasped the Prince, coming to his senses. 'Sheriff, we are undone. The King has escaped from prison.'

At these fateful words, the barons, one and all, high and

low, took a step backwards, and glanced fearfully at one another. Already one or two slunk away from the Prince's side. The Sheriff turned as white as his master.

'It cannot be true!' he gasped. 'It is some enemy who has sent this message.' He hissed in the Prince's ear, 'Take heart, Sire, dismiss this news from your mind and try and behave as if nothing had happened. Look how quickly your barons are melting from your side, and only those who are deeply committed in villainy, like Oswald Montdragon and Guy of Gisborne, are standing by you. Rally yourself, Sire, and try to save the day.'

The crowd eagerly watching the Prince's strange actions from their seats in the well of the hall, saw him recover himself, return to the royal chair, drink a goblet of wine straight down and manage a weak smile.

'Sad news, sad news indeed,' said the Prince. 'Alas, our poor brother is still in prison. Yonder minstrel has just brought me further tidings of him. Would that he might return to us!'

Not a man present was deceived by this pretence of affection for King Richard. The Normans were also uneasily aware that something momentous had happened up there behind the arras. The Saxons muttered in their beards that the day of deliverance must be at hand for Prince John to be so affable towards them.

So the evening wore on, with the Prince growing ever paler and more restless, yet trying hard to act as if nothing had happened, the Sheriff casting about in his mind how he might yet save the situation, and Oswald Montdragon wondering whether by any possible means he could disassociate himself at this late hour from the Prince's cause. Only Guy of Gisborne remained unmoved by all this disturbance. He at least had the courage of his villainy.

'You show a poor spirit, Sire,' said the mighty Baron of Gisborne. 'And it is a mistake to try and curry favour with the people at this late hour. Grind their faces still further into the mud with your taxes – that is the way to convince them that you are still master of England.'

'Ah, Gisborne,' sighed the Prince, looking at the rest of his timid, white-lipped barons with contempt, 'you are the only man here. Your advice has given me new heart. Sheriff, impose new duties upon the people of Nottingham. Montdragon, issue an edict ordering a levy of gold upon the whole country. This message is surely false, and if it is not, at least I will be prepared against the King's return with a rich store of gold.'

It was Oswald Montdragon, fired by the Prince's words, who suggested that the best way to celebrate this dismal piece of news would be to demonstrate the Prince's strength in one particular direction.

'Let's make an end of the outlaw!' he said. 'Let's finish once and for all with Master Robin Hood. And I have a plan which will both effect his capture and demonstrate your strength.'

His speech was greeted with loud cheers from the rest of the barons. The colour began to steal back into their cheeks. The whole assembly became considerably more cheerful.

NEWS FROM NOTTINGHAM

''Tis true, I swear 'tis true,' exclaimed Friar Tuck to Little John. 'There is to be a tournament in Nottingham once

more. And that rascal of a Sheriff is having the impudence
to offer once more as first prize the very silver arrow
which Robin won, and which he did not – er, stay to
receive!'

The fat friar had just returned from a surreptitious visit
to Nottingham, with this remarkable piece of intelligence.
Immediately the merry band were all agog to know what
it might mean. Robin Hood, reckless as ever, vowed that if
his own prize was to be offered again, then he would show
the Sheriff what sort of man Robin Hood was, by winning
it all over again.

Maid Marian protested, and Will Scarlett added his
pleas and cautions to hers, but Robin would not listen to
them.

'I have not had an adventure for many a long year,' said
he gaily. 'I am beginning to think the Sheriff has forgotten
all about his old friend Robin Hood. A little visit to
Nottingham will serve to remind him of my existence.'

Forthwith Robin began to sort out his festive clothes,
and brush the feathers of his famous green arrows.

'A trap – it is another trap,' groaned Will. 'How many
times have I warned you, friend Robin?'

'Prudent Will!' exclaimed Robin. 'But you are too
prudent for your years. I am young and the red blood of
adventure flows in my veins. Do not try to check me, I
pray you, for we cannot quarrel after so long a friendship.'

Reluctantly Will put aside his fears, and agreed to plan
Robin's escapade with him.

'At least visit Nottingham in some sort of disguise,' said
Will gloomily. After a long argument, he prevailed upon
Robin to adopt the disguise of an old man, and not to
flaunt his well-known striped jerkin in his native town.

All this time Marian sat dolefully wringing her hands and mourning Robin's obstinacy. However, when she saw that Robin's mind was made up and that nothing would sway him from visiting the tournament, Marian took Will Scarlett aside.

'If Robin dies, then I have no wish to live,' said she. 'So, dear Will Scarlett, think of some way by which I may stay near his side, and accompany him secretly to Nottingham.'

'Never!' cried Will, still more horrified at the thought of a fair maid imperilling herself in the very heart of the enemy stronghold. But he soon discovered that Maid Marian could match Robin for obstinacy. It was not long before poor Will found himself offering to go with Marian: he suggested that she should disguise herself as a boy in order that she might be less conspicuous by her youth and beauty.

The day of the tournament dawned fair and free. Unaware of Marian's plan, Robin bade a tender farewell to his love, and mounted his horse. Skilfully he disguised himself with all the trappings of old age. Only the muscles in his bare arms revealed that here was no old man but the formidable bandit of Sherwood Forest. Then with a gay wave to all his merry men, he set forth for Nottingham.

'Adieu, my brave fellows,' he cried. 'When I return, I shall bear with me the silver arrow.'

The moment that Robin's back was turned, Marian and Will made haste to carry out their plans. Marian adopted the attire of a boy, and slung over her back a quiver of arrows and a bow. She hoped to pass as one of the many competitors who would be flocking to Nottingham.

Not for these two conspirators a rousing departure – they were anxious to keep it as secret as possible. Unobserved, with beating hearts, Will and Maid Marian stole from the camp.

Robin's last and greatest adventure was about to begin: and they were determined not to be far behind.

14

THE GREAT TOURNAMENT

NOTTINGHAM HAD never been in such a state of joyful excitement. It seemed as if the joyful days of King Richard had come again. Many-coloured pennants fluttered gaily in the wind and highest of all fluttered the royal pennant of England, signifying that Prince John himself was honoring the tournament with his presence.

The market square was already packed by the time Robin Hood reached Nottingham. He saw Prince John, with the Sheriff at his right hand and Oswald Montdragon at his left: quickly he lowered his eyes, lest his keen glance might arouse their suspicions. Around the square, each in their box, sat the town worthies, and the knights and ladies from the neighbouring castles, who had brought with them their children, waiting-women, squires, pages and even hounds, all eager to see the fun. Tier upon tier of seats for spectators of lesser degree ran round the two far sides of the square.

The fields around were bright with coloured tents, some of which had been pitched by competitors who had come from a distance and had been unable to obtain lodgings in the town. There was a goodly number of men with five-foot bows on their backs, waiting at the open end of the square, suggesting that the competition for the silver arrow was likely to be keen. The windows which over-looked the square were also bright with hangings, and out of them peeped those fortunate families who lived there and consequently had a view of the tournament for nothing.

Through the busy crowd passed hawkers and beggars and peddlers, jostling and shouting at each other, adding to the confusion which the unaccustomed crowds had already brought to Nottingham: Robin Hood felt his spirits lift.

It would be easy to pass unrecognized in a hurly-burly such as this!

Then he turned his attention to the target. It was made of straw, two or three inches thick, and faced with a cloth, upon which rings were painted in black and red. The aim of every archer was to transfix the very centre of the target: but in order to make this more difficult still, the target sloped backwards from the archers. Robin noted that the distance was not so great for one who was used to shooting at the elusive deer of Sherwood: and by now he felt positively cheerful, for he was convinced that the silver arrow would not be snatched from him this time.

'Zounds, Sheriff,' he said aloud, 'you shall not rob me of my prize a second time!'

A few curious onlookers stopped and stared at the old man muttering to himself. Fortunately a diversion, in the shape of a herald blowing his trumpet, distracted them: for now all ears were strained to hear the announcement of the competition.

Nearly sixty tall fellows stood forth to shoot. Among them was the same ragged old man, whose curious muttering had aroused attention. When he went up with the rest of the competitors to give his name to the clerk, there was a great shout of derisive merriment from the crowd.

'Ho there, grandfather!' shouted one wit. 'Hast got out of thy grave to come and shoot thy palsied arrows at us?'

Even the clerk looked at him doubtfully.

'I doubt if you have strength enough left to draw a bow,' he said, 'and therefore it is hardly worth you wasting our time by entering. Be off with you, old man, and leave the competition to younger men.'

The ancient shook his fist feebly in the clerk's face: and to the onlookers it seemed as if even that effort was too much for him.

'I am as good as any young sprig with a bow,' he quavered. 'Take my name, clerk, and no more of your impudence.'

Reluctantly, the clerk inscribed the name 'Hodden of Barnsdale' upon the roll, while the crowd turned from jeering the old man to jeering the clerk who had given way to him. Several high-spirited lads began to imitate old Hodden: they hobbled up to the clerk, and in cracked, quavering voices, asked that they too might be admitted.

'For I am not more than a hundred years old, master!'

Angrily the clerk shooed them away, and in surly tones bade them take their foolery elsewhere.

Now Prince John, seeing this ragged old man among the stout fellows drawn up to shoot off for the first round of the prize, leaned forward in his seat and called down the lists.

'Clerk, what mean you by admitting yonder greybeard to this tournament? Do you mean to make a mockery of us all?'

The clerk flushed and said in a surly voice:

'Sire, I was instructed to admit all comers. Pray pardon me if I have done wrong.'

'Yea, all comers!' quavered Hodden of Barnsdale, shaking his bow in a tremulous hand to show that there was still strength left in his arm.

The Saxon crowd, for ever looking for some opportunity to show their resentment of the Norman dominance, started to grow restive: there were faint hisses from one quarter, and a few shouts which sounded suspiciously like 'Down with Prince John!'

'Let the old fellow shoot,' bellowed one lusty fellow from the common stands, shaking his large fist in a menacing fashion towards the royal box.

'The crowd is growing angry,' murmured the Sheriff in the Prince's ear. ''Twere best to let them have their way and permit the old fellow to take part. After all, he will not get further than the first round. Then, when he has been defeated, and the Saxons have lost interest in him, we can have him soundly whipped for his pains.'

'Your advice is good, Sheriff.' With a cold smile the Prince signified that the tournament might proceed and Hodden of Barnsdale be among the competitors.

HODDEN OF BARNSDALE SHOWS HIS SKILL

It was decided that the sixty stout fellows – or rather fifty-nine stout fellows and one weak old man, for Hodden of Barnsdale did not look in the least bit stalwart – should shoot off in twelve rounds of five. The fellows jostled to shoot in the early rounds, where they felt they would attract the favourable attention of the judges, and it happened that Hodden of Barnsdale, by reason of his age and feebleness, got pushed into the very last round of all. So that in fact fifty-nine fellows had shot off before the aged man so much as pulled his bow. There had been good shots – which the crowd greeted with Oohs and Aahs of delight – and bad shots, which were greeted with rough words and cries of contempt. It was noticeable that the Saxons always got acclaimed from the common stands, whereas the Norman men-at-arms, such as Walter of Weybridge, were cheered from the royal box, or the boxes of the lords and ladies of the neighbouring castles. So marked was the distinction that the Sheriff observed to the Prince:

'The nation is divided in two, Sire.'

The Prince scowled angrily.

'I am master of both halves,' he observed.

At that moment Hal o' the Mill, a stout Saxon archer from Belmoor way, scored the nearest ring to the centre with his arrow. A great huzza went up from the Saxon crowd, and a multitude of caps were tossed in the air, regardless of the attempts of the stewards to restore silence for the next competitor.

'Hoorah for the Saxon hero!'

'Down with the Norman dogs!'

These lusty cries seemed to give the lie to the Prince's proud assertion that he was master of the nation. Hal's shot bid fair to beat all the rest – that is to say, until Walter of Weybridge stepped forward in the eighth round. Now Walter of Weybridge knew well that he could outshoot any man in the north, with the exception of Robin of Locksley. He had scrutinized the competitors carefully, and satisfied himself that the outlaw was not among them.

So it was with an air of complete self-confidence that he stepped forward, a fine upstanding manly figure, the cynosure of Norman eyes, and drew his bow.

Straight as a die it flew: and landed a shade within Hal o' the Mill's. Now it was the turn of the Normans to cheer, and toss their caps in the air: and this time the stewards allowed it to happen without interference, because they could see from the Prince's smiling face that he was well pleased with Walter's success.

'My man will win the day!' exclaimed the Sheriff. He too was delighted that Walter had represented him so well, for he hoped that Walter's glory would be reflected upon him.

'He certainly shoots well,' commented Oswald Mont-dragon. 'But it happens that I have a man-at-arms who has been in foreign parts these twelve months, and he also draws a fine bow. See, he steps forward yonder.'

The Sheriff shot a look of hatred at Montdragon. Then the Sheriff remembered that only once in his life had Walter of Weybridge been defeated, and that by Robin Hood himself. Let the Montdragon man do his worst: Walter of Weybridge could still outshoot him.

The Montdragon man was a dark avised, burly fellow, broad in the shoulder, with great muscular arms, which bulged and knotted like a wrestler's. When he drew his mighty bow, the wood seemed to crack beneath the strain which was imposed upon it.

'How do they call him?' inquired the Prince.

'Lewis,' replied Montdragon. 'But they call him the Blackamoor for his inky brows, and also I fear for his savage temper – for he is so arrogant that none dare gainsay him for fear of a blow from those mighty arms or a cuff from those strong fists.'

The Prince looked with new respect at the archer.

'Hmm. I could do with a man like that about me,' said he. 'If Lewis wins this tournament, Montdragon, I will pay you any price you like to name for the services of such a stout archer.'

Montdragon smiled, well pleased: he felt convinced that Lewis would carry off the prize, and that would make his master, also, the richer, if the Prince stuck to his word.

'May you be the victor, Lewis the Blackamoor,' thought Oswald Montdragon to himself.

It looked as if his wish would be granted: for in the first fifty men, none had shot better than the Blackamoor: his arrow landed even nearer to the centre of the target than that of Walter of Weybridge, to the great chagrin of the Sheriff and his men. Glancing cursorily at the rest of the competitors, Montdragon did not think that they would provide much excitement: for the most part they were stolid Saxon yeomen, who could draw a reliable bow in a battle, but lacked the skill of the Norman archers, essential for a test of this sort. As for the old dotard, now trimming his bow, his beard waggling up and down in his excitement – if Montdragon spared him a thought, it was only to reflect derisively on the foolishness of old age.

Imagine his astonishment then, shared indeed by the whole assembly from Prince down to the meanest beggar whining beside the lists, when the dotard actually scored a shot exactly the same distance from the target as the Blackamoor's. To say that Montdragon was stupefied would be no exaggeration; the Sheriff's jaw dropped open; the clerk's pen dropped from his fingers; and for a second no sound at all was heard from a single spectator.

Then, all at once, a mighty roar burst from the throats

of the Saxons, who decided that the old man's success was a personal triumph for them. How they cheered him, and how they laughed in the faces of the Normans, regardless of the fact that Hal o' the Mill also had been outshot. In the twinkling of an eye, Hodden of Barnsdale had become the most popular man at the tournament with one half of the audience, and the least popular with the other half.

THE FINAL ROUND

It was now time for the twelve men left out of the sixty to shoot out the tournament. Now, it was one of the rules of the tournaments of that day, well known to all present, that he who had shot best in the first round should have the right to shoot first in the final round. Consequently, the Saxons in the common stands and standing beside the lists, confidently expected that the clerk would toss a coin between the Blackamoor and Hodden for the first place, in view of the fact that they had both shot equally well. To their indignation, the Blackamoor calmly stepped forward and drew his bow, as if the first place was his by right!

'Stand back!'

'Norman knave!'

'Upstart!'

The angry cries filled the air, and many fists were shaken in the direction of the royal box, where the Prince sat with set lips and pale face, listening to the indignant murmurings.

'I will not be browbeaten,' he muttered to the Sheriff. 'The Blackamoor shot with true skill whereas the old fool's shot was a fluke.'

The Sheriff was torn between the desire to spite Oswald Montdragon and his own dislike of the quavering old man, whom the crowd had made their favourite.

'Why not let Walter of Weybridge shoot first?' he suggested. 'That way no one will be offended.'

The idea commended itself to the Prince, who leant forward and bade the clerk alter the order of the shooting, so that the Blackamoor shot eleventh and the old man last of all.

Walter of Weybridge, conscious that the eyes of his master were upon him, drew himself up to his full height, and with a powerful sweep of his bow, launched his arrow towards the target. Zing! It landed on the very line which ringed round the bull's-eye – a skilful shot, indeed, and one which would be very hard to beat.

Well satisfied, the plump Sheriff leant back and permitted himself a small complacement smile in the direction of Oswald Montdragon. Let the Blackamoor beat that if he could.

The next nine contestants, including Guy of Gisborne's retainer, who was no mean archer in his own right, shot off without in any way rivalling Walter of Weybridge. Even Hal o' the Mill failed to score a better shot, and since he represented the Saxon hopes, a groan went up from the crowd at his failure.

'The prize is Walter's already,' said the Sheriff, airily.

'You speak too soon, Sir Sheriff,' intervened the Prince, motioning to Oswald Montdragon to check the hasty retort which had sprung to his lips. 'Let no man call the prize his until the very last arrow has been fired. Why, who knows, masters, Hodden of Barnsdale may be the winner yet!' And the Prince laughed merrily at the very idea.

As he laughed, the Blackamoor stepped forward and stood, resplendent in the full pride of his strength, with the sun gleaming on his black curly head and his fine black beard. He flexed his great arms twice, so that the muscles rippled, and acknowledged the cheers of the Normans with a disdainful bow of his head, as if such plaudits were mere flies on the flanks of a mighty horse. The Norman ladies sighed with admiration for the handsome archer, and several white kerchiefs fluttered down from boxes, as tokens of their favour. The Blackamoor acknowledged these with the same superb disdain.

'Will the mighty lord deign to shoot his arrow soon or must we stand all day waiting for him?' said a waspish voice behind him. The Blackamoor whipped round angrily and saw Hodden of Barnsdale standing behind him. He raised his hand as if to strike down the old man, but the clerk bade them angrily to desist.

'Fire your shot, Lewis the Blackamoor,' added the clerk, for he, too, was becoming impatient of the big man's airs and graces.

'What rank impertinence!' exclaimed the Prince, who had overheard the interchange. 'Sheriff, see to it that that old fool is soundly whipped when the tourney is over.'

Now at last the Blackamoor was ready to make his shot. His bow drawn back, his whole body expressive of his careless confidence, he loosed the arrow . . . the crowd held their breath while it flew through the air . . . then gradually a great 'Oooh' went up from between closed lips – for the arrow had landed plumb in the centre of the target itself!

How the Normans roared and cheered, stamped their feet and pelted the Blackamoor with coins and flowers and anything else they could think of to mark their favour. Their cheers must have been heard as far away as York, and as for Oswald Montdragon, he threw a whole bag of gold down at the feet of his man in his enthusiasm and excitement.

'Mine, mine indeed, this man must be mine!' exclaimed the Prince joyfully. 'Montdragon, I am grateful to you a thousand times for training such a right royal archer in your service. Clerk, bring forward the silver arrow. With my own hands I will bestow it upon the victor.'

The clerk obediently picked up the silver arrow from where it lay gleaming in the sun, and made as if to hand it to the Prince.

'One moment, fellow,' said a quavery voice behind him, and the clerk felt a hand pluck at his sleeve. He turned round impatiently, only to see Hodden of Barnsdale standing plaintively behind him, with bow in hand.

'Be off with you, old man!' exclaimed the clerk angrily. 'This is no time for your foolery. The Prince is about to present the prize to the winner. Get you home before the Sheriff sees you and trounces you soundly for your impudence.'

'Nay, my young jackanapes,' answered Hodden. ''Tis my right to have my shot, and have my shot I will!'

Before the clerk could gainsay him, the old man stepped forward, and bent his bow. The Prince's breath was quite taken away by this effrontery.

'Seize him, seize the fumbling old fool!' he shouted. 'Throw him into a dungeon! A thousand devils take him! Does he think he can beat a shot like that?'

It was Oswald Montdragon who plucked at the Prince's sleeve and persuaded him to calm himself.

'Sirrah, it can do no harm to let the aged fellow make a fool of himself,' he said peaceably. 'Perchance the people will be angry if you seize him in front of their very eyes.'

'Intolerable effrontery!' muttered the Prince again. But he let Montdragon have his way, and no further attempt was made to check Hodden of Barnsdale then and there, although various dark threats were issued by the clerk as to what would happen to him later.

'Save your breath, master,' replied the old man. 'I can look after myself as well as any of these Norman knaves; they will look in vain for Hodden of Barnsdale once this merry tournament is over. He will vanish into thin air, as if he had never existed.'

With these strange words – which gave the clerk much food for thought afterwards, although he dismissed them as the ravings of an old man in his dotage at the time – Hodden of Barnsdale stepped forward for his final trial of strength. He seemed half the height of his bow, so bent and wizened was he, and indeed it was scarcely credible that such a decrepit figure should have enough strength to pluck the arrows from the quiver, let alone pull the bow itself. Nevertheless, there was a sort of confidence about the tremulous old man which was strangely impressive. Even Prince John, impatiently drumming his fingers at the delay, found himself leaning forward as Hodden was about to release the arrow, and watching the result with an unaccountable interest.

'A hundred crowns that he does not even hit the target!' jested the Sheriff.

'Taken!' said one of the bold sparks about the court.

It was at that exact moment that Hodden of Barnsdale's arrow transfixed that of the Blackamoor, with the ease of a knife cutting through cheese, and by splitting it clean in half, landed plump in the centre of the target! The two halves of the Blackamoor's arrow fell useless to the ground. Hodden's arrow alone quivered proudly in the bull's-eye.

'Huzza! Bravo! A Hodden! A Hodden!'

The frenzied cries of Saxon triumph rent the air. A deep-throated roar of satisfaction, from the very heart of the Saxon people, echoed across the whole city of Nottingham.

Meanwhile, in the royal box, the Sheriff turned first white then red. Guy of Gisborne snapped the stem of his wine glass in his astonishment and dismay. Oswald Montdragon started back from the edge of the box, and bit his lip until he drew blood. The Prince himself, in an excess of fury, choked and spluttered and cursed and screamed until his retainers feared that he would give himself a fit.

The Sheriff was the first to recover himself.

'Pull yourself together, Sire,' he hissed. 'The people must not see your discomfiture. You must present the prize as if nothing had happened.'

For all Prince John's faults – and they were many – the royal blood of England flowed in his veins. Visibly he drew himself up, and with a great effort mastered the rage which convulsed his features.

'You are right, Sheriff.' He ground the words out from between clenched teeth. 'I shall give the old fool the prize. But *afterwards*. . . .'

Behind the Prince's back, one of the pages drew his finger across his throat, as if to show that he knew well the sort of fate that awaited the unfortunate winner.

The Silver Arrow

So Hodden of Barnsdale half hobbled, half dragged himself on his stick towards the royal box, amid the cheers of the Saxons and the derisive hoots of their Norman enemies. Impossible to believe that this shapeless, forlorn figure had really defeated Walter of Weybridge, Hal o' the Mill and Lewis the Blackamoor himself in a fair contest! Yet, for all his lameness and seeming crippled walk, it was notable that Hodden covered the distance between the lists and the box quite as fast as any young gallant.

'Grammercy, Sire,' quavered old Hodden. 'Who'd have thought I would shoot better than any of these young bucks? Still, they say blood will out, and one old Saxon can shoot better than a dozen young Normans!'

The Prince, who had creased his face into a cold smile of welcome, began to frown angrily at this impudent speech.

'Old fool—' he began, when the Sheriff and Oswald Montdragon together each plucked one of his sleeves, and said in unison:

'Patience, Sire!'

At this, the Prince recollected himself and drew back haughtily within the box.

'I will not demean myself by presenting the arrow to this babbling Saxon,' he whispered in a frenzied undertone. 'Guy of Gisborne, for you are the senior baron present, do you undertake this loathsome task on my behalf.'

Guy of Gisborne, slightly taken aback at the request, nevertheless picked up the arrow from where it gleamed on its bed of velvet and went to the front of the box to present it to the aged beggar. Hodden of Barsdale, crouched low on his stick, looked up in surprise at the unexpected sight of the Baron of Gisborne, when he had anticipated seeing the Prince himself.

It was at that moment that some bright gleam in those keen blue eyes, some faint hint of laughter in the firm mouth half hidden by the folds of the old man's hood, something altogether too youthful and muscular about the pose of the figure, first aroused Guy of Gisborne's suspicions. Memory rushed to his aid. Where else had he seen an aged figure such as this, which, if it had been unmasked, would have revealed a young man in the prime of life? A wedding! Thunder and lightning! His own wedding – the wedding that had never in fact taken place . . . the old harpist, yes, that was it, he had it now, the old harpist in the corner of the chapel. *That* was who Hodden of Barnsdale reminded him of. And that aged harpist had been in fact none other than Robin Hood himself!'

All these thoughts had taken but a second to flit through Guy of Gisborne's darting mind. So that Hodden – or Robin Hood, as we must now call him – had scarcely any warning of the baron's intention when, instead of handing him the silver arrow, Guy suddenly leant forward and tugged at his long white beard.

Robin leapt backwards. Too late. The beard had come away in Guy of Gisborne's hand! There it fluttered in the breeze, the undeniable proof of his disguise.

Consternation in the royal box! The Prince flinched backwards, as if he thought the outlaw would murder him on the spot, in spite of all his guards. The Sheriff uttered inarticulate sounds and only managed to point one shaking finger at the enemy in their midst.

The Saxons in the common stands craned their heads

forward to see what had occasioned the disturbance, and the Norman lords felt for the swords at their belts, although it was noticeable that not one of them actually rushed forward to beard Robin Hood where he stood, alone, in the lists.

Guy of Gisborne, who did not lack courage, whatever his faults, made the first move. Leaping the edge of the box, he flung himself upon his ancient enemy. But Robin lithely stepped sideways from his furious rush, and drawing his sword from beneath his ragged clothing, defied the Normans to apprehend him.

Alone? He was not quite alone. For when Guy of Gisborne plucked the beard from his face and unmasked him, two figures had rushed from the crowd, two figures in jerkins and hose, and well-hooded faces, who had watched the whole proceedings from afar with their hearts beating fast. Now they stood beside him, and each had a sword in the hand.

Their unexpected support, by confusing the Normans, enabled Robin to feint from their clutches, and like a fox pursued by hounds, run for cover amid the loyal Saxons. A hundred friendly hands were there to help him on to a horse. A hundred hostile daggers thwarted the Norman advance. But Robin had not finished with the Normans for one day; he wheeled the horse, and at full gallop, with Will Scarlett close behind him, made for the royal box.

'Take heed, Robin!' cried the loyal Will, but Robin did not seem to hear him.

As he reached the royal box, he bent low in the saddle and plucked the silver arrow from its cushion, where Guy of Gisborne had roughly thrown it down.

'You shall not cheat me of my prize a second time,

Prince John!' he shouted, then turned his horse and headed for the gates, with the sun sparkling on the arrow firmly clenched in his fist.

'Not so fast, outlaw!' The ominous words came from Guy of Gisborne, himself mounted on a powerful horse, who barred Robin's way. 'The time is come for my revenge.'

'Willingly do I give it to you,' cried Robin joyfully, for the prospect of a fight against the cruel baron filled him with zest. 'On guard, tyrant of Gisborne!'

THE FALL OF THE TYRANT OF GISBORNE

With only their swords to protect them, the two men rushed upon each other. There had never been a worthier match than these two – blow for blow, cut for cut, thwack for thwack, they went at each other, until each streamed with blood. Yet neither would relent or give way in the slightest.

'Bandit! Take that, and that!'

'Usurper! Norman thief! Ah, you would, would you – take that, and that, and that!'

Robin slashed his way behind the baron's defences. Then Guy of Gisborne rallied and delivered two mighty blows which nearly shook Robin from his saddle. He swayed first one way when the other, and even the crowd could see that he was faint from lack of blood.

'Ooh, Robin Hood falls, Robin Hood is falling!' The long sigh went up from the common people.

It seemed as if Robin Hood had heard them; for suddenly he rallied, grasped his sword more tightly, and rushed upon Guy of Gisborne in one last assault, so fierce, so savage, and so unexpected, that the baron had no resources left to meet it. He quailed, he staggered under the impact of Robin's sword, then with a mighty crash which reverberated round the stands, he fell to the ground.

Robin Hood's weapon had pierced his heart.

The Lord of Sherwood waited for no more than to see that the cruel tyrant was dead. At once he was away for the forest at full tilt, with Will Scarlett steady behind him. The silver arrow gleamed at his saddle, like a beacon, mocking the Norman soldiers who pursued him in vain.

THE HOSTAGE

But what of Maid Marian? What part had she played in all this turmoil, since first she stepped forth from the crowd at Will Scarlett's side? Will Scarlett imagined that she had made her escape conveniently quickly, for he had seen her vanish among the Saxons, and he imagined that some friendly soul had provided her with a mount.

Alas, the very opposite was true, and while Will and Robin rode confidently towards the forest, full of their fresh triumph over the Prince and the Sheriff, Marian, the queen of the band, languished in the hands of Oswald Montdragon! As yet, however, Robin and Will were ignorant of the fact. They talked pleasurably of Marian's cunning in eluding the enemy, and the joy of seeing her again in Sherwood.

'What courage she showed to come to Nottingham in the guise of a boy!' exclaimed Robin, full of admiration.

Unfortunately, even the guise of a boy was not enough to avoid detection by the sharp eyes of Oswald

Montdragon. As the two allies had stepped forward to Robin's side, at the beginning of the mêlée, he had suddenly recognized one of them as his stolen bride, Marian of Whitby. While Guy of Gisborne fought and was slain by Robin Hood, Oswald Montdragon concentrated on capturing Marian. In vain she squirmed and struggled in his grasp. His iron fingers kept her firmly beside him and guided her remorselessly towards his tent where his retainers bound her firmly hand and foot.

'A hostage!' said Oswald Montdragon, grimly. 'We have a hostage in our hands. Let us see what Master Robin Hood makes of that!'

It was Much the Miller who had the grievous task of breaking the news to Robin. As the leader of the band combed the camp distractedly for Marian, asking first one man, then another, whether he had seen her, and always receiving a sad shake of the head, Much went up to him and pulled him by the sleeve. One glance at the Miller's woeful expression told Robin the worst.

'They have got her,' he said dully. 'Oh, Marian, Marian, why did you ever come with me? Tell me, faithful Much, tell me it is not true?'

Two tears trickled down the Miller's rosy cheeks.

'Notices are posted in the town,' said he, 'and the heralds proclaim the news at every street corner. Marian of Whitby lies in the deepest dungeon of the castle and' – his voice faltered – 'and, oh Robin, forgive me that I have to tell you even this – she dies tomorrow at noon, unless Robin Hood and all his band surrender.'

15

THE STRANGER IN
THE FOREST

ALL THAT NIGHT Robin Hood could not sleep. He tossed and turned for an hour or so on his couch, then rose impatiently to his feet and began to pace restlessly through the camp. Soon his aimless steps led him beyond its boundaries into the cool green darkness of Sherwood itself. There at least there was some comfort to be found in the trees and shadows which had nursed him so long.

What was he to do? The tormenting question rang in his head like a bell which would not be stilled. He could not leave Marian to die – that was out of the question. Yet, if he gave himself up, what guarantee was there that the Normans would release her, and in any case how could he betray his band, the men he loved so well, even for the sake of Marian? Suppose they tried to rescue her, as they had done once before – but what chance was there of a rescue now? Not one in a million. Robin knew that well enough. Forewarned, they would guard night and day, nor let her out of their sight until the moment came for her execution.

Robin groaned aloud.

'Help me!' he cried. 'Help me to think of some way.' And he smote his temples with his fists.

'I will help you if I can,' said a cool voice behind him.

Greatly startled, Robin whipped round, and found himself face to face with a knight in armour, mounted on a horse. His visor was down and there was no possible way of knowing whether he was friend or foe. From the cross on his breast, he was evidently a pilgrim, yet even Prince John's barons had been known to go on pilgrimages, and the pilgrim garb was unfortunately no longer a guarantee of good faith. Robin felt for his trusty sword.

'Nay,' said the stranger, 'you have no need of weapons. I come in peace. I heard your cry for help and asked myself what manner of man was this, walking alone, without a horse in the forest, and calling on the trees to help him.'

'What may your business be in Sherwood, Sir Pilgrim?' Robin counter-attacked. 'As you say, the hour is late, and honest fellows are in bed.'

The stranger laughed behind his visor.

'Then we are neither of us honest fellows, and if both are rogues, then we may get on very well together. Here's my hand to it.' The mailed stranger stretched forth his hand, and Robin, feeling some strange sympathy for the unknown, took it in his.

'I like you well,' said he. 'Welcome to Sherwood!'

The stranger seemed slightly taken aback by this greeting. He did not exactly withdraw his hand, but there was a certain reserve about his manner which had not been there before.

'Why do you say – "Welcome to Sherwood"?' he inquired. 'Is this forest yours that you welcome me to it? Methinks it belongs to the King.'

'We have no King in England,' replied Robin bitterly. 'Only a weakling prince who calls himself the Regent and is in fact ruled by his barons. Would that Richard the Lionheart would return and see that justice was done!'

'I have been away from England some years on a pilgrimage,' observed the stranger. 'Tell me the news, fellow, for I am mighty curious to learn all that has been happening in my native land. Spare nothing in your telling, neither good nor evil.'

Nothing loth to air his indignation at the state of England, Robin plunged into his sorry tale of Norman wrongdoing and Saxon distress. In the course of it he naturally revealed the part which he himself had played, and the many skirmishes which he had had with the Prince and the Sheriff, although he tried to make light of them.

'Hmm,' murmured the stranger. 'So you have been dwelling here in the forest, you and all the men you call your band.' He paused, and with a faint question in his voice, added: 'No doubt the royal deer have played their part in providing you with food?'

Robin laughed without a trace of embarrassment.

'We are right grateful to the Prince for his hospitality,' he said. 'If you come back and rest awhile in our camp, we will give you venison for breakfast, so that you may taste his hospitality for yourself.'

'I thank you for your kindness,' replied the stranger. 'And gladly do I accept it. But one thing, Robin of Locksley, you have not revealed to me. You have not revealed why you were wandering thus mournfully alone in Sherwood's dark glades.'

Robin sighed deeply. Talking to the stranger, he had momentarily forgotten the dire straits in which he lay. Already an hour had sped by in conversation with the pilgrim – and he was an hour nearer to the time when he must decide whether to sacrifice himself and all his men or let Marian die.

With a shrug of his shoulders, he decided that no harm could come of telling the sympathetic stranger his sorrow. It was late now for any mortal to save Marian, and their situation could not be made any worse by a further betrayal. So recklessly, with all the passion at his command, he poured out his tale of woe.

Robin puts his Faith in the Stranger

A long silence followed when Robin had finished. The stranger, sitting upright on his horse, might have been an empty suit of armour for all the sign of life he gave.

Then suddenly he stretched out his hand for the second time, and touched the outlaw on his shoulder. It was a curiously royal gesture, as if the man who made it was used to command.

'I will help you, Robin of Locksley,' said his strange friend, and so astonished was Robin at his words that he did not notice that the pilgrim had addressed him by his proper title instead of by the name he had given him – Robin Hood. 'Fear not, and look not amazed. Of all men in this country, I alone can save Marian of Whitby. You have only to trust me completely and follow my instructions faithfully. I promise you that Marian will not die, nor will the merry band of Sherwood be sacrificed.'

These words, said in a calm tone of authority, flabbergasted Robin Hood. How could a mere pilgrim promise such a thing? The Castle of Nottingham was impregnable. The Prince was Regent of England and all-powerful.

What could a stray pilgrim do against forces such as these? And yet . . . there was something in the Pilgrim's whole bearing which inspired confidence.

Against his will, Robin found himself saying:

'It shall be as you say, Sir Pilgrim. God grant that you do not fail me.' Half mesmerized, he knelt down before the visored stranger and kissed his hand.

Once they reached the bandit camp the stranger announced that he intended to lie down and have a few hours' sleep. He advised Robin to do the same.

'Sleep!' exclaimed Robin, his new-found confidence waning. 'How can I sleep when I am racked with anguish!'

'You promised to follow my instructions,' said the stranger. 'This is the first order that I have given you. Do as I say!'

Reluctantly, for it was the first order to which the Lord of Sherwood had ever been subjected within the domains of the forest, Robin obeyed, and laid himself down. Exhausted as he was by the exertions of the day, and suffering at the thought of Marian's plight, he soon fell into a deep and mercifully dreamless sleep.

When he awoke, he found the men of Sherwood grouped around him in a circle. To his surprise, they had their bows and quivers on their backs, and their swords at their belts. They were evidently equipped for some expedition. For a moment Robin could not think what had happened. Then he caught sight of the pilgrim, still masked in his visor, and the strange events of the night before came back to him. Robin sprang to his feet.

'What do these arms mean?' he exclaimed. 'Will Scarlett, Little John, what does this mean?'

Will Scarlett pointed silently to the pilgrim.

'They have obeyed my orders,' said the pilgrim in the same deep, imperious voice. 'We march to Nottingham.'

Robin's first instinct was to rebel against his calm assumption of his own position as leader. But he had promised to obey the pilgrim, and he could not in loyalty break his oath. So, silently resentful, he took his place behind the pilgrim and followed in the wake of the new Lord of Sherwood towards the great castle of Nottingham.

THE MARCH ON NOTTINGHAM CASTLE

The march was long, and the hearts of the men of Sherwood were heavy. There were no merry songs now, as in other marches in the past: even Friar Tuck felt no urge to bellow forth a jovial ballad. He trudged along with the rest, dour and anxious. Nor did the pilgrim give them any hint of what they were to do once they reached the Castle of Nottingham. Were they to attack it? Impossible to believe that he would counsel an attack by so few men against such a mighty stronghold.

The men trudged on, wondering secretly what the future held in store for them. It was now eleven o'clock, and at noon Marian was to die.

At length the great castle towered above their heads. The sentries were thick upon the battlements, and from every slit in the wall an arrow poked out its ugly head. Evidently the Prince was taking no chances!

At the sight of the outlaw band, a great shout of warning went up from the sentries.

'The bandits! The bandits are here!'

Their outcry reached the ears of the Sheriff and the

Prince, sitting in council. Oswald Montragon heard it, as he sat, with his arms crossed and his dagger on his knees, before the nail-studded door of Maid Marian's dungeon. He, too, was taking no chances this time. Calling to the soldiers to guard the prisoner with their lives, for he would surely execute them if she escaped, he rushed on to the battlements and saw for himself the outlaw band – looking pitifully small and helpless there on the green sward before the castle.

'Shoot them down!' he yelled to the sentries.

'Nay, Montdragon!' cried the Prince, who had reached the battlements a moment later. 'You take too much upon yourself. Let us first parley with these impudent scoundrels. We have them in our power and it should be good sport. Make them admit that they have come to give themselves up and taste the humiliation of defeat before we slay them.'

He beckoned to his vassals to follow him, and descended to the drawbridge. There, well guarded by a score of archers, the Prince surveyed the rebels with satisfaction.

'So you have come to surrender, outlaw!' he shouted. 'It was prudent of you, for sure enough the girl would have died at noon!'

'Knavish Prince! False tyrant!' cried Robin. 'I shall never surrender. Hand over Maid Marian, else one of my green arrows will find its way to your heart.'

Amazed at Robin Hood's impudence, the Prince drew back in some confusion and consulted with the Sheriff as to what this strange answer might mean.

' 'Tis a trick of some sort,' said Oswald Montdragon. 'How can he harm us with his little band of archers, when

229

we have a veritable army within our walls. Order the men to shoot them down!'

'Do not for ever be giving orders to your ruler,' said Prince John petulantly. 'I want to have the satisfaction of hearing the rascal admit defeat, after all we have suffered at his hands. Besides, it will be good for the men's morale to hear him cringe and beg for mercy.'

He stepped forward again.

'Robin Hood! I give you the time the bell takes to strike noon to surrender, and if you do not, we shall shoot you down like the Saxon dogs you are!'

As the Prince's words died away, the great bell of the castle began to toll for midday.

The Stranger unmasks at Noon

One, two, three, four – still the outlaws did not stir. The sentries readied themselves for the assault. The Prince held his breath, while the Sheriff trembled slightly at his side. Only Oswald Montdragon felt genuine joy at the prospect of the slaughter of the men of Sherwood: to the others, however cruel their nature, there was something pitiful about the little band pitting itself gallantly but in vain against the strength of Nottingham's great castle.

Seven, eight, nine – would Robin Hood not even bow his stiff neck to save his men? Did he care nothing for Maid Marian? Nothing for Will Scarlett, Little John, Alan-a-Dale, Friar Tuck and the rest?

Ten . . . eleven – and now the great bell was about to strike twelve, tolling the hour of noon to the good citizens of Nottingham. Prince John lifted his white handkerchief to give the signal to fire.

'For the last time, outlaw, do you surrender?'

'Never!'

'Then you die!'

Even as the Prince spoke, the bell tolled out deep and sonorous the final note of the hour, and the white handkerchief fell from the Prince's hand.

'Hold your fire, John of England, unworthy of the name!'

With these dramatic words, spoken in a loud, resonant voice, the pilgrim stranger suddenly stepped forward and confronted the Prince, at the very moment when a hundred arrows were about to transfix Robin Hood and his men. His visor was up: all could see his face clearly now. What features were these which made the Prince start back, white and trembling? Why did the Sheriff sink to his knees in fear? And Oswald Montdragon, too, fling himself abjectly to the ground? The answer came in the deep roar which went up from every man present at that fateful scene:

'Richard the Lionheart! King Richard has come back to us!'

And one and all, they flung themselves on their knees before the King, while the outlaws around him kissed the hem of his robe.

'Yes, it is indeed your King,' replied Richard, acknowledging their cheers with a majestic wave of the hand. 'Rise, good people of Nottingham, and let each man in turn do homage to me on my return.'

The long procession of loyal subjects filed past the King. Each placed his hands between the King's and swore fealty to him anew, to signify that he abjured the false rule of Prince John for ever. Last of all to perform homage was Robin Hood himself.

'Ah, Sire,' he cried. 'Forgive me for my words to you in the forest. I would not have spoken thus freely had I known that I was speaking to my King.'

'Fear not for your boldness, Robin of Locksley,' replied King Richard. 'England has need of brave spirits like yours. Freely I pardon you and all your men of your outlawry, and also' – he paused and smiled – 'I pardon you for those royal deer which you have purloined so lavishly from my forest!'

'God save King Richard!' cried all the merry men together, flinging their caps in the air with loud huzzas of joy.

'Furthermore,' continued the King, 'forasmuch as your father, whom I loved well, and was my loyal companion on the Crusade, died in the Holy Land, fighting against the heathen – in token of his services and of yours, I create you, Robin, Earl of Locksley.'

So Robin Hood, the erstwhile outlaw, knelt before his King, and received the earldom which had belonged to his dead father, together with the restitution of all the manors and lands which had been unfairly snatched from him by his enemies.

THE ROYAL VENGEANCE

'But for you, Sheriff,' said the King, turning suddenly on the cringing man, still kneeling suppliantly before him. 'For you, and for Oswald Montdragon, there shall be no mercy. As you have dealt with others, so will I deal with you. You have trodden the faces of the poor, persecuted the widows and orphans, and made the name of my government stink in the nostrils of honest men. You shall both die!'

Thus Oswald Montdragon and the Sheriff of Nottingham were hauled off, shrieking curses and imprecations, to the very dungeons where they had imprisoned and tortured so many victims. The next day, at dawn, unmourned by any, the two villains met their death at the hands of the public hangman.

'As for you, Barbara Nevill, rightly named Black Barbara,' said the King with a terrible frown, 'you shall atone for you wickedness by abandoning this world for ever. You shall spend the rest of your days immured in a convent.'

Shrieking and groaning, Black Barbara also was borne away.

The King then turned to his brother.

'John Plantagenet,' he said sternly. 'In your veins flows the royal blood of England, and I may not spill that blood. Be thankful that your lineage has saved you, for had you been of common birth, you too would have died. Now begone from my sight, and do not darken my court again!'

Trembling, cringing, bowing, Prince John stumbled to get away from the furious gaze of his royal brother, and was seen no more.

THE MARRIAGE OF ROBIN HOOD

Once he was gone, Robin Hood dropped on his knees before his King.

'Sire,' he said. 'One last favour may I beg from you?'

'Name it, Robin, Earl of Locksley!'

'Grant me the hand of Marian of Whitby in marriage. For many long months have I loved this maid, and could not wed her, inasmuch as I was an outlaw without lands or fortune. Now I am restored to wealth, and further emboldened by my new rank, I seek her as my bride.'

The King smiled graciously and forthwith ordered Marion to be brought before him. Pale and dishevelled from her imprisonment, Marion was still further confused and amazed by the sight of King Richard standing there before the castle, holding his court, for all the world as if he had never left England's shores. There was no sign of Prince John, the Sheriff, or Oswald Montdragon, and with tears of mingled happiness and relief, Marian fell to her knees before the King and did homage.

'Marian of Whitby,' said the King. 'It is our gracious pleasure that you should be wedded, and as your husband we have chosen our noble Earl of Locksley, whom we love well. Make ready, for your nuptials shall take place immediately!'

'The Earl of Locksley!' cried Marian in dismay. 'Nay, Sire, it shall not be. I would rather die than wed any other man than Robin Hood!'

At these words, spoken with such fervour and courage, for all Marian's youth and frailty, the King smiled broadly.

'Well spoken, Maid Marian,' he said. 'Your loyalty does you credit. Then learn that I have this day created Robin Hood of Sherwood Earl of Locksley!'

With a glad cry Marian turned and perceived for the first time Robin Hood and his band standing beside her. How happily then she embraced her lover, and swore that it was now her keenest desire to be wedded to the Earl of Locksley as soon as possible.

Friar Tuck stepped forward and offered to perform the ceremony immediately; and a most splendid wedding followed, fit for the Lord of Sherwood Forest. The men of Sherwood sang lustily in the choir, remembering the day when they had had to sing in real earnest, in order to rescue the Lady Lucy from the clutches of Guy of Gisborne. Lucy pressed Alan-a-Dale's hand, thinking of their wedding day in the Forest of Sherwood; and as for Marian and Robin, they gazed into each other's eyes and swore to remain true to each other until the day of their death.

16

THE LAST
ARROW

ENGLAND NOW LIVED at peace within herself, and Norman no longer strove with Saxon, the poor no longer groaned under the exactions of the rich. Robin of Locksley rose high in the favour of the King, and full of years and honours, became one of the most important barons at his court. He lived in great contentment, with Maid Marian at his side, and a goodly brood of handsome sons and daughters all around him.

Yet, although the merry band of outlaws was scattered, and the forest itself no longer the lawless place it had been in the time of Prince John, Robin did not quite forget the carefree days in Sherwood. Will Scarlett, his faithful friend Will, still dwelt in a manor house on its outskirts, and oftentimes when Robin was sad or depressed by the bustle and worldliness of life at court, he would pay Will Scarlett a visit. Together the two friends would ride through the forest, talking of the old days, and re-living the many adventures which they had had together. They would revisit the site of the camp, now deserted and overgrown with greenery; they would put flowers on the grave of Dickon Barleycorn; and perhaps towards evening on their way home, they would pay a call on the little hermitage where Friar Tuck now dwelt in great contentment. As the years passed, the fat friar's girth grew no less, but his smile was cheerful and welcoming as ever, and he was always ready to put his best ale on the table for the sake of Robin Hood and Will Scarlett.

Alan-a-Dale and his Lady Lucy now ruled their estates in the North country, with Tom Turpin as their bailiff. But Little John found he liked the country round Nottingham so well that he had found himself a farm not far from Will Scarlett's manor, where he toiled away, using his mighty muscles for more peaceable pursuits than in the days of his brigandage. Thus all the merry men had found the fortune and contentment which they deserved.

But this is not quite the end of the story of Robin Hood. When Robin was old, his hair turned grey, his fair face lined, his arm no longer so strong to draw a bow as in the days of his youth, he set out at Michaelmas to pay one last visit to Will Scarlett, fearing lest the chills and fevers of the coming winter might part the old friends for ever by death before they had exchanged a last word of farewell.

Marian waved him good-bye from the window of her bower with a feeling of foreboding. Yet she forced herself to keep silent and smile in spite of the feeling of anxiety which obsessed her. Would that she had given her fears voice! For Robin had not quite reached Will Scarlett's house when he suddenly fell ill of a violent ague, which weakened him so greatly that he could not proceed a mile farther, without tumbling from his horse altogether.

He looked desperately around for help. Fortunately he had fallen right at the gates of a convent, standing by itself on the outskirts of the forest, with murky trees growing right up to the edges of the grey forbidding walls. Robin resolved to seek shelter there. He dragged himself to the gates and rang the rusty bell. After a few minutes a nun appeared, cautiously opened the gate a tiny crack, and peered out.

'What is your business?' she asked, in a hushed whisper. 'We are women of God, and have naught to do with this world.'

'Gentle Sister,' gasped Robin. 'I have fallen sick of a fever. I pray you give me shelter for the night, and in the morning my true friend, Will Scarlett, will bear me from your convent. But it is growing dark, and I fear that I can go no farther by myself.'

The nun looked at him with compassion and distress.

'Alas, Sir, we have strict rules to admit no strangers within our walls.'

Robin groaned. He felt his senses failing.

'At least tell your Reverend Mother that Robin of Locksley, one who ever loved the Church and kept her laws, lies helpless at the gates and begs for succour.'

The nun pattered away. Robin was left alone, with the wind blowing eerily through the trees around him. Ten minutes later, to his surprise, he heard the rustle of gowns, and a great deal of whispering. The gate opened wide, and half a dozen nuns lifted him up and bore him within the precincts of the convent. Not a word was spoken. He was laid gently on a straw pallet, in a small cell with only one narrow window, out of which he could just glimpse the forest.

Time passed, and Robin half fainted, half dozed. When he awoke he felt burning hot and feverish. Suddenly he sensed that he was not alone in the tiny cell. He turned his head and perceived a nun sitting beside him.

'Water!' he gasped.

Without a word the nun rose to her feet, filled a beaker and handed it to him. She did not look at him at all, and all the time she ministered to him, she kept her eyes fixed on the ground. But when she saw Robin was comfortable, she suddenly observed to him in a low whisper that it was necessary to let his blood, and from the capacious folds of her gown produced a sharp knife.

Robin did not flinch. He knew that the leeches were always prescribing blood-letting for fevers, and although it was extremely distasteful, it was nevertheless often necessary.

He bore the incision of the knife patiently, and saw the red blood seep out. The loss of blood made him feel faint. To his disordered mind, it seemed that hours passed, and still the nun made no move to stem the flow. He felt himself growing rapidly weaker, and closed his eyes. Suddenly, some terrible instinct of danger warned him. He looked up.

Oh terrible sight! For out of the white wimple stared not the meek features of a holy nun, but the burning eyes, the diabolical features, stamped with hatred and vengeful joy, of Black Barbara herself! Black Barbara grown old, her beauty withered, her tresses scraped back behind her coif, but still clearly recognizable for who she was.

'Murderess!' cried Robin.

With all the strength still left to him, he snatched the knife from her hand, and then began desperately to staunch the wound.

'Too late!' exclaimed Black Barbara triumphantly. 'Too late! You will die. All these years have I wanted to revenge myself on you, and now at last fate has brought you into my hands. The years I have spent in this convent fall from me: once more I am Barbara Nevill, whose love you scorned and who swore to kill you. It is Barbara Nevill who has revenged herself on Robin Hood!' And laughing hideously, the villainess rushed from the room.

Robin knew that his end was near. Scarcely conscious, he took the bugle from beside the bed and blew a faint despairing gasp. Faint as it was, it was still enough to reach the ears of Will Scarlett. The faithful lieutenant, wandering through Sherwood, searching for his old friend who had failed to arrive at the appointed hour, caught the tremulous notes.

'Robin!' he thought. 'Robin in danger!'

Again the soft note sang in the forest, and this time Will Scarlett traced it to the convent. Disregarding the fluttering protests of the nuns, he forced his way in, and scouring the corridors and cells, discovered Robin at last, by now nigh unto death.

'Oh Will,' gasped the dying leader. 'Black Barbara has – got me.' He gasped, and only managed to get out the words, 'The Reverend Mother,' before his head sank back.

'Robin, you cannot die like this,' cried Will, and he attempted in vain to staunch the wound, whose blood was now staining the mattress red.

'My bow, bring my bow, Will.'

Will placed the bow in Robin's hands and gently fitted the arrow to it. Then, with the last remnants of his strength, the Lord of Sherwood bent back the mighty weapon and loosed the arrow through the narrow window. The green-tipped arrow flashed against the trees and vanished.

'Bury me where it lands!' whispered Robin. 'And now, Will, my time has come. Tell Marian that I loved her dearly till the end – and to all the merry men' – the whisper grew fainter, so that Will Scarlett could scarcely catch the words – 'bid them remember the days in Sherwood Forest.'

With a cry of despair, Will flung himself forward across the body of his dead leader. Robin Hood was no more.

When the first violence of his grief had subsided, he rose to his feet, eager to cut down the murderess who had taken Robin's life. With sword in hand he flung open the door of the cell and shouted through the corridors of the convent:

'Barbara Nevill, Black Barbara rightly named! Show yourself!'

Suddenly he remembered Robin's last words:

'Bid them remember the days in Sherwood Forest!'

What oath had they sworn so long ago, if not to cherish the weak? And was he now, with Robin scarcely dead, to break that oath and cut down a woman in cold blood? There was no way to avenge his death. Let Black Barbara wallow in her crime, for she had damned herself. Will Scarlett put away his sword, and tenderly carried Robin's body out into the forest.

There, where the green-tipped arrow had landed, he dug a grave, and buried Robin deep within the earth of the forest which he had loved. Then he mounted his horse and set forth, slowly and sadly, to break the news of Robin's death to Marian. As he rode, the autumn leaves blew around him and the wind soughed sadly in the branches, as if to signify that the Lord of Sherwood was dead.

'Robin Hood is dead!' the wind seemed to say. 'Robin Hood is dead!'

And yet, thought Will Scarlett proudly, his spirit lives on in Sherwood Forest and he will never be forgotten while the memory of his daring adventures lives in our hearts.